Abundant Rain

Abundant Rain

Vanessa Miller

www.urbanchristianonline.net

Urban Books, LLC
78 East Industry Court
Deer Park, NY 11729

ISBN 13: 978-1-60162-797-1
ISBN 10: 1-60162-797-1

First Mass Market Printing August 2011
First Trade Paperback Printing November 2008
Printed in the United States of America

10 9 8 7 6 5 4 3 2 1

Distributed by Kensington Publishing Corp.
Submit Wholesale Orders to:
Kensington Publishing Corp.
C/O Penguin Group (USA) Inc.
Attention: Order Processing
405 Murray Hill Parkway
East Rutherford, NJ 07073-2316
Phone: 1-800-526-0275
Fax: 1-800-227-960

PROLOGUE

We wrestle not against flesh and blood,
but against principalities, against powers,
against the rulers of the darkness of this
age, against spiritual hosts of wickedness
in the heavenly places.

Ephesians 6:12

There was so much commotion on that twelfth day of September that no one noticed the two, tall-enough-to give-Shaq-a-crook-in-his-neck, figures that descended from on high. They walked through the eerie streets of New York passing many mournful and tear-soaked faces.

One man's knees buckled under the weight of his grief. His wife would not be coming out of the World Trade Center. He bowed his head low as he fell on the ground screaming, "Oh, God, why her? Why, God?"

Another grief-stricken victim shook her fists at the heavens and said, "You've never looked out for us. Do you even exist?"

Nathan turned to Brogan. "The people's faith has wavered."

"Yes," Brogan answered. "Many saints will fall away from God because of yesterday's tragedy."

They continued on. Some assignments were harder to pull off than others. Nathan had a sinking feeling that this one would be a doozy. The prayers of the saints had risen to the heavens concerning Kenneth and Elizabeth Underwood. Aaron, the captain of the angelic hosts, had given Nathan charge over the safety and well being of Kenneth. Likewise, Brogan had charge over Elizabeth.

Brogan pointed at the rubble. "You got any idea how we can get Kenneth out from under all that?"

Nathan shook his head. "We'll think of something."

"Why do you think the Almighty sends you on impossible assignments?"

"I don't know."

Their destination lay before them as a desolate wasteland. What was once beheld in awe was now the object of pity. Billowy smoke still rose from the ruins. In the place that was famous for buying and selling, body bags were now the commodity being exchanged, as executives and tycoons were lifted from the rubble.

Nathan pointed at a shadow that filled the air. "We've got company."

"You didn't think the evil one would miss the opportunity to see so much death and destruction, did you?"

Nathan surveyed the layout. He wasn't surprised at what his heavenly vision displayed. "His demons are all over this place. Just keep your head down. Let's find Kenneth and get out of here." They moved quickly through the wreckage, each tossing aside stones that would have normally taken three or four men to lift.

Nathan and Brogan split up as they tirelessly worked hour after hour, removing rubble and pulling bodies from the debris. Brogan moved to the south side and continued sifting through the debris.

Nathan yelled, "I found him!"

Brogan ran back to the north side just in time to witness two hulking spirits standing over Nathan, growling and snarling. "Put him back, pansy boy."

Nathan had Kenneth in his arms. He looked up to see who had just called him a pansy, and was face to face with two of the biggest, grizzliest-looking demons he'd encountered in years. Their heads were like bats and they had ten-inch fangs. Nathan turned to Kenneth. He was bruised and bloody. Nathan couldn't feel a pulse, but his body wasn't cold yet. He had to be alive. Instead of getting his charge to a hospital right away, he was going to have to contend with Bif and Bof. "Get out of my way," Nathan told them. "I'm on an assignment from the Lord!"

Bif and Bof burst out laughing. "You better put him down or I'm gon' send you back to your Lord crying like a pigtail-wearing girl," Bif told Nathan while massaging his fist with his scaly fang.

Brogan had already stripped out of his workman's disguise and was now in full glory. Wings extended and sword drawn, he was ready for battle.

Nathan tried one more time. "Look, can y'all just get out of the way? I'm not in the mood for kicking demon butt today. Okay?"

The one with jaundice eyes spat brown mucus on the ground and snarled. "Punk, please. You're the one in disguise, trying hard not to be noticed for who you are." He puffed up his scaly chest. "We come as we are, 'cause we ain't scared of," he poked Nathan in the chest, "you or nobody else."

"That's right," his beady-eyed, bat-faced cohort said. "Boy, I'm gon' whup you so bad, you gon' beg the Ancient of Days to make you human, so you can go on and die."

Nathan laid down his charge, praying that he wouldn't become a casualty of 9-11. But if he didn't spank Bif and Bof's fang-extended behinds, he wouldn't get Kenneth out of there anyway. Nathan took off his construction hat and a bright light shone above his head. The demons green-eyed it and got fidgety when he pulled off his workman's clothes. They really got mad when they had to behold his massive wings and white garment trimmed in gold. "Yeah, you miss this gear, don't you?"

Jaundiced eyes told him, "We're going to beat it off you, then we'll wear yours."

"Never again will you wear the Lord's armor," Brogan said.

The demons turned their intimidating stares on Brogan. "That's all right," Nathan said. "They talk like those big-bad fallen angels that got their wings clipped, but they fight like Sodomites." Nathan pulled out his golden sword. "Come on with it."

When the ruckus exploded and the fight was on, friction from the heavenly and hellish blows caused fire to spring up as rubble and debris were kicked out of the way. The firefighters got busy extinguishing the flames, while the rescue workers pulled countless half-dead and lifeless bodies from the ruins. None of them were aware of the struggle at Ground Zero, but a certain tension hung in the air.

Nathan and Brogan gave as good as they got. One blow after another was dealt to the adversary. Nathan was feeling pretty good about his performance, considering he hadn't been in battle in at least a century. Then he saw one of the rescue workers kneel down by Kenneth. The rescue worker looked at another guy, then said, "I don't think this one is going to make it."

Nathan swerved around his opponent. He knelt down at Kenneth's side and whispered in his ear, "You've got to make it. You've got too much to live for. Don't give up now."

Jaundiced eyes grabbed Nathan by the back of the neck and threw him into a pit of rubble. Brogan soon followed. Nathan shook his head and looked at his comrade. "Come on, we can't let these monkeys whup on us like this."

Brogan stood and stretched his wounded body. "I know, man. They've gotten stronger since we last met."

"Don't look now, but here they come, and they brought friends." Nathan looked around the pit for something to knock off the heads of those demons. Several steel beams had been tossed into the rubble when the buildings collapsed. Each beam was already constructed in the form of a cross. That was all the sign he needed. He stood up and grabbed one of the beams. "You slice 'em and dice 'em with your sword and I'm going to have some batting practice with these beams," Nathan told Brogan.

The demons descended upon them. Bif, Bof and friends lived through the night, but by morning, they regretted their folly. Nathan picked up beam after beam and smashed one rotten skull after the next. Brogan then drove his sword through their hell-possessed bodies. The demons that Brogan didn't get with the sword had steel beams driven through them. The beams were firmly planted in the ground. The deed took all night. Nathan and Brogan wearily ascended from the pit, too tired to notice the construction worker that walked into the World Trade Center looking for any sign of life and found hope.

The man stood in front of the crosses that Nathan had erected, and bellowed, "Abba, Father! You are here!" He ran past Nathan and Brogan as he spread the word of what he had found.

Firefighters and rescue workers followed him back to the sight. He carried a can of spray paint, and with it. he wrote GOD'S HOUSE, and drew a directional arrow. The firefighters looked at the shards of steel that formed crosses standing in perfect symmetry. In a place where everything else was in complete disarray, they bowed down and began to weep and pray to God.

"Where is Kenneth?" Nathan asked.

"I don't know," Brogan replied.

Nathan lifted his head to the heavens and asked, "Where is he, Lord? Please give me some direction."

The heavens were silent.

Nathan fell to his knees, snatched gray debris from the ground, and threw the ashes on his head. "Not again. Oh, God, no, no, nooo!"

Covered in soot and ashes, Elizabeth Underwood opened her eyes. She spent the night amongst the rubble and debris at Ground Zero, waiting for news of her husband. When none came, she stood up and ran her soot and ash stained hands through her tangled hair. She tried, unsuccessfully, to wipe some of the dirt from her clothes as she walked to one of the firemen. "How long is this going to take? I need answers. I need my husband!" she demanded.

He turned away, unable to meet her pitiful gaze. "We're working hard. We're going as fast as we can."

Elizabeth walked away. She wanted to tell him that today was her tenth anniversary, and that she and Kenneth had plans. But God had conspired against her. She woke up to a world that did not contain her husband. She was forced to inhale and exhale without him. She could now answer the question Jesus asked, "Oh, death, where is your sting?" The sting was felt by loved ones; the people left behind. She, Elizabeth Underwood, had been stung.

Four years of her college life had been spent dating Kenneth; another ten years of marriage, loving and adoring him—making him her world. Even through their bad times, she had loved that man.

Forget all the waiting, she would find her husband herself.

"Ma'am, you can't go in there," one of the firefighters told her.

Elizabeth kept walking.

"Look, lady," he said, grabbing her arm. His grip was tight. "This is not a safe area. Just let us do our job, okay?"

"All right," she said. He released her arm and Elizabeth took off running.

"Grab her!"

Two men in gray T-shirts and jeans grabbed Elizabeth and tried to pull her away from the rubble. "No!" she screamed. She dug in her heels and fought against their grip. "Please, please let me go. I've got to find my husband."

They finally managed to pull Elizabeth out of the way. They sat her down on a piece of the tower that had flown a hundred feet away from the building. "It's for your own safety, ma'am. We don't want you to get hurt."

Both men were white, young and athletic. One of them had a mustache. The other was clean-shaven.

"But it's my anniversary," she whimpered.

The clean-shaven gentleman said, "Aw, dag," sadness clouded the man's eyes as he continued. "Just hold on. We'll find your husband."

Her shoulders slumped. How could she hold on? Didn't he know that her world had collapsed? *Why have you done this to me, Lord? We were faithful to you. My husband loved you—I thought you were supposed to rebuke the devourer?*

Two firemen pulled a man's body out of the rubble. Elizabeth put her hand to her mouth and gasped. "Kenneth?" Well, she couldn't just sit on this rock and wonder.

She watched them lay the body on the ground. Elizabeth barreled through the onlookers and workers. She fell after tripping on a rock, got up, and didn't bother to brush the dirt from her clothes. She ignored the pleas of, "You can't go in there," and "Ma'am, come back." Nobody was going to stop her.

By the time she reached the body, tears had welled in her eyes. Elizabeth collapsed to her knees. As she looked in the face of this dead man, she let the tears flow. He wasn't Kenneth, but someone would miss him. She cried for that person, another victim of the sting of death.

"Ma'am, is this your husband?" one of the workers asked Elizabeth.

She shook her head. The workers bent down to pick the man up.

"Wait!" Elizabeth screamed.

The clean-shaven man she had talked to earlier said, "We have to move his body. I'm sorry."

"But, but—his family. They shouldn't see him like this." The man's shirt and pant leg had been torn. She reached over and buttoned the jacket of his navy blue suit. They took the body into a building that had the word DEAD spray painted on one side and ALIVE on the other. Had Mr. Navy Blue Suit also trusted in the Lord for his safety?

Brogan stood over Elizabeth, desperately trying to find a way to comfort her. Nathan was out scouring the city in search of Kenneth. Brogan looked toward the same building at which Elizabeth was staring, and prayed that Kenneth was not in there. At least, not on the same side they had just laid Mr. Navy Blue Suit.

He put his hand on her shoulder. Elizabeth looked around, immediately feeling a change in her environment. She shrugged, shifting away from this comforting feeling that was trying to overtake her and moved back into her state of misery. A night's sleep on the hard dust-covered ground had not changed anything for her. She still prayed for lightning to strike, or for a bull-dozer to run her over. Funny how death ignores you when you crave it.

1

Tommy Brooks sat at a back table in the Belanté Club going over his nightly receipts, his mail, and paying bills. Empty glasses from the night before lined the bar and some of the tables. The club had been good to him. This was the Friday and Saturday night home to hustlers, gold-diggers, punks, and thieves. At least, that's what the *Dayton Daily Newspaper* reported. Tommy didn't care. Thieves paid their liquor bill just like well-educated businessmen. Oh, he'd had a few run-ins with the law because of his clientele, but cops and news cameras added to the appeal. The best thing that ever happened to the Belanté Club was the night Isaac Walker got shot. Tommy shook his head. Ray-Ray was the poster child for stupidity. Take on Isaac Walker? Hah, many had tried, but few lived to tell about it. Well, Ray-Ray's soul was now being tormented in hell for the effort.

At least that's the story Isaac was telling everybody. Isaac was on a letter writing campaign; determined to tell everybody about his so-called hell experience. Who would have thought big, bad Isaac would get jailhouse salvation?

Tommy guessed it was his turn to hear the story as he picked up his letter from Isaac and opened it.

Tommy, December 10, 2001

Man, I just wanted to drop you a line and tell you how sorry I am about how things went down in your club. I've been rethinking a lot of stuff lately.

You're not going to believe this, but I took a trip to hell. I saw Ray-Ray. Do you remember my girl, Valerie? She was also there. They were being tormented like nothing I've ever seen. And, I've seen a lot, man. Whew. I don't know. My head is still messed up behind that whole scene.

Anyway, how is everyone doing on the outside? Was the 9-11 attack as big a shock to you as everyone else? Do you have any family members in New York? Nina's best friend, Elizabeth Underwood, went to New York with her husband to celebrate their tenth wedding anniversary. He was in the tower when it collapsed. She lives in Dayton. If you know her, you might send some flowers or something. I hear she's not doing too well.

I don't want to take up too much of your time. I just wanted to let you know that I'm a better man in prison than I ever was on the street. God has graced me with a second chance and I'm taking it. May the peace of God reign in your life, Isaac

Tommy laughed so hard he had to wipe the tears from his eyes. "Alert the warden! Somebody is selling drugs in prison." Tommy slapped his knee and tried to calm his chuckles. "Whew. I got to have whatever Isaac is taking."

He finally stopped laughing, sat back in his seat, and thought about Elizabeth. Yeah, he knew her. How could he forget the best vocalist he'd ever heard? The only time he'd ever considered giving up his precious Belanté Club was due to the emotions she sparked in him. Five years ago, Elizabeth had auditioned to be the lead singer at his nightclub. Her voice was like warm honey. He still dreamed about the sway of her body, as she bellowed tunes that made him want to close his eyes and float away. Impressed, he called some cats he knew from the music industry, had them listen to her audition tape, and was about to sign her to a contract when she turned Jesus freak on him. Years had passed and he still hadn't been able to get her off his mind.

He'd had countless lovers since the day she walked through his door. He rubbed his goatee with his thumb and index finger. Women couldn't get enough of this Mandingo black brother, and he gave them all the loving they could handle. There was only one woman he couldn't stop thinking about. The one he had never touched because she was married. At least, she had been married. Maybe, just maybe . . .

Lillian Edwards didn't take kindly to able bodies lying in bed all day. "Elizabeth, child, I swear you're going to end up with bed worms if you don't get out of that bed. Adjust your position, or something."

Elizabeth figured the only way to shut her mother up was to sit in the living room. So here she was, in flannel pjs and Kenneth's old terrycloth robe. Her dark brown eyes carried the same vacant expression they had for the past two months, as she put her feet on the couch and hugged her knees to her chest.

"Do you want me to get you anything, honey?" her mom asked.

Elizabeth shook her head. Her shoulder-length hair swished lightly across her deep chocolate face. Elizabeth didn't speak much, and never initiated conversations anymore. Sometimes she would lie in bed real still, staring into space. Drifting away.

"You have got to snap out of this, Elizabeth. Your children need you," her mom told her.

"Don't you think I know that?" Elizabeth wanted to scream at her mother. She wanted to kick, throw something. Anything, but be trapped in this world of despair. Her children were suffering. She wanted to hold them, tell them everything was going to be all right. But how could she when she couldn't even figure out how to wake up without wishing for death?

"Real hard to watch my baby drift away like this," Mrs. Edwards told Nina.

Elizabeth looked at her friend. Well, Nina was not just a friend. Since the day they met at a new members' meeting at The Rock Christian Fellowship, they had been best friends. Five years. Whew, where did the time go? They learned to lean on each other and count on their friendship to get them through tough times. But this was the toughest situation they'd ever faced.

Nina nodded in agreement with Mrs. Edwards. "Real hard."

Tears rolled down Elizabeth's face. Her mother grabbed the Kleenex. "I swear, sometimes I don't think she knows that she's crying." She wiped her daughter's face and kissed her on the forehead. If only forehead kisses made it all better.

Elizabeth ran her hand through her hair, then reached out and touched her mother's hand. "They never gave me a body, Mama. How can I move on if I can't even bury my husband?"

Nina knelt down in front of her friend and whispered, "Elizabeth, would you like to pray? Do you want me to read the Bible to you? That might be comforting, huh?"

Elizabeth lifted her head. She was going to tell Nina what she could do with her Bible readings. For two months, Nina had come to her house toting her Bible, quoting scriptures, talking about the joy of the Lord and His strength. Elizabeth had had enough. She opened her mouth to blast her friend when the doorbell rang.

Elizabeth sunk into the couch and pulled the cover over her body. She wanted to pull it over her head. Better yet, she wanted a pair of earplugs. That way, she wouldn't have to listen to another do-gooder tell her to let Kenneth's memory rest in peace. "Get over his death and move on. Live for the Lord again," as one of her visitors had told her. She wanted to know why they thought she should get over Kenneth's death, when no one had ever produced his body. And why should she live for the Lord? What had He done for her lately?

"I don't want to see anyone else from the church right now," she told her mom, then turned to Nina's disapproving stare. "All they do is judge me. Don't you think I know they're talking behind my back?"

"Elizabeth—"

"I know how they feel, Nina," Elizabeth said. "They think I should get over it. They've told me that I should allow God to take away my pain. Well, I don't know how to do that, and I'm tired of listening to them preach at me."

Nina replied, "All right; you lie down and rest. I'm gonna check on the kids."

Before Nina could stand, Mrs. Edwards walked in the living room with a large bouquet of roses. Two dozen to be exact. "That was the florist. Here, read the card." She handed Elizabeth the card, then placed the roses on the mantel.

"They're from Tommy Brooks," Elizabeth told them after opening the card.

"Tommy Brooks?" Nina rested her chin in the palm of her hand. "Isn't he the owner of the Belanté Club?"

"That's him." Elizabeth presented her friend with a sorta-kinda smile. "I auditioned for him a few years back. I was going to be his lead singer at the club."

"Good thing you found Jesus," Nina joked.

Elizabeth's lips curved downward. She sunk back into the couch and mumbled, "Yeah, good thing."

2

Tommy Brooks had been Elizabeth's life preserver. While everyone in the church tried so hard to help her forget about Kenneth's sudden and untimely removal from her life, Tommy Brooks, Mister Night Club Owner himself, stepped back into her life with the idea of visiting the place she took her last notable breath—Ground Zero. Everything else had just been activity—something for the lungs to do.

Elizabeth, Erin, and Danae gladly rolled with Tommy. It was action, rather than retreat, which she had grown accustomed to these last three months since Kenneth's disappearance.

"Mama, we're going to find Daddy, and then everything will be okay again," Erin informed her mother.

"Okay, baby." Elizabeth said and smiled at her first-born daughter, but her heart wasn't in it.

"No, Mama. Smile at me with your eyes. Like Daddy always liked for you to do."

Elizabeth closed her eyes for a moment. The pain that dwelled behind those lids brought forth tears. How could one human being hold so much water? Surely her well should have run dry by now—but the tears were just like menstrual cycles. They kept flowing no matter how inconvenient or painful. And now, her baby was asking for a real smile. But how could she produce it, when to do what Erin asked, she would have to inform her heart that something just occurred that made her happy? She hadn't known happiness since her husband plunged to his death from the World Trade Center. And now she was going back there, armed with flyers that read: LOST SEPTEMBER 11, 2001. A picture of Kenneth was in the middle with a plea that simply read, "If you see this man, please call Elizabeth Underwood." She gave several telephone numbers and added at the very bottom, HE'S ALL WE HAVE. WE NEED HIM.

Her children were eight and five. Way too young to be without a father. With deep chocolate skin, long hair, and a pencil thin body, Erin looked like Elizabeth. Erin was always grooming herself. Her hair had to be just right, and a mirror was always just to the left of where she sat.

Danae, on the other hand, looked like Kenneth had spit her out. Light-bright, with freckles covering her high cheekbones, Kenneth couldn't have denied Danae if he wanted to. While Erin was constantly in the mirror, Danae was in the refrigerator. Within the past year, Danae had gotten a pouch that didn't look to be leaving anytime soon. Elizabeth didn't care. She loved her children just the way they were. If only she could find a way to show them what she felt in her heart.

Arriving in New York did nothing to cure Elizabeth's smiling-eye problem. They left the car at the hotel and took a cab over to the area of her husband's demise. Walking through Battery Park, Elizabeth viewed the memorials of the firemen and policemen that had been lost before America knew anything about this war against terror.

Their family and friends had done the same thing for them as she came to do for Kenneth. Pictures of these heroic men and women covered each wall. Poems lamenting the sorrows of the Love Jones could be found on the wall of the dead, but not forgotten.

Erin wanted to put Kenneth's picture on the Firemen's Memorial. Elizabeth had to calm her down. "Not here, honey. I'll let you know when you can post your picture."

Erin and Danae were running and jumping. This was the first time she'd noticed their playful motions since she returned from New York three months ago.

"Here, Mommy?" Danae asked, gesturing toward the Policemen's Memorial.

"No, baby. I'll let you know."

Tommy patted Danae on the shoulder before she took off running again. "They miss their father, don't they?"

"They're not the only ones," Elizabeth said as that glaze returned to her eyes. Just like menstrual cramps. She could handle the regularity of her tears, if the pain that accompanied them wasn't so all consuming.

"Here we are, girls." They stood in front of the public viewing area. Thousands of people had already been through this place. They'd posted information on the walls; names, poems, and pleas for help in finding family members. Elizabeth put a piece of tape on the girls' poems and let them post them on the wall. She walked around showing Kenneth's picture to the visitors of one of New York's many wailing walls. "Have you seen this man? Please, can you look again?" And on and on she went.

Tommy grabbed her arm and guided her away from a frightened Mexican woman that she had asked to look at Kenneth's picture four times. "Post one of the pictures right here." He pointed to an empty spot on the wall. "And let's go on to the family memorial area."

Elizabeth started to protest. She wasn't leaving this place until she had talked to every single person there. Her children started pulling on her. "Come on, Mama. We want to see the family area."

The family viewing area was similar to the public one, but more personal. On the back wall were the names of every country that had experienced loss during the 9-11 attack on the World Trade Center. Flowers, flags, and banners were placed throughout. What caught Elizabeth's eye was a poster with a flag on it that read GOD SHED HIS GRACE ON THEE 9-11-01. Elizabeth wanted to find the maker of that poster and ask them how they could see grace or justice in what happened to her family. She wanted to snatch that poster down. God's grace indeed. God must have been caught unaware. He must have been asleep. How else could an attack of this magnitude have occurred? Why else was Kenneth still missing? No body to bury, no face to look upon one last time. Nothing!

Elizabeth picked up Danae. "Here, baby. Put your other poem on this pole. There's an empty spot right here." Elizabeth pointed at the spot and Danae obeyed with a smile. Elizabeth turned to the wall that was littered with pictures of missing or dead loved ones. With tears in her eyes, she lovingly placed her last picture of Kenneth next to one of a smiling lady with pale skin and long flowing auburn hair. Elizabeth never met this lady, but she had a lot in common with her family.

The tears were rolling down her cheeks as she stepped away from the wall of loss and pain. Tommy handed her a handkerchief as they walked out of the family viewing area. He put his arm around her, but Elizabeth moved out of his reach. "I'm okay," she told him as she wiped away the tears.

I'll make it. I'll get through this, she told herself over and over as they walked up the street. She had almost convinced herself of rising suns and shooting stars when she spotted the temporary Red Cross facility just two blocks west of the Trade Center ruins. Spray painted on the wall of this building that used to be some type of fast-food joint were the words ALIVE and DEAD. Next to each word, an arrow pointed in the direction of where the volunteers laid the bodies of countless victims. She had seen this building the last time she was in New York, but it never occurred to her to go inside and look around. Where had Kenneth's body been laid? She took off running toward the building. Tommy picked up Erin and Danae and followed after her.

Elizabeth peered wildly through the window of the temporary Red Cross facility. Her eyes darted back and forth as she yelled, "Where is he? Where is he?"

Tommy put his hand on her shoulder. "He's not in there, Elizabeth. This place hasn't been used in a while."

She turned cold eyes on him. "I don't believe you! You're trying to keep my husband from me."

"Elizabeth, calm down. Kenneth is not here."

"You liar," she spat as she pushed Tommy out of her way. "He's here. You can't keep him from me." She strutted over to the facility and started banging on the door.

Tommy calmly sat the children down on the sidewalk. Just as he told the kids, "Wait right here, everything is going to be all right," Elizabeth started practicing karate on the door.

"Elizabeth, you have got to calm down." He tried to pull her away from the building.

Was he mad? How could she calm down when her husband was being held in this building against his will? "Noooo!" she screamed as she pulled away from Tommy, spouting a profane name at him. Then she said, "You aren't going to get away with this."

"Elizabeth! *You* don't curse!" he told her, as if trying to convince her to get back in character.

"If you touch me again, I'm going to do more than curse your lying behind out," she told him with a soul-piercing glare. She walked back over to the building, cracked her neck like a prizefighter, then did the Bruce Lee thing again. "Open up! I want my husband out of this place right now."

The children huddled close together, crying. Elizabeth went to them. "Don't worry, I'm going to get Daddy out of here." She walked over to the door and started laughing.

"Any minute now, her head is going to start spinning around," Tommy mumbled to himself.

"I'm giving you three seconds to open this door. One, two—"

Tommy turned toward the street and raised his hand as a police car cruised down the street. "Help! I need help!"

The police drove Elizabeth to the hospital. They made sure she was admitted to the floor where the patients played with their lips and ate checkers. For the first week, she didn't remember who or where she was. The next week, as the memories flooded her existence, she cried her eyes out. Her brother, Michael, and best friend, Nina Lewis, prayed by her bedside from morning to night.

One morning, as she opened her swollen eyes, she saw them in prayer and told them, "Stop praying for me. I just want to die."

Michael walked over to her bed. As he looked down on his sister, his eyes filled with tears. "Not on my watch, little sis."

She grabbed her brother's shirt as her tears gushed out again. "Don't you understand, Michael? I can't live without him. I've tried. I . . . I've tr . . . tried."

"Try harder," Nina said from the other side of Elizabeth's hospital bed.

Elizabeth slumped back in her bed. "You don't understand," she cried. "He was everything to me."

Nina softly rubbed her friend's hair. "You're wrong, Elizabeth. Only God is the first and the last. That makes Him everything."

Elizabeth moved away from Nina's gentle touch. She stared at her friend. The short cut of her feathered hair accentuated her hazel eyes and olive skin. Elizabeth always felt lacking around her. Not only was Nina prettier than she, but Nina also trusted and loved God more than she did. Elizabeth lashed out. "Nina, you may be living and breathing the Holy Ghost, but everybody ain't there."

"Elizabeth!" Michael chided her.

"No, Michael. I mean it." She lifted her hands. "Just go. Please, I need to be alone."

Nina and Michael exchanged worried glances. Michael patted Elizabeth on the shoulder. "We're going to the cafeteria to get a bite to eat. Okay?"

"Yeah, yeah. Just go." Elizabeth didn't care how rude she sounded. All they wanted to do was pray and tell her about the goodness and faithfulness of God. She wasn't buying it. Not this time. God hadn't been there for her when she needed Him most, and she wasn't going to sit there and pretend that she was okay with that. She would go to church and do her duty, but she was through trusting in a God that just didn't seem to care about her broken heart.

On the eleventh day of her captivity, while Michael and Nina were in the waiting area communing with God, Tommy paid Elizabeth a visit. He told her that she needed to get back in the game, and he had the perfect solution to her problems. "If you concentrate on getting your singing career off the ground and doing a tour, you won't have time to notice the hours and days that pass while you wait on word of Kenneth."

He had a point. If she must continue to take in air, might as well be doing something productive. "A singing career, huh?" she replied.

"Not just any career, Elizabeth. You will be one of the greatest."

"But all I know is gospel."

"Hey," Tommy said with a smile. "Move over Yolanda Adams and Cece Winans, here comes Elizabeth Underwood."

"But where will we get the money to fund a CD?"

"Don't worry about anything but getting out of this place. I'll sell my nightclub. That ought to provide us enough to get started."

Elizabeth smiled. "You'd do that for me?"

"No, Elizabeth. Not just for you, but for me too. I'm tired of the nightlife. I think I'm ready to come back to church." Tommy really hoped he meant everything he was saying; he was really going to try.

Elizabeth wanted to tell Tommy not to put all his eggs in one basket. Because if God didn't come through for him, he would end up just as sad and disillusioned as she was. But she wouldn't say that to him. She wouldn't tell anyone that her faith and trust in the Almighty had been shattered. She would cover her funk of depression with Mac make-up, St. Johns dresses, and this singing career that Tommy promised. "When do we get started?"

"I don't know," he said, as he rubbed his goatee with his thumb and index finger. "Do you think we should ask your brother to pray for us, so that we handle all this the way God would want us to?" Tommy couldn't believe those words were coming out of his mouth. He wasn't even sure that he trusted God, but he knew that he wanted to be with Elizabeth. Tommy had no doubt that he would be able to convince Elizabeth to forget about Kenneth and marry him, so for that reason, he was willing to try this God thing.

Elizabeth chewed on her lower lip as she thought about that. God hadn't been interested in what she wanted. Why should she give a fig what His Holiness preferred? Wasn't it enough that she would sing gospel rather than secular music? But then again, she might need Michael to talk her doctor into letting her out of this funny farm. She painted a smile on her face. "I think that's a great idea. Yes, let's ask Michael to pray for us."

In the years to come, Elizabeth would perfect the art of outward smiles and inward death. The masquerade she'd perform would devastate a multitude of believers.

3

Two and a half years later

On the last leg of her tour, Elizabeth sat in one
of her favorite Los Angeles restaurants waiting
on Tommy to arrive. He had promised to treat
her to lunch. While she waited, she continued to
work on a song that had been playing in her head
for months.

Tommy rushed over to her table. "I've got
good news!" he told her in his disgustingly good-
natured fashion.

Elizabeth raised a hand to silence him. "Don't
tell me. I don't want anything to take away this
bad mood I'm in."

He grabbed the paper she had been writing
on. "What's this?"

"Just a song I'm toying with."

"May I?"

"You've got it in your hand. You might as well
go on and read it."

He looked down at the paper and tried to imagine Elizabeth singing as he read aloud:

You've been in this thing awhile; your desire has waned away. You cover up with plastic smiles. Offering up to God a phony praise. The masquerade is just a game we play, while our lives are wasting away. No longer trusting in the Lord, no. Taking for granted His amazing grace. For we don't recognize the deceit, placed upon us by the enemy. Get all dressed up to play charades. Welcome to the masquerade.

Sunday morning, time to let the games begin. Praise the Lord, girl, how ya doing? Well I'm just blessed girl, how've you been?

What an empty exchange, offered from a heart that's grown so very cold. I can't tell you that I'm hurting, I'm broken, and I'm empty—'cause I cannot let the truth be told.

Tommy slowly put the paper down and looked at Elizabeth. "I'm not finished yet, but what do you think so far?" "You make a mockery of the church with this song.

That's what I think." She shrugged. "It's how I feel. Why shouldn't I tell the truth?"

"Elizabeth, honey. You've got to snap out of this." He sat across from her and lifted a hand to signal the waitress.

"Or better yet, why don't you tell the world to take the month of September off the calendar?" It was the ninth of August. Almost three years had gone by since that terrorist group had taken Kenneth's love from her. Since then, America had experienced Anthrax, the search for bin Laden, and the war with Iraq. None of it had brought her pain or peace. How could she snap out of it?

The waitress arrived with two glasses of ice water. As she set the water down, her eyes widened. "Hey, aren't you Elizabeth Underwood?"

"Yeah, that's me," Elizabeth told her without an ounce of enthusiasm.

"Oh, my God, oh, my God!" the woman shrieked. "I have all your CDs. Wait, let me get it." She set her pad and pen on the table. Her micro braids swung back and forth as she ran out of the restaurant.

"All?" Elizabeth raised a questioning brow as she took a sip of her water. "I only have one CD for God's sakes."

"Elizabeth, the girl is excited." Tommy threw up his hands in agitation. "Will you allow her that, please?"

Elizabeth set her glass down. "The *girl* needs to get some more lemon for my water or do I have to get up and do it myself?"

Tommy rolled his eyes.

Elizabeth did the sista-sista neck move and sucked her teeth. "Like I care that you have an attitude. It's your job to make sure that I have everything I need."

Tommy's hands tightened into fists as he laid them on the table. "What don't you have, Elizabeth?"

She put her water glass in his face. "Lemon."

The waitress rushed back in with 'God's Got It' clutched in her hands. "Will you autograph it for me?" she asked, while shoving the CD in Elizabeth's face. Elizabeth took the CD. "Autograph it to your number-one fan."

"While she's autographing your CD, can you please get Mrs. Underwood some more lemons?"

"Coming right up. Not a problem," the waitress replied.

Elizabeth signed the CD as the waitress ran to the kitchen, brought back a bowl full of lemons and sat them on the table. "Thanks for all your support," Elizabeth said.

"Are you kidding?" The waitress beamed down on Elizabeth. "Thank you, Mrs. Underwood, for all the joy you brought back into my life. I can't begin to tell you how much your music has blessed me. I was at a really low point in my life when I heard you sing about the joy of the Lord." Tears welled up in the woman's brown eyes, as she touched her heart. "That song gave me hope."

Mmph, the only thing that song ever gave me was royalties. "I'm glad it helped you. Now, do you think we can get our menus? I'm kind of hungry."

"Oh my God." Her hand went to her mouth. "I'm so sorry, Mrs. Underwood. Right away." She grabbed some menus, came back to the table, and took their orders. She began to walk away, then turned back. "Mrs. Underwood, I hope you don't mind, but I also wanted to tell you how sorry I am about what happened to your husband."

Elizabeth bowed her head, ready for a good cry. Maybe her number one fan could go and get her some Kleenex. The woman kept talking.

"It really blessed my soul to see you serving the Lord in spite of your pain."

Elizabeth looked at the woman. She wanted to tell her that she was weary and just about ready to give up. Instead, she flashed her famous smile and said, "Thank you."

When she was gone, Tommy covered Elizabeth's hand with his own. "See. All of America knows who you are."

God had blessed her singing career. There was no doubt about that. Elizabeth sang to thousands. Every time she opened her mouth, people gave their lives to the Lord. Some nights she just wanted to cry out to the crowd and beg them to help her. On those nights, Elizabeth would have much preferred that God mend her heart and leave the soul winning to someone more qualified. Yes, God had gifted her with a great ministry; still, she felt as if she was on a slow ride to hell.

Tommy caressed Elizabeth's hand. "Honey, come on. It's been long enough. Can't you let him go? Can you find room in your heart for someone else?"

Elizabeth sneered. "Someone else?"

"For me, Elizabeth. Me."

Whoever said 'there's no free lunch' must have dined with Tommy Brooks. She looked at her manager, her friend. She had nothing to give him or anyone else. She thought he knew that. Had she somehow given him false hope? "Tommy, I—"

He raised his hand. "I know you don't love me. But I—I'm sure I love you enough for the both of us. You're everything I've ever wanted. You're what I need, Elizabeth."

The waitress couldn't have picked a better time to bring Elizabeth's turkey sandwich that she'd ordered before Tommy arrived. She picked it up and stuffed her mouth.

Tommy continued, "I would be good for you, honey. I'd help you forget."

But I don't want to forget, she said inwardly. She put her sandwich down and wiped her mouth. "The memories I have of Kenneth keep me alive."

He brought her hand to his mouth and kissed her fingers. "Oh, baby, your life could be so much more. Let me in. Let me love you."

Her eyes scanned the *GQ* physique of Tommy. Mocha man had it going on, with his smooth silky skin, thick eyebrows, goatee, and that washboard belly was something to see. Elizabeth had worked out with Tommy a few times at the gym and was rewarded for her diligence with a view of his abs. Those muscle-shirts revealed everything.

The man was no blue-light special, that's for sure. Yet, she could not give him her heart. Another already possessed it. "So, what's this good news you have?"

"Elizabeth, don't do this. Don't change the subject. I need an answer from you."

She wiped her hands and mouth before telling him, "I can't give you an answer right now. At least not one that you would be happy with."

Tommy rubbed her arm. "Will you at least think about what I have said today?"

She gave up a weak smile. "I promise I will think about it. Now, what's this good news?"

"The limo is waiting. Our plane leaves in thirty minutes. We've got to get moving."

"I thought we were staying in Los Angeles tonight?"

"I decided that you need to rest, so I booked us on a flight home. We're going back to Atlanta, baby."

She looked straight through him. "The only time you want me to rest is when you've got something else planned for me. So spit it out. What's really going on?"

Tommy smiled sheepishly. "I'll tell you all about it once we're on the plane, okay?"

Elizabeth grabbed her purse and walked out of the restaurant as Tommy paid the bill. On their way to the airport Tommy tried to make small talk, but mostly there was dead air. Once seated on the airplane, Elizabeth turned to Tommy. "Okay, what's this big surprise?"

Tommy smiled. "I'm glad you used the word 'big'—because it's the only way to describe this." He took a deep breath, hesitated briefly, then told her, "You've been asked to perform your hit single "In Your Arms" in New York during the 9-11 ceremony this year."

Elizabeth's mouth hung open.

Tommy mistook her expression for happiness and said, "I know, baby. Isn't it wonderful?"

Even though Elizabeth didn't open her Bible much these days she knew that the book of Proverbs said something about a soft answer turning away wrath; but she wasn't hardly trying to be nice right now, and she sure didn't want to keep the peace. "Are you drunk?"

"No, why would you ask me a thing like that?" He quickly looked around to make sure no one else heard her.

"Maybe I'm crazy, but I thought, that as my manager, you would know that New York is the last place I want to be next month. And to make matters worse, I hate that song. I don't ever want to sing it again."

"Why don't you want to sing the very song that will win a Grammy for you?"

Elizabeth's hands moved in the air in complete frustration. "I don't want a Grammy, Tommy. I'm a gospel singer. I should never have allowed that song on my CD in the first place."

"Come on, Liz—"

"Don't call me that," Elizabeth snapped. "Only my *husband* called me Liz."

He held up his hand to surrender. "Look, *Elizabeth*. New York wants you, and 'In Your Arms' is hot on the charts right now. We should be there. The world will be watching this event."

When would he ever get it? "I do not want to go to New York, and I do not want to sing that *secular song*."

Tommy smirked at her. "Don't get spiritual on me now, sweetie. You didn't seem all that interested in 'coming out from among them' when you co-wrote the song."

She stared out the window. The clouds appeared light and fluffy, pillowy soft. She wished she could jump out of the window and land on one. She'd ride it all the way back to Jesus and beg Him for a second chance. "It was not meant to be a secular song, but you let the radio stations think whatever they wanted. You let them do whatever they wanted with my song."

Tommy rolled his eyes and let out an agitated sigh. "The bottom line is you're under contract with New Destiny Music and with me. They like the idea of the show and so do I. So, baby, you might as well put those morals of yours in a bag and use 'em at a later date. You're doing this show!"

She kept looking out the window. *Lord Jesus, why don't you just take me now?*

"I don't see what the big deal is anyway. Your last single is being played in nightclubs all over the world."

She turned to face him. "That was *your* idea. You told me not to use the name of Jesus in that song, and look what it got me."

He smiled like the cat that swallowed the canary. She could almost see it between his teeth, or was that a reflection of herself?

His words dripped with venom as he asked, "Did you think you could cross over without paying the price?"

Elizabeth looked right into his eyes. She had almost forgotten everything she had learned at The Rock, but now she knew. This battle was not between her and Tommy. Satan was after her. Her hands went to her face, her eyes opened in horror, and before she knew it, she was screaming. "You can't have my soul!"

Tommy laughed, "I don't want your soul, baby. I just want you to do this show, okay?"

The plane landed smoothly in Atlanta, but Elizabeth didn't notice. Passengers moved off the plane. Elizabeth stayed in her seat. *I have sold out*, she thought. Tommy pulled at her sleeve to get her attention. She looked up at him, wanting desperately to blame him. But the truth was, her life was in her own hands, and she would pay dearly for every decision she made.

4

He walked through the foyer of the house and looked out of the window. A lady and two small children stood on the front stoop. He opened his mouth and said, "You don't live here anymore. I told you that."

She gave him a questioning glare, then looked at the key in her hand. "You said you were moving in on Monday."

He hunched his shoulders. "The locksmith was available today."

He watched her ball her fist. She was fuming. And in his mind's eye, as he watched this scene evolve in his head, he thought, *This must be my house, but who is this angry woman?*

"Oooh, you better open this door!" the angry woman spat.

"Leave my children here and go find yourself a place to stay."

The woman bellowed, "You think you can just put me out of my own house, huh?" The brick sailed through the front window and landed on the foyer floor.

He opened the front door and menacingly moved toward the woman.

The little girls screamed, "Daddy! Daddy!"

He ran past them as the mad lady picked up her second brick.

"You lunatic! Only a fool destroys her own property."

She shook the brick in her hand. "I don't live here anymore, remember?" She reared back, ready to send another brick flying through the window.

He grabbed her arm and snatched the brick out of her hand. "You are the most selfish woman I have ever met. God, I can't stand the sight of you!" He moved back, trying to put some distance between them.

Only weak men beat their women. Yeah, maybe so, but he still wanted to smack the taste out of her mouth.

The fury in his eyes blinded his vision. He couldn't see his wife's face. If he could get a glimpse of her face, maybe he could grab her throat. Then he remembered a vow he made as a kid. He was never going to cheat or beat on his wife. He had already broken one of his vows by cheating on her, and now he was about to break the second vow. Instead, he turned and walked away.

"Don't you walk away from me." She strutted up to him and put her finger in his face. "I bet you feel like a big man today, don't you? Put your wife and defenseless kids on the street with no place to go."

"Get out of my face."

She grabbed his arm as he tried to move away from her. She balled her fist and busted him in the mouth. His daughters were crying as he stepped back and raised his fist to retaliate.

"Nooo!" he screamed as he jolted from his sleep. Sweat drizzled down his face as his heartbeat quickened. He lay in bed, reeling in the shock from the subconscious ordeal. Once he calmed down, he put his hands under his head. "Mmh, I have a wife," he mused. "A very unhappy wife."

5

By the time Tommy dropped Elizabeth at home, she had calmed her wrath. He was, after all, a good man. He had been there for her and helped her through some really painful times. He was a good friend.

"You know," Tommy began as he opened Elizabeth's door and handed her back her keys. "I could stay here tonight."

She softly touched his cheek. "Tommy, you know that is out of the question."

He leaned into her and placed a simple kiss on her lips. "Baby, I'm what you need. Let me into your heart."

She really wished she could. But she had been carrying Kenneth around in her heart for so long, she didn't know how to make room for anyone else. She opened her mouth to speak, but a lump caught in her throat.

Tommy held up his hand. "You don't have to answer me now." He dug in his pocket and pulled out a small box. "If you ever decide that you want a real man in your bed, rather than a ghost, let me know."

He turned and walked out. Elizabeth opened the box, stunned to find a three-carat, princess-cut diamond ring. "He would have bought a platinum band. Dag, he thought of everything," she said as she covered her mouth. She put the ring on the glass-top coffee table, sank into the soft cushions of her love seat, and gazed up at the life-size picture of Kenneth that hung over the fireplace. Tears flowed down her face as she turned from Kenneth's picture to Tommy's ring. Her hands trembled as she looked at the ring that still held a place of honor on her left hand.

"I can't deal with this," she said as memories of Kenneth swelled in her mind.

The children were in Ohio with her mother so she wouldn't have them to distract her. Sometimes, she longed to have her children with her, but her schedule was grueling. Three cities every week was really beginning to wear on her. Pursuing her dreams wasn't all caviar parties and limo rides. It was work.

Elizabeth kicked off her shoes, undressed and headed toward the master bath. As her bare feet touched the cold ceramic floor, she shivered. She adjusted the thermostat to heat the floor tile.

Hot, steamy water in her Jacuzzi would soothe her. As the water ran, she leaned against one of the Grecian columns that stood bold and tall on either side of the Jacuzzi. The sandy brown walls complimented the taupe columns and tile surrounding the tub. She thought the combination would give this room a feeling of warmth. But it was cold in here, cold everywhere she went. She lit a few candles around the tub, inhaled the vanilla scent that fragranced her bathroom, turned the lights down, and unintentionally created a sexy and alluring atmosphere. She sighed as she got into her Jacuzzi alone.

Relaxing her head on the air pillow, she allowed herself to remember. As the bubbles swirled, she was swept into the world where she lived, rather than the one in which she breathed. Elizabeth was enjoying breakfast in bed, prepared by Kenneth, as he sat with her asking, *"So what's on your agenda today? I was hoping I could hang out with you."*

She choked. Kenneth hit her on the back a few times before the bacon dislodged from her throat. "You want to spend the day with me?"

Kenneth rubbed her back. "Not just today, baby. Tomorrow, next week, next month, next year. Ah heck, let's just spend the rest of our lives together and call it quits when we're so old and decrepit that no one else will want us. What do you say?"

Elizabeth pulled herself away from the painful memory of promises too sweet, too endearing to be real. They wouldn't spend their lives together. They wouldn't grow old together. She had believed every word he told her back then, but now knew it to be nothing more than lies. How could he guarantee her something he had no control over?

"Baby, I'm going to run back to you," he had told her the last time she saw him.

But he didn't run back to her. He would never again run to anyone. "Why?" Tonight, she would face reality. Kenneth was dead. That's the only reason he hadn't come home. Her fingers gripped the edge of the Jacuzzi. She rocked her head from side to side and cried. "How am I supposed to live without him? I can't go on like this."

Once, she thought she had it all. An MBA, a husband who was the CEO of his own business, two beautiful little girls, and love. At times, their love overflowed. It rocked her world, consumed her. She raked her hands through her hair. "What's the use of dwelling on the past?" She leaned back against the tub and cried. Tears and sadness had become her friends. She woke up with pain and went to bed with sorrow.

She was almost a prune by the time she pulled her weary body out of the tub, but she had gotten a good cry. Still, what was she going to do about her predicament? She dried herself off, put on Kenneth's old terrycloth robe, and walked into the kitchen. She poured some grape juice into a glass and walked back into the living room where she again stared at the big rock that Tommy had given her. It was much bigger than the one Kenneth gave her. And, as an added bonus, Tommy was alive. Elizabeth picked up the ring and escorted it to her bedroom. Tonight she would lie alone in her four-poster king-size bed. She would sink into the pillow-top mattress, close her red-rimmed eyes, and dream of the only man she'd ever loved. But tomorrow, something other than dreams would fill her bed.

6

He got out of the bed and limped over to the mirror. He looked at the left side of his face. Deep and jagged scars ran from his ear lobe to the cleft of his chin. Old news to him, but frighteningly new to everyone who looked at him for the first time. This morning, he couldn't dismiss his scars. What would his wife think of his face? Would she see him as a monster? Would his children run at the sight of him?

What was her name? He already knew she was an angry woman. What were his children like? Does that angry woman beat on my children? "Oh, God, please help me remember. If my children are in danger, I've got to get to them." He looked around his meager surroundings. Where would he put two children and a wife? He was living in a small studio. The bedroom, kitchen, and living area were one room. A tattered curtain separated the bathroom.

He didn't know what to do. His mind was so jumbled. Well, not really jumbled, it was . . . well, blank. All he knew was two years ago, when he awoke in a hospital bed, his face was bandaged and his body in a cast. The nurse told him that he had been in the World Trade Center when it crashed to the ground. The doctor promised that after a year of physical therapy, he would walk again. No one could tell him why he couldn't remember who he was, or when he would regain his memory. They called it amnesia. He called it prison. His whole life was locked up inside his head. Since his mind didn't seem to be getting an early release, he decided to make the best of his situation. As soon as his bandages were taken off, he asked his nurse to bring him a Bible.

He devoured it. He couldn't explain it, but somehow, reading the Word of God helped him to not feel so lost. How could he be alone when he had Matthew, Mark, Luke, and John to keep him company? Some days, King David or King Solomon came for a visit. Other days, he sat down for a chat with Apostle Paul. Jesus became his center. Somehow, he filled the hole that had been left vacant in his life with the Word of God.

He took Jesus to physical therapy with him. His nurse always had a question for him about the things he'd read. One day, Debra Minion asked, "Are you going to pick a name for yourself, or do you like being called John Doe?"

"Mmh, I really hadn't thought about it. But if I were going to pick my own name, I think I'd go with Andrew."

Debra crinkled her small nose. "Out of all the names in the world, why would you pick Andrew?"

"In the Bible, there's a story about Jesus using two fish and five small loaves of bread to feed about five thousand people. Andrew was the one who spotted the little boy who carried the meal for five thousand and didn't even know it." He shrugged. "I don't know. There's just something about Andrew helping out during desperate times that caught my attention. Some of those people were probably lost or torn away from their family."

Debra lifted him out of his wheelchair. "You read that Bible a lot, don't you?"

He grabbed hold of the walking bars and stretched his legs. Pain etched on his face as he told her, "It gives me comfort."

She bent down and positioned his feet. Her long blond hair hung close to the ground. "Andrew, would you pray for me?"

He took a labored step, then another. Stopped. Sweat was dripping from his forehead. He was breathing hard when he asked, "Wh—what do you need prayer for?"

"My husband and I have been trying to have a baby for twelve years. We've tried everything," she told him as a lone tear rolled down her oval shaped face. "We've spent all our money on doctors. We're in debt up to our eyeballs, with two miscarriages, but no baby to show for all we've been through."

He put her hand in his and gently squeezed. "I'll pray for you."

A couple of months later, Debra came into his hospital room. The grin on her face spanned from Mississippi to Ohio. She told him that she was pregnant, and that she and her husband knew this miracle occurred because of him and him alone. Her husband wanted to meet him and thank him personally.

He actually didn't know if he wanted to meet the man who thought he was responsible for his wife's pregnancy. "Please tell your husband that the thanks belong to God. All I did was pray."

"Oh, don't be modest. You were sent straight from God."

Another couple of months passed and the hospital staff informed him that they had run out of funding for the victims of 9-11. He understood. After all, he had been in the hospital for nine months. "Oh, Andrew," Nurse Debra said with a sigh during one of their sessions. "If only you could remember who you are. Your family might have enough money to pay for your physical therapy."

He shrugged. The entire hospital staff called him Andrew now. So, he too, began to think of it as his name. "I will pray about it. God will show me where I am to go. Maybe He will have mercy on me today and lift the cloud from my mind."

Debra smiled. "God has already shown me where you are to go."

He took his hands off the rails and sat down in his wheelchair. "And where is that?"

"I have a mother-in-law cottage behind my house. You could live there, and my husband and I could continue your physical therapy. You will walk again, Andrew. I promise you that."

"But I have no way of repaying you."

"God has already paid us," she told him while patting her stomach.

He had moved into the Minion's mother-in-law cottage a year and a half ago. Day by day, his body began to recover. He walked with a limp and a cane—but he walked. His face was scarred, but he reminded himself often that his eyes had not been affected, so he could see. And now, to-day, he had a glimpse of his family.

He hobbled outside. He needed to share this news with someone. Debra was in the backyard standing at the barbecue pit. Brad and little Brad, the miracle baby, were lying on the lawn chair waiting on the food.

Debra smiled and waved him over. The Minions thought of him as some kind of lucky charm. They wouldn't take rent from him for the cottage. Debra told him that since he moved in, Brad had received two promotions on his job. Their bills were all paid, and they hadn't had an argument over money in the last year. So, free rent was just their way of blessing him for blessing them. He tried to explain that he wasn't the blessing giver, that it was God.

Debra just smiled and said, "Ah, yes, but God gives His blessings to the people around you."

He smiled back at his hostess as he walked over to the pit, but his mind danced over a wicked memory of another barbecue he attended.

His wife was serving him a plate in their backyard. She had an anything-you-want-honey expression on her face. He thought things might turn around for them. Then he looked at his plate. Charred pieces of pants and suit jackets that looked like some of the things he owned were on the plate. "What's this?" he asked, dumbfounded.

"Oh, I'm sorry, you need a fork." She pulled a plastic fork out of the box and put it in front of his plate. *"Eat up,"* she told him.

With a horrified look on his face, he declared, "She burned my clothes! Oh, my God! She actually burned my clothes!"

Debra put the lid back over the steaks and hamburgers and turned to Andrew. "Who burned your clothes?"

Startled, he looked up at Debra. "Huh?"

"Your clothes. Who burned them?"

"Oh nobody. Nothing, don't worry about it." He turned and walked back to his little house. As he opened the door, he told himself, "I'm married to Satan."

7

Determined not to sleep another night with only dreams to keep her company, Elizabeth knocked on Tommy's door. She waited for him with a smile, and his ring on the third finger of her left hand. What was a woman to do? Kenneth was out of the picture. Doggonit, she needed to know what it felt like to be held again. She had trusted God with her and Kenneth's life. So much for trust. What did it ever get her? A dead husband and two fatherless children, that's what.

Knock, knock. "Come on, Tommy. What's taking you so long?"

Tommy opened the door. He quickly tightened the belt on his oriental silk robe. His eyes darted back and forth. "Elizabeth, what are you doing here?" He held the door close to him as he knuckled down on the doorknob.

She studied him for a moment. *He probably doesn't have anything on under that robe. How sexy.* "I need to talk to you. Why are you hugging that door so close?" She pushed him out of the way and barged in. In the living room, standing in front of him, she lifted her left hand so he could see his ring on her finger. "Well, say something," she demanded.

He turned away from her gaze, put his head in his hands and shook it. "I really wished you had called before you came over."

"Why?" she asked as she scrunched her eyebrows. "I'm here now and that's all that should matter. I don't want to spend the night alone, Tommy. I want to stay here with you."

He sat down on his sofa and put his head in his hands. "I really wish you had called first."

Elizabeth knelt down on the floor next to him. "Tommy? I thought this was what you wanted. You've been asking me to marry you for over a year. What's wrong?"

Tommy held Elizabeth's face in his hands. Sorrow filled his eyes. "I love you, Elizabeth. Please believe me."

"I do believe you, Tommy. What's wrong?"

A sultry voice from the back room of Tommy's apartment called, "Come back to bed, baby. How long are you going to keep me waiting?"

Elizabeth's mouth fell open. "You've got a woman here?" She stood up to go to Tommy's bedroom and check things out as she thought, *that woman better have a cold and be hoarse right about now; cause she sounds like . . .*

She threw open the bedroom door and burst in the room like Miami Vice. Mmph, mmph, mmph, she couldn't get a break. In Tommy's bed was some Albino-looking brother, posing as if he were waiting for the clickety-click from one of Hugh Hefner's cameramen. She was going to be sick. "You have got to be kidding me!" *If this ain't something straight out of an E. Lynn Harris novel.*

She strutted into the room yelling, "Get your nasty butt out of this bed, and get out of here!"

He/she put his hands on his hips. "I don't know who you think you're talking to, Miss Thang." He snapped his fingers. "But I will bust your head if you don't get out of my face."

She pulled off her earrings, and kicked off her shoes. Elizabeth couldn't believe that she was getting ready to go toe to toe over a man she wasn't even sure she was in love with. But Tommy had asked her to marry him, so as far as she was concerned, he was her man; and nobody was sleeping with him but her. Putting up her fists and poising herself for a fight, Elizabeth said, "Come on wit' it. Bring it on."

"Oh, you don't want none of me." He had that sista-sista head bob down pat.

"Now that's where you're wrong." She picked up the glass ashtray from the dresser. *That Negro told me he stopped smoking*, she thought as she emptied the ashes on boy-toy's head.

She leaped on him and hit him with the ashtray again. He was about to swing on Elizabeth when Tommy grabbed his arm. "Nigel, man, you need to go."

"Let my arm go, Tommy. You just gon' let her hit on me like this?"

Tommy grabbed Elizabeth and tried to pull her off Nigel. She had a firm grip on Nigel's locks. "Let go, Elizabeth."

"No!" She pulled harder. She'd scalp him if she could.

"Man, you better get her off me!" Nigel screamed.

Tommy grabbed Elizabeth's fingers, uncurled them from around Nigel's hair and pushed her behind him. "I'll see you later, Nigel."

Nigel poked out his lower lip and huffed, "What do you mean, *you'll see me later*? Miss Thang over there is the one interrupting us."

Tommy picked Nigel's shirt off the floor. "Like I said, you need to go."

Elizabeth stood behind Tommy mimicking him. "Yeah, like he said, you need to go."

"I don't take orders from you!" Nigel told her, then looked back at Tommy and sneered, "Unlike some people."

She clenched her fist and got in her wolf-ticket stance. "Boy, I will bust you—"

"Elizabeth! Let me take care of this, then I will explain everything. Okay?"

She hit Tommy in his back. "What kind of mess is this? How are you going to explain asking me to marry you when you know you like boys?" She needed this mess like she needed a hole in her head.

"I got ya boy," Nigel told her while zipping his pants.

Elizabeth pointed at him. "You need to get your little confused behind out of here and let me and this man handle our business."

Nigel twisted out, opened the front door, then looked back at Elizabeth with a sneer. "That's all right. You might control the purse strings, but you better believe I control the man. He'll be back." Nigel slammed the door behind him.

Elizabeth looked at her manager, her friend. She looked at the ring that glistened on her left hand. How could she know him so well, and yet, not know him at all? "So is that it, Tommy? You only wanted to marry me because I control the purse strings?"

He turned toward her, but could not make eye contact. "No, baby, never that. I love you. I've never lied about that."

She smacked him. "You don't love me." She pounded at his chest with her fists.

When she started crying and slid to the floor, he sat down next to her and just held her. "I'm sorry. I'm really sorry."

"How could you do this to me?" She rocked back and forth, tears pouring from her confused eyes. "You don't look gay. How can you be gay?"

"I'm not gay," he told her as he brushed hair out of her face.

Elizabeth pulled herself out of Tommy's arms and looked at him with disgust. "If you're not gay, explain *Nigel*."

"Elizabeth, I love women. The majority of the time I want to be with women. I want to be with you." He reached for her, but she pulled away again. "There are occasions when I need something . . . different." He shrugged.

"Something *different*," she spat. "Negro, you were with a man! Don't you have any shame? Do you listen to the pastor's sermons?"

"Oh, so did you come over here to have tea and shoot the fat? Where is your shame? What do you think the pastor would say about you coming over here to sleep with me tonight?" He stood and paced the room. "Look, I'm sorry. Just don't mention the church and what it frowns on to me. Okay?"

She stood. "Why not, Tommy? Don't you attend church every Sunday? Didn't you tell me you were turning your life over to the Lord when you sold your nightclub?"

He grabbed her shoulders. "Look, Elizabeth. The church is the reason I'm the way I am."

"Oh, no. Don't you blame the church. They teach against this mess."

Tommy snarled, "Well, they must've forgot to teach the deacon who raped me when I was nine years old."

Elizabeth's hands covered her mouth. She shook her head as she moved away from Tommy. "No," was all she could mumble.

He thought he had forgotten. Thought he would never conjure up that memory, but here it was again, like a bad dream. Always turning up, always haunting him. Tommy closed his eyes tight. But as he spilled his guts to Elizabeth, he couldn't stop himself from becoming that nine-year old helpless little boy again.

Sitting on his mother's porch, head hanging down, basketball in his hand. "Mama, do I have to go?"

"Boy, what's wrong with you? You think Deacon Grid-ley don't have more important things to do besides spend time with you?"

"I still don't want to go." He walked down the driveway, kicking rocks and cursing his mother. He contemplated running to the park. He wanted to shoot hoops; he didn't need anybody to play with. Yeah, that's what he'd do. Why should he wait on fat ol' Deacon Gridley to come and hug all on him? The man sweated like a pig. Every time he hugged him, Tommy would have to wipe Greasy Gridley's sweat off his cheeks and arms. He started walking toward the park and Greasy Gridley pulled his 1969 leaning-to-the-left Oldsmobile in the driveway.

Grinning, he told Tommy to get in. Why anybody with two rotten front teeth would grin so much, Tommy didn't know. He just wished Greasy would close his mouth, back out of his driveway, and never come this way again.

His mother was in the doorway. "Go on, boy," she shoed him with a wave of her hand. "Deacon Gridley don't have all day to wait on your narrow behind."

Tommy got in on the passenger side and hugged the car door to his side. Greasy's fat sweat-laden hands clutched the steering wheel. Two days ago when Greasy took him to a base-

ball game those fat hands had rubbed his shoul-
der. Tommy didn't like how that felt. But most
of all, he just didn't like Greasy Gridley. Why his
mother thought he needed some grown man he
knew nothing about to pal around with him was
beyond understanding.

They pulled up in Greasy's driveway. Tommy
didn't know why, but he started sweating. "I
thought we were going somewhere. Why are we
at your house?"

Greasy smiled. "I've got something to show
you inside." He got out of his car smiling as he
walked up the drive. "Come on, boy," he said,
when Tommy hadn't budged.

Tommy silently prayed, "God, please don't let
this man put his hands on me."

But God must not have been listening. The
minute Tommy got out of the car and walked
into the house, Greasy was squeezing his shoul-
der. "I'll be right back." Tommy ran to the bath-
room, locked himself in, then pulled the switch-
blade out of his pocket. "Praying didn't work. I
wonder if slashing will do the trick." He cut the
knife back and forth in the air a few times, then
put it back in his pocket.

He stepped out of the bathroom. Greasy said
the surprise was in the den. Tommy walked to
the den holding his back pocket. They sat down

on the sofa. Hot dogs and popcorn were on the coffee table. Greasy pointed to the TV. "Baseball. We can watch it here."

"Why we gotta watch the game on your TV? Why can't we drive to the game like before?"

"I didn't want to be bothered with all those people. I thought we could just relax here." The words were innocent enough, but the hand that touched his thigh and lingered was not.

Tommy jumped up. "Don't put your sweaty hands on me no more." He started reaching for his switchblade.

Greasy threw his hands up in surrender. "Hey, little man, be cool. I didn't mean no harm. Come on and sit back down." He patted the sofa. "Let's watch the game."

Tommy hesitated. He wanted to slit this sucka's throat just on GP, but his mama would start tripping again; Raving about how he was a juvenile delinquent and was going to end up just like his daddy. Sometimes, he wanted to ask his mother, if his daddy was so bad, and she was so good, why in the world did she lie down with him?

He didn't want to think about all the drama with his mama right now. So he forgot about his knife and sat back down. He liked baseball, but Greasy grabbed Tommy and hugged him tight. Real up close and personal.

"Let me go."

"I just want to hold you for a minute."

Tommy tried to reach for his blade but couldn't move his arms. "Please let me go." Tears rolled down his face.

"Don't be so fidgety, I'm going to let you go. I've got something to show you first."

Tommy tried to push Greasy off of him. When the weight of the man wouldn't budge, Tommy screamed. He screamed several times that afternoon.

Tommy looked away from Elizabeth as he finished his story. "He told my mother that he wanted to help us. A single woman couldn't possibly raise a boy up to be a man without some help." He made a disgusted grunt. "He took me to a couple baseball games, and to the YMCA to play basketball." He shook his head. Tears ran down his face as he turned back to Elizabeth. "I never told anybody this story before. But you need to remember this, Elizabeth, it was the deacon of my church who took me to his house and showed me what disgusting old men do to innocent little boys. So yes, I did say that I was turning my life over to the Lord, and I've been trying. But how can you blame me for having certain urges when the church introduced them to me?"

"Tommy, you still had a choice. You don't have to become a part of what was done to you."

He shrugged. "I don't know. Maybe we do what we were born to do."

Elizabeth walked over to her friend. The tears on her face were no longer for herself, but for the child that had been tainted. For the pain and the shame Tommy had carried all these years. She hugged him and allowed him to cry on her shoulder, as she thought about injustice and broken spirits. She thought about Kenneth and how he was taken away from her. She shook her head in disgust. God should have protected them from it all. Reality struck her like an overdue bill.

"I guess the great Watchman in the sky failed to look after you too," she told Tommy as her tears dropped onto his lap.

At home, Elizabeth sat on the floor in the middle of her living room. She lived in the Sandstone development with Kelly Price and other well-known celebrities. That fact had always made her proud. Tonight, she didn't care. Tommy followed her home and asked to come in, but she refused. He finally gave up and went back across town to his apartment. Elizabeth felt numb and sick to her stomach at the same time. The only thing that comforted her was the silence, the fact that she was all alone in this big house; no one talking to her, no one asking her questions.

Despite herself, she laughed at the irony of it all. The quietness and loneliness of this place was the reason she decided to marry Tommy, but he was too confused for her. So now she longed for silence once again.

"Oh, Kenneth, why'd you have to leave me?"

She could see Kenneth lying in bed with her. Telling her how much he loved and needed her.

"Not just today, baby. Tomorrow, next week, next month, next year. Ah heck, let's just spend the rest of our lives together, and call it quits when we're so old and decrepit that no one else will want us. What do you say?"

Elizabeth grabbed at her heart. Tears freely rolled down her face as they had so many nights before. "I'd say you're a liar, Kenneth. You, Tommy, and all the rest. Nobody ever means anything they say. They're just words."

"You've got to go on. You've got to do the work the Lord has anointed you for," Nina would tell her, as Elizabeth lay frail and dying inside in that miserable hospital room a couple of years ago. Many people from her church in Dayton told her that Kenneth had encouraged them to be better Christians. For that, she was glad. She only wished that someone could tell her how to get over this empty feeling. "This is not the program I signed up for, Lord!" she screamed at her Savior.

The untimely ringing of the telephone caused Elizabeth's hands to go to her head. She hated that telephone. People were always calling at the worst times. She stood and walked the distance to the telephone, now feeling the weight of an enormous headache.

"Hi, Elizabeth," Nina said.

"Oh, how are you?"

"I'm well. I've got a few projects that I'm working on, but I called to check on you. Is everything all right?"

"Why wouldn't it be?"

"Okay. Let me put it this way. Tommy just called me. He said that the two of you just had some kind of blow up."

Elizabeth massaged her temples. "Did he tell you what the blow up was about?"

"No, he didn't. But he did tell me that you just wrote a song called 'Masquerade.' In the song you make comments about hurting, and being empty, but not being able to talk to anyone about it. Elizabeth, you do know that you can talk to me, don't you?"

She was fuming. "Tommy is making a big deal over nothing. It's just a song and, besides, he needs to worry about his own problems."

"Why don't you come home for a little while?"

"My home is in Atlanta now, Nina."

Silence filled the line, as if Nina was trying to find the best way to say something to her friend. "But your children are in Dayton. Your mom has had them for three months now."

"I *know* that."

"They miss you. They get upset when you leave them. That's all I'm saying."

"Mind your own business," Elizabeth told her friend, then hung up the phone. She walked toward her bedroom holding her head. "I need some sleeping pills." She took six at one time the other day. Maybe she would finish off the bottle tonight.

"I'm a wreck." She sucked on her bottom lip and threw her hands in the air. "Couldn't you have looked out for my family? Oh, God, how do you expect me to keep going? Every day is a struggle for me. Three years hasn't changed anything. I still wake up wishing for death."

She found the pills and tightened her grip on them. "I go to bed hoping that I will just stop breathing. How can I take care of my children when I am so messed up?"

Elizabeth sat down on her bed, picked up the phone and dialed her mother's house. Erin answered on the first ring. "Hey, baby how's it going?"

"Oh, it's you."

"What's that supposed to mean?"

"Nothing. Why are you calling? You bored or something?"

Elizabeth had had all the disrespect she could take. The older Erin got, the worse her mouth became. "Now look here, young lady, I'm not up for your mess. So cut it right now."

"Whatever."

"Why are you upset with me, Erin? You know I've been on tour."

"Well, go back on tour. We don't need you," Erin said, then slammed down the phone.

Elizabeth clutched the phone to her chest and sobbed. "I can't do anything right. Even my children hate me."

She pulled herself off the bed and went to the bathroom to fill her glass with tap water. Sorrow enveloped her as she looked at the pills in her hand. *No one would miss me.*

She opened the pill bottle and poured the contents in her hand. She walked into her bedroom, and through tear soaked eyes, she stared at the life-size portrait of her husband. "If only I could be with you," she said as she swallowed the pills.

Now peace would come. She was sure of it.

Brogan, Elizabeth's angel had his back against the wall. Literally. Two massive demons with outstretched fangs were whupping on him like he stole something. Brogan kept hoping that Elizabeth would pray—prayer gave him more power. He would have been able to stop her from taking those pills if she had just prayed before taking them. But demonic forces were blocking him from helping his charge because he didn't have the strength to fight them off.

8

He woke up panting. "Aha, aha, aha!" He frantically searched the room. Something had happened to his family. Just what, he was not sure of, but something had gone terribly wrong.

Nathan, Kenneth's angel stood at the head of Kenneth's bed. He had been there most of the night massaging Kenneth's temples; bringing back to his remembrance the things he should never have forgotten.

He had been plagued with nightmares. Always something following or tracking him in his sleep. He had gotten used to scary images visiting him at night, but this dream was different.

He threw back the covers and jumped out of bed. "Aaarrrh!" he screamed as the sudden move jarred his injured leg. He struggled to get on his knees despite the pain. "Lord, my God, something is wrong. I don't know what has happened. Please, Father God, look in on my family. And Lord, please help me to remember where I belong. My children need me."

They need me more.

"Then go to them, Lord. Be to them what I cannot." Getting off of his knees was a slow, painful process. As the pain seared through his body, he wanted to scream out loud. He sat on his bed and felt an incredible need to cry for himself and his family. Years of unshed tears brimmed in his eyes. He tried not to release them. "Buck up," he told himself. Then he saw one of his daughters. She was so excited. Couldn't have been more than five years old.

"Daddy, you're home!" His daughter ran toward him.

He put his briefcase down and knelt to pull her into a tight bear hug. "Yes, baby, Daddy's home."

He let the tears flow. Oh, how he wanted to be home. Needed to be near his children. They were in trouble, and he was lost in the labyrinth of his mind.

A knock at his door pulled him out of his thoughts. "Come in."

Debra stepped into his small quarters. "Hey, I just stopped in to check on you."

Silence.

"What's wrong?"

He wiped his face. "Everything, but nothing that I can fix."

"Andrew, is there anything that I can do? You know that Brad and I would do anything for you. Just tell me what's wrong."

Debra was a good person. She had helped him in his time of need, but only God could help him now. Still, he told her his troubles. "It's my family. Something has happened to them."

She plopped down on the bed, eyes wide, mouth open. "I don't understand, Andrew. You don't remember who your family is, how can you know they're in trouble?"

He sighed. "I didn't tell you, but for quite some time now, I have been having more frequent flashbacks. I know that I have a wife and two little girls, but I still don't know who they are."

"Andrew, that's wonderful news," she said cautiously. "But if you're only seeing flashbacks and you still don't know who they are, how can you know they are in trouble?"

"God speaks to me through dreams. As I slept last night, I saw my wife and my children. They were falling off a . . . a cliff. I tried to reach out to them, but I was too late."

Debra lightly put her hand on his shoulder. "Don't worry, Andrew. God will take care of your family."

"There's something else," he told her, looking away. "My wife. I'm worried that she might have done something to my children."

9

She couldn't even kill herself right. Tubes were in her arms. As she awakened, she started to pull them out, but her attention was drawn away from the tubes in her arm to the wall. Several poster-sized messages had been hung around her hospital room. One of the posters read:

Beloved, think it not strange concerning the fiery trials that come to try you, as though some strange thing happened to you, but rejoice to the extent that you partake of Christ's sufferings, and if you suffer with Him, you will also reign with Him.

Elizabeth turned from that poster to read yet another:

For I wreckon that the sufferings of this world are not worthy to be compared to the glory which shall be revealed in us.

"What glory can come from my suffering?" she spat the question in the air. She turned away from the offending poster and saw two more plastered on the opposite wall:

For I have been young and I have been old, but I have never seen the righteous forsaken nor His seed begging bread.

The other read:

A man's heart deviseth his way: but the Lord directeth his steps.

She closed her eyes, determined to shut God out. Wasn't it enough that she had failed to kill herself? She was still alive, still breathing. Couldn't God just leave her alone and let her suffer through this the best she could?

"So, how's our patient today?" a too cheerful nurse in a Sponge Bob smock asked as she walked into the room.

Elizabeth kept her eyes shut, hoping she would take the hint and go away.

No such luck. "I've got some medicine for you, Mrs. Underwood. You need to sit up so you can take it."

"I don't want it," Elizabeth told her without opening her eyes.

Still too cheery for Elizabeth, and probably the rest of the depressed world too, the nurse said, "Oh, but this will make you feel better."

"What part of *I don't want it* don't you understand?"

The nurse stood her ground. "Doctor's orders. Now open wide."

"I said no! Do you understand English? No means no!"

"Whew! What's up with all that 'tude?" Nina said.

Elizabeth glared at Nina as she stood in the doorway of her hospital room. "Did you put all these posters on my wall?"

"Michael made the posters. I helped him put them up."

"Take them down."

"I can't. You're going to have to speak to your brother about that."

Elizabeth shook her head. "If you're not going to help me, why did you even bother to show up?"

Nina walked over to her bed and the nurse seemed to take that as her cue to leave. "I'm here because I care about what happens to you. Now look, I've got to get back to Dayton tonight, but before I leave, we're going to talk about some things."

"I don't want to talk right now, Nina. I'm mad, and I want to stay mad."

"It's okay to be mad, Elizabeth. But it's no reason to try and kill yourself."

"I didn't mean to do it," she lied. "I just wanted to sleep. Maybe sleep forever, I don't know."

Nina bent down and hugged her. As Elizabeth embraced her friend, she began to sob. "What happened to me, Nina?"

"Oh, the same thing that's happened to us all: life."

"Mmh, ain't that the truth."

Nina moved a chair closer to the bed and sat down. "It's more like a kick in the head."

They both laughed, then reminisced on days gone by. They talked about how unsure they were of this Christian walk in the early days, but they had been able to see the work that God had performed through them. They talked about the changes in their lives. They laughed some more, and then Elizabeth began to cry.

"I miss him so much, Nina."

"I know you do."

"He was so good to me." She grabbed some tissue, wiped her eyes, and blew her nose. "I can still hear him saying, 'Hey, beautiful.'" Her eyes filled. "It's just so hard to keep waking up every morning, knowing that he won't be there."

"I know it's not easy, honey, but Kenneth wouldn't want you to go out like this." Nina hugged her friend and sighed. "Your first experience with the sovereignty of God is a real trip."

"If only I could wipe away all these years, and go back to the day when I first received Jesus."

Nina produced a weak smile. "To the place of innocence."

"Yeah, before we knew anything about the sovereignty of God." Elizabeth started crying again. She turned away from her friend and snuggled into her pillow.

"Don't shut me out, Elizabeth. Don't *ever* shut me out again." She pulled at Elizabeth's shoulder and made her face her. Tears welled up in Nina's hazel eyes. "I mean it, girl. If you're feeling lonely or sad or just need to talk, call me. Don't let things build up like this."

"Why are you crying?" Elizabeth reached up and wiped a tear from Nina's cheek.

"I just can't imagine this world without you, and I sure don't want to be in heaven without my home girl."

When Elizabeth took those pills, it didn't cross her mind that suicide was one of those do-not-pass-go-do-not-collect-a-hundred-dollars-just-take-your-butt-straight-to-hell kind of sins. "I just felt so tired, Nina."

Nina stood and kissed her friend's forehead. "Think of it this way. Your situation, everything you're going through just means that God found you worthy to be considered."

"Considered? What do you mean?"

"Remember the story of Job? When Satan came to God, God asked him, 'Have you considered my servant, Job? How there is none like him?'"

That revelation put Elizabeth in a snit. "So are you saying that God is playing Russian roulette with my life?"

"No, I'm not saying that. But what I am saying is," she pointed to one of the posters on the wall, "think it not strange concerning the fiery trials that come to try you."

Elizabeth closed her eyes. Sometimes it helped to shut out the pain, but not this time. "I'm hurting, Nina. Can you understand that? I don't know how to live without him."

"Mmmh, but you are going to make it. You will live."

"Yeah? How can you be sure?"

"Because if you try something like this again, I'm going to beat you down."

Laughter was good for her, like a medicine.

Debra handed Andrew a tabloid newspaper. The woman on the cover was beautiful. Deep chocolate skin tone and sad eyes. And no wonder, he thought, as he read the caption:

Christian singing sensation attempts suicide after catching her fiancé in love tryst with another man.

He looked up at Debra, a question in his eyes.

"Her name is Elizabeth Underwood," she told him. "Your name is Kenneth Underwood. She's your wife."

Kenneth sat lifeless, momentarily dumbfounded. He looked back at the picture, then shook his head in disbelief. "But, she's engaged."

"She must have finally given up on finding you, assuming you were dead."

He shook his head again. "What do you mean? How do you know all this?"

Debra handed him another piece of paper. This one had his picture on it. The words on the paper tore at his heart. *Lost September 11, 2001. If you've seen Kenneth, please call Elizabeth Underwood. He's all we have. We need him.* He pulled his gaze from the paper and looked at his caregiver, the woman he called friend. "Where did you find this paper?"

She wouldn't meet his gaze. "At the family memorial site."

He stood up, grabbing his cane for support. It clicked on the uncarpeted floor as he paced back and forth. He rubbed his left temple with his thumb and index finger. "When did you find it?"

Her eyes were downcast as she opened her mouth to answer his question. No sound exited. She closed her mouth and looked up at him. He stood in front of her, waiting. "Andrew, I mean Kenneth, I—I'm sorry—truly sorry for what I—"

"How long have you known?" His words vibrated against the walls of his small cottage.

She jumped. "I found several flyers taped on poles and the walls of the viewing areas not far from where the Trade Center used to be a little over two years ago. Actually, I found them the same day I discovered I was pregnant. I thought about telling you." She reached for his hand, but he pulled away from her. "You've got to believe me. I know I was selfish, but I wanted my baby so badly. I was so worried that if you weren't around to pray for me I might miscarry again."

"How could you be so cruel and thoughtless?"

"I didn't intend to keep you away from your family forever, Kenneth. As soon as I had my baby I called your wife."

Kenneth's eyes blazed with interest. "What happened? Why didn't she come to get me if," he held up the flyer and continued, "they needed me so much?"

"I never talked to her," Debra confessed. "Her manager answered the phone. He flew into New York the same day I spoke with him." Debra put her hands to her face to cover her eyes. "Oh, God, Kenneth please forgive me. That man gave me twenty thousand dollars to keep you with us and never call Elizabeth again."

He lifted his cane to pummel her. *I'll just plead insanity*, he thought. *Yeah, that'll work. No judge in the world would convict me.*

Debra lifted her arms to protect her face. "Andrew, no!" She scurried across the room. "I never meant to hurt your family. How was I to know that this would happen? He told me that Elizabeth had sold all of your possessions and embarked on a singing career. He said she didn't want you in her life anymore. I'm so sorry, Kenneth, but that's what he told me."

He moved away from Debra and stood at the window, looking past the confines of her small home. His children were out there somewhere. They were probably scared and feeling alone right now. His precious wife had shown how little she cared about their children. She'd evidently preferred death to living without her fiancé. "So to keep your child, you sacrificed my whole family," he said to Debra without looking her way.

10

Elizabeth couldn't sleep. She lay in bed thinking over the conversation she'd had with Michael and her mother earlier that day. They told her it was time to forgive God and move on. Michael had said that she needed to realize that bad things do happen to good people. Or to put it more biblically, God caused the rain to fall on the just and the unjust. Or was it the sun? Ah, she didn't know—but one followed the other anyway. If God causes the sun to shine on all, then He also lets the rain fall on all.

"I know what happened to Kenneth threw you for a loop. It would have thrown me also. But it's been over two years. Please, please try to understand. God never promised us that the rain wouldn't fall. But if we trust Him through the storm, He will bring us peace," Michael had explained.

"I don't know, Michael. I just don't know if I can trust God with my life anymore."

Michael scooted his seat closer to the bed. "Elizabeth, I love you, but right now, I need to tell you something that may cause you not to like me very much."

Elizabeth shrugged. "That never stopped you before."

"Whatever, big head." He harrumphed, then loosened his tie. "I believe that your life is a representation of the story Jesus told in the book of Luke concerning seed falling among thorns."

"That is ridiculous, I have been in—"

Michael raised his hand. "Just think about the description Jesus gave of this type of Christian. First of all, we both know that the seed is the Word of God. Jesus told His disciples that when the Word of God is received, he or she who receives it would then go forth into ministry. But the cares of the world eventually choke the Word, and the person becomes unfruitful."

Elizabeth looked away, but found herself staring at another of her brother's dag-blasted posters.

Although they knew God, they did not glorify Him as God, nor were thankful, but became futile in their thoughts, and their foolish hearts were darkened.

"I guess what I'm trying to say is, when you accepted Jesus into your heart, you were converted. But now it's time for you to be transformed."

Elizabeth rubbed at her temple. "I don't know what you're talking about."

"It's simple," Michael said as he sat up straight assuming his usual soldier position. "When you got saved, you were converted from making your own decisions and doing everything your own way. You have a Savior that you're supposed to pray to, and receive direction from. But being transformed is the process of becoming more like Christ. It's when you begin to desire the things that God desires. And to be quite honest, Elizabeth, when you are truly transformed, you will know the peace of God, even for what you are going through right now."

Tears cascaded down Elizabeth's face. "Don't you think I want peace, Michael? I just don't know how to get it."

"Ask God for it."

Elizabeth shifted in her bed. "I'm still waiting on God to do the last thing I asked Him for."

Michael rubbed her shoulder and sighed. "Have you forgotten about the heroes of faith in the book of Hebrews? They died in the faith, believing God, even though they never received what they wanted."

"You don't have to worry about seeing my name mixed up with Abraham's or Moses'. God will have to earn my trust before I start believing in Him again."

"Elizabeth, don't stop believing. Don't stop trusting God."

Elizabeth crossed her arms around her slim body. "God and I are at a stand still. It's His move," she said with a smirk.

Later, when she was alone, she didn't feel much like smirking. She wanted to cry out to God and beg Him to provide her with His peace. She looked up to heaven and demanded, "Why couldn't you give me the one thing I asked? No, I didn't just ask, I begged you for Kenneth's safe return—why didn't it happen?"

During the early years of her walk with the Lord, God actually talked to her as she prayed. But she hadn't heard from God since Kenneth's demise. Elizabeth hadn't noticed when God stopped communing with her. Hadn't cared. She lived a lie. But tonight was different from the last two years of midnight storms that she suffered through alone. Tonight, she needed to be God's beloved. Even if He wasn't her beloved, she needed God to care enough to make her His again. Tears sprang to her eyes as she realized that she not only wanted God, but also desired His presence more than anything else. "Why don't you speak to me anymore? Oh, God, do you know how miserable I am? Do you know that I cry myself to sleep almost every night?"

Silence.

"When is it going to end?" She gave the Lord a weak smile as the tears continued to flow down her face. "I tried to end it. When I took those pills, I didn't expect to wake up—I thought it would all be over. But I know Nina's right." She wiped away some tears to make way for the current of new ones bubbling in her sorrow-filled eyes. "If I . . . I had killed myself, I wouldn't have p—peace from my situation, because I would be in hell right now. I know that it was nothing but your mercy that kept me out of hell. I don't know how to thank you for that. I don't even know if I want to thank you just yet. But Lord, if you could just give me peace from my problems tonight. Help me to sleep and not desire to die before I wake. Then maybe, I'll be ready to thank you for your kindness to me."

She pulled the covers up and turned over in bed. Michael had left his Bible on her nightstand. It was open to Psalm 29. She picked it up and read:

The Lord sits enthroned over the flood; the Lord is enthroned as King forever. The Lord gives strength to His people; the Lord blesses His people with peace.

Tears rolled down her face as she closed the Bible and snuggled into her pillow.

Tommy shook his head as he shredded yet another grocery store tabloid that had a picture of him and Elizabeth on the cover with the caption, *Gospel singing sensation attempts suicide after catching her manager/fiancé in gay love tryst.*

It wasn't fair that reporters could print this trash. That punk, Nigel! Anything for a fast buck. He should have known. They were making matters worse for Elizabeth. It wasn't fair that Elizabeth was in the hospital after crumbling under the weight of his sins. He should be the one in the hospital right now. He should be dead. All of this was his fault. If he hadn't paid that woman off years ago . . .

"God, why are you never here when anyone needs you?

Why do you choose to ignore our pain?" Tommy roared, deciding that this was all God's fault.

God had been ignoring him for years, and he knew why. He had the Bible right next to him. He opened it and turned to the first chapter of Romans and read the offending words that had separated him from God. His lips formed a snarl as he slammed the Bible shut. "Nothing's changed there," he said. He turned his venom on God. "So that's it then? You have given me over? You have turned me away from your sight? I am offensive to you!" He stood up and flung the Bible across the room. "Fine, I don't need you."

"What did you ever do for me anyway? I'm the one that was molested by one of your church people. And now you condemn me. You turned your righteous back on the things that were done to me!"

Tommy made his decision. He wasn't going to hell by trying so hard to do right. Slipping and falling, then feeling miserable about the sins he'd committed was getting old. Forget that! If he was destined to dwell with the grim reaper after six feet of dirt swallowed him up, he was going in style and with a smile. "Don't look now, *my* Lord. 'Cause if you think what I've done so far was bad, I'm going to really shock your sanctimonious system." Tommy picked up his keys and strutted out of the house. Hotlanta hadn't seen nothing yet.

He cruised the streets with a predatory eye, watching and waiting for his heart's desire. He was free, no longer bound by God's unjust laws. Yeah, he was going to enjoy his fast and furious ride to hell.

11

Elizabeth awoke the next morning, refreshed. Her demons had not plagued her through the night. A strange feeling washed over her with the morning light. A kind of knowing. A separation from what was, to what is. She smiled. God had answered her prayer—she was at peace.

Peace. The word, the emotion was foreign to her. Maybe it wasn't foreign anymore, because she was definitely caught up in this emotion now. She had only experienced glimpses of this thing called peace in the thirty-five years she'd been on earth. Always too worried about what somebody thought about her deep chocolate complexion to ever relax around anyone. Always had to show them that she was all right. No. She was better than all right. She was the best at whatever she put her mind to doing. She had almost succeeded in convincing herself too. After all, she had a bachelor's degree and an MBA. She had snagged a top-notch corporate job, when so-called friends told her that all her credentials wouldn't mean a thing against her dark skin.

Well, she got the last laugh on them, but she stopped laughing after she married Kenneth. Seven years into their marriage, he up and cheated on her with a white woman. All those you're-not-good-enough-darky thoughts came tumbling back like the dawn crashing into a sunset. No, she hadn't known much peace with Kenneth, even after he'd left his girlfriend, came back home, and rocked her world. Her doubts and mistrust clouded the love that ran hot and bold between them.

But today was new and fresh. Today, she woke up trusting God. She finally believed that God had the power to see her through. He had shown her mercy, hadn't He? First, by not letting her die when she foolishly took more than a dozen sleeping pills, and later, by granting her peace to make it through the waking hours. And if she awoke in peace, maybe, just maybe, she would also find some peace to lie down with tonight.

Tonight, she thought with a smile. Elizabeth was going home today and would sleep in her own bed. Her children would be there. She missed holding them, being with them. And even though she knew it wouldn't be the way it was when their father was alive—it could still be good. She would make it good. Elizabeth could hardly wait for Michael to arrive and take her home.

The words of a song by Tonya Baker, a wonderful new gospel artist, crippled her heart: *You still show mercy. Every time I wake up, new mercy I receive.* She needed God's mercy. No way could she make it through all of this drama without it. "Oh, God, please forgive me. I thought the only reason I was miserable was because Kenneth was no longer with me. But maybe my misery stems from the disintegration of my relationship with you. I used to pray, Lord. You know, I used to pray all the time. But when things happened the way they did, I thought, what's the use?"

Elizabeth put her hands over her face. "I'm so tired of being miserable. Help me!" She thought over what Michael said about being transformed rather than just being converted. She pleaded, "Transform my life, Lord. I need to know what that feels like."

She got out of bed and walked over to the window. A whole world was just outside this hospital that she had yet to experience. Yeah, she had been many places. Touring to promote a new CD was necessary, but she had yet to really experience any of the places she visited. She had never tasted the peaches in Georgia, never noticed the sleepless nights in New York, and never witnessed the gusty winds of Chicago. She was so busy being rushed from plane to cab and from building to limo, that she didn't have a chance to experience anything.

Her nurse walked into the room and eyed her standing by the window as if she thought Elizabeth might jump.

Elizabeth tried not to laugh at the nervous looks her nurse, Ronda, gave her. She smiled as she asked, "Do you think it would be okay if I took a walk around the hospital? I feel like getting out."

Ronda gave her an uncertain look. "I-I'm not sure."

Elizabeth raised her hand. "Look, I'm not suicidal, if that's what you're worried about."

Ronda laughed. "Actually, that's exactly what I was worried about," she confided.

"Death is not what I crave anymore. I'm going to live," Elizabeth pronounced out loud. In her heart she said, *without Kenneth*. Her heart finally accepted that she could live in a world that did not include the man who had claimed her love. As long as the One who claimed her soul was a part of this world, she would stay. "But I need to figure out what living means to me. I'm just not content with mere lung activity anymore." She turned back toward the window and stared longingly at a world she was a part of, but still did not know. "I need to know what's out there. You know, smell some roses or something."

Ronda ran her thumb along the gold chain around her neck. "Yeah, I know what you mean. Being given a second chance at life is like waking from the dead, isn't it?"

Elizabeth cocked her head and rubbed her chin. "In a way that's true, but it's much more for me. Not only have I been given a second chance at life—I feel like I've been given a second chance with God. And that feels like waking from a fate worse than death. It's like climbing out of the pit of hell."

Ronda fidgeted around the room, wrote a few notes on Elizabeth's chart, looked around the room, then played with her gold chain some more. Elizabeth could tell something was on her mind. She just wished Ronda would spit it out.

Finally, Ronda spoke. "I know that you are getting out of here today, Elizabeth, but I wanted to invite you to a Bible study I attend on Mondays."

"I have Bible Study at my church on Wednesday evenings." Elizabeth lowered her head and confessed, "With my tour schedule, I don't get to attend very much, though."

"This is different than Bible Study," Ronda told her. "It's for people with dependency issues."

Elizabeth put her hand on her hips and turned to face her nurse. "Just because I took a few pills does not mean that I'm a dope addict."

Ronda twirled her short, layered hair. "These classes are not just for people dependent on drugs. Elizabeth, you could be addicted to your career, dependent on men—it's anything that you rely on more than God. Those are the things we need to be delivered from."

Well, she had depended on Kenneth, more than she had on God. Wasn't that why she was in the hospital, because she didn't know how to cope with life without Kenneth? "Let me think about that," Elizabeth told her as she pulled off her hospital robe. "Do I have any regular clothes in here?"

Clouds hung in the sky just waiting to release the rain that had become commonplace in Elizabeth's life. The chrysanthemums and tulips bloomed nicely, much different than last year's tulips and lilacs. The air was dry last year. Grass turned to straw and flowers wilted under the heat. Like those tulips, she had wilted under the heat.

The wind blew softly as she bent down to take in the fragrance of a flower—up close and personal. She smiled. Even the smell of this simple flower made her think of God. She couldn't get away from Him now. "You created this beautiful thing," she said, head tilted upward, toward her God. The wind blew harder. Lightning slithered through the heavens. Elizabeth sniffed the air, taking in the clean smell of the soon coming rain. She sat on the ground next to the flowers that bloomed so beautifully and the oak tree, so sturdy and magnificent. If the rain never came, she would not be able to enjoy the beauty of nature or the wonder of God's creation. The rain must fall. But even if it fell in abundance, the afterglow of the wind and the waves, the roar of thunder and the crackle of lightning brought forth the rainbow. No pot of gold waited for her beneath all those colors, but something much more important.

Elizabeth sat on the ground and remembered the storms that shot through the small two-bedroom house she lived in as a child. Storms liked the nighttime best. When they came, she would run to her parents' bed and snuggle under the covers. Her mom would hold her and say, "Don't be scared, baby. The rain is just God's way of washing away the old to make way for the new."

"But it's so much rain, Mama," she would whimper as she snuggled closer to her mother.

Lillian would squeeze her a little tighter and rub her hair. "Sometimes the rain falls in abundance, baby. Sometimes, one area receives more rain than another, until it can't take another drop. But when the sun shines through, we forget the wrath of the rain."

When the rain stopped, and loud booms and slithering streaks of light no longer controlled the night, her mother would nudge her and say, "You hear that?"

"I don't hear anything, Mama."

Her mother kissed her softly on the forehead. "That's right, baby. 'Cause when God wipes away all the old bad stuff, there's no need for noise. Newness brings peace, and with peace comes a sweet quietness."

Tears brimmed the edges of Elizabeth's eyes as she thought of the storms she had weathered. She released the tears. How right her mother was! God had given peace to her soul. Rain splattered on her head. Instead of running for cover, Elizabeth welcomed it. She reveled in it. What could be the harm in a storm that ushered in newness and sweet, sweet peace?

She stood and stretched out her arms. The thunder roared and she roared right back as she stood in the midst of the storm. This was her baptism, her rebirth. She smiled as she declared to God, "I love you, Lord. There is none like you."

I've been waiting for you, Elizabeth.

The voice she heard was that of a whisper. She didn't need to wonder who had spoken to her. It was God. His voice couldn't be heard by human ears. No, God's voice could only be heard with the heart. "I need you. I can handle anything as long as you are with me."

The wind blew stronger, angry. The thunder roared at her again, but Elizabeth stood planted. Never would she run from the storm again.

Visitors and hospital employees frantically scurried for cover. Ronda grabbed Elizabeth's arm. "Come on, we've got to get inside."

Around her, people tried to escape the rain. Hurry was etched across their faces. Children were screaming and crying. Ronda was holding Elizabeth's arm. Her brown eyes darted back and forth. Worry lines stretched across her mocha chocolate face. What was she worried about? The slither appeared in the sky again. Ronda looked at the sky and then at the tree that stood a few feet away.

"We're not going to get struck by lightning," Elizabeth told her.

She pulled at Elizabeth again. "I hope you don't mind, but I'd rather not stand out here and discover that your prediction was wrong."

Elizabeth brought her arms down and allowed herself to be tugged through the hospital doors. She wanted to alleviate Ronda's fear. Wanted to tell her that storms are different when God rides the waves with you.

As soon as they entered the hospital, the rain stopped. Elizabeth walked over to the window. Ronda followed her. "Let me get you to your room so you can put on some dry clothes."

"Do you hear anything outside?"

Ronda looked around, then shrugged. "No, I don't hear anything. It's not raining anymore."

"I know. After the rain, God brings peace."

12

Kenneth was on his way home. *Home*. The word sounded alien to him. In truth, he still had no idea where home was. His memory was still lost in the fog of his mind with only occasional glimpses at the life that once belonged to him. That life was terrifying, to say the least. His wife was a she-devil, who apparently lived to torment him. And to add insult to injury, that demon tried to commit suicide over her gay lover.

She was undoubtedly a selfish, inconsiderate woman. She never gave a second thought about his children when she decided to do a nosedive into hell. "Well, that's it. I'm going to collect my children, and may God have mercy on my wife's wicked soul."

Debra offered to pay for Kenneth's plane ticket, but her betrayal had sickened him. He didn't want anything from her. Nor could he bear to be in her presence more than the time it took to pack his meager belongings. He wanted nothing more from her, nothing but to be left alone. Let her find herself another lucky charm. She was too crazy for him anyway. After all this time, she still didn't realize that God was the giver of gifts. Now that he thought about it, he should have made Debra rent him a car. They owed him that much. Pride and anger sent him tearing out of the house of his captors without a backward glance.

Kenneth felt as if he were at enmity with everyone. So, he decided to do penance to God by hitchhiking to Atlanta and telling everyone he met about the God he served.

As the rain beat down on his black windbreaker, he wondered if he had lost his mind, in addition to his memory. He had been thrown out of three cars already. The one at the Jersey Turnpike was still moving when he was told to go. Apparently, the name Jesus on the lips of a hitchhiker screamed "lunatic" to some people. Now he walked the roads of Richmond. Actually, today, they were muddy roads. His stonewashed jeans and used-to-be white tennis shoes could testify to that.

Kenneth desperately wished to turn back time and snatch the money for his plane ticket out of Debra's lying, conniving hands. He would have been in Atlanta by now, in pursuit of his children, so he could rescue them from that twisted excuse for a mother. Instead, taking a mud bath in Richmond, he wiped raindrops from his eyelids and drizzle from his nose. Kenneth decided that this tell-every-stranger-you-meet-about-Jesus idea of his was for the birds.

A red Sunbird with tinted windows pulled up alongside him, just as he was about to give up and find shelter. The driver rolled her window down. Kenneth noticed her fiery red hair and reddish-brown skin as she yelled, "It's pouring out here. Do you need a ride?"

"I sure do." Kenneth jumped in the car. "Thanks."

"No problem," she told him. "Where are you headed?"

"Atlanta."

"Well, I'm going as far as Chattanooga. If that's okay, you're welcome to ride."

Was she kidding? "Thanks, I appreciate the lift." He started feeling bad about being so weak. How could he give up on God's Word so quickly? *Because you prefer a dry car to a wet and muddy road, that's how,* he told himself. He rationalized that no one would be on the road anyway. With all this rain, common sense folks would be at home. He knew it was true, still his lips curved into a frown at the thought of missed opportunities.

She turned to face him, when she stopped at the light. "Oh, by the way, my name is Faith."

Kenneth undid his frown and smiled like a sixteen-year-old boy on his first unchaperoned date. "What a coincidence," he told her, "I'm of the faith."

Tommy strolled into Visions with one thought— find himself some used-to-be-fresh meat. He didn't care if it came free or had a 'for sale by owner' sign on it. He sat down at the bar and scanned the crowd.

"What'll it be, mister?" the beer-bellied bartender asked, while pouring beer into a mug for a customer on the opposite end of the bar.

"Bacardi." The bartender fixed the drink and put it on the bar. Tommy grabbed his drink and took a big gulp. "Aaaah." He hadn't had an honest drink in over two years. The taste was soothing, like coming home. "Hit me again."

He turned to face the crowd. The party was jumping. Sistas with good jobs and no men were finger popping on the expansive dance floor. The dance lights flashed across the room. Tommy got a glance of some serious bootie-bouncing action. "Mmph, mmph, mmph. Sistas, don't hurt a brother."

He left the bar and prowled the room. All the fly sistas were already in conference with

Mister I'm-Just-Trying-To-Come-Up, or Mister Baby-Baby-Please-Have-Mercy-On-A-Brother. The women leaning against the wall, waiting on him to speak to them would be waiting all night, because he was out. "I'm going to Strokers." He pulled out his keys and smiled, had some strippers on his mind.

Tommy wanted so badly to enjoy himself. He needed to wipe the past few days from his mind, but Elizabeth kept invading his space. He would have gone to see her by now, but he just couldn't shake the feeling that he was the reason she was in that hospital bed—the straw that broke the camel's back, so to speak. Maybe he should call her. Just check on her to make sure she was all right. He ordered a drink as soon as he walked into Strokers; downed it, pulled out his cell phone, stood up as if he were getting ready to recite the Pledge of Allegiance, and dialed the hospital.

Elizabeth answered on the third ring. She sounded groggy, but not sad. Not suicidal. He had missed the signs a couple of days ago when she left his apartment. Better to check and be sure. "Hey you, how'ssss it g—g—going?"

"Tommy?"

"Yeah, it's me." He twisted his lip. "You still mad?"

"No, I'm all right. Why are you calling so late?"

He looked around the room. A brunette in a Cinderella outfit was on stage doing her thing to *It's Gettin' Hot in Here.*

"That's right, Cinderella, take off all your clothes," the drunk at the front table yelled.

Obedience, and having pride in what her mama gave her, must have been the golden rule in this place. Cinderella was stripping down to her birthday suit—and what a glorious birth that must have been.

Tommy wanted to scream, "Dollas, dollas over here."

Then he remembered that Elizabeth was holding up the other side of this phone conversation. "Had to know that you were all right. Couldn't rest without knowing." As an afterthought he asked, "You still thinking 'bout offing yourself?"

"Tommy, are you drunk?"

A nappy blonde strutted by him. Tommy winked and patted the seat next to him. "Why I gotta be drunk? Elizabeth, I swear! I can't do nothing right in your eyes, can I?"

"Whatever, Tommy. I'm going back to sleep. Call me when you sober up." Tommy heard the click, put his phone back in his jacket pocket, and turned to the nappy blonde standing in front of him. "Looking for a seat?" he asked, patting the seat again.

Her three-inch heels were kicking her butt. "I'll sit. What's up with you?" She crossed her legs.

Tommy licked his lips as he looked at her luscious thighs. "I'm trying to find someone to spend the night with. You up for that?"

"I just finished my last show for the night. I'm available."

"What costume did you strip in?"

"Little Bo Peep."

Tommy smiled. "Why don't you get that outfit and let's get out of here."

She raised her hand, slowing Tommy's roll. "Wait a minute. What's in it for me?"

"Baby, if you bring that Little Bo Peep outfit, you can name your price."

13

"Thank you. Thank you so much!" Faith said as she cried.

"The Lord has saved you. Do you believe that?" Kenneth asked.

"Yes! Oh, yes, I believe it. I've never felt so good in all my life."

Kenneth smiled. If nothing else good happened for the rest of this trip, he would be grateful that God allowed him to meet Faith. She told him the tragic story of her life. She had been molested as a child, beaten and used by boyfriend after boyfriend, and experimented with drugs. Her dad had been evicted from his home and was now living in a shelter.

"I can't wait to tell my dad." Her smile brightened as she looked at Kenneth. "Would you come with me to pick him up?"

Kenneth hesitated. They were in Chattanooga. It was getting dark, and he still had another ninety-minute journey to Atlanta.

He opened his mouth to decline.

"If you come with me, I'll drive you all the way to Atlanta. Come on, I would love for my dad to meet you."

"Well, okay."

At the Chattanooga Street Mission, Kenneth and Faith got out of the car and stared at the no-frills, no-windows building. "Well, let's go on in." Kenneth took Faith's arm and allowed her to guide him up the steps. They opened the door and stepped back as a gush of urine and funk assaulted their nostrils. They held their noses and braved their way into the great hall of the homeless. Walking through the mission dulled their smell glands, so they released their noses and started looking for her father. About sixty cots littered the room. The mission workers were in the hall with the temporary residents. Some were sitting, talking with the inhabitants, Bibles in hand. Others were busy changing the sheets on the beds. Would dirty feet men appreciate the clean sheets they were blessed with tonight?

Kenneth hadn't thought of himself as homeless. But surrounded by rows of cots, mission workers, and the unmistakable smell of urine, he realized that he had been homeless. His captors allowed him to stay in their small cottage, under the guise of physical therapy, but he was homeless, nonetheless.

Desperately, he yearned for home now. What did it look like? One of the residents opened the bathroom door and Kenneth put his hand back to his nose. What did his home smell like? Good God, nothing could be worse than this. Even if Elizabeth no longer wanted him, he would beg for her to allow him to stay in their home until he could buy one of his own. What type of work had he done? Would he be able to afford his own place?

"Hey, Mac."

Someone touched him. His skin crawled as he turned toward the man. "What can I do for you?"

Greenish-yellow teeth protruded from his bony face as he said, "Help a brother out, man. I just want something to eat."

"Don't they feed you here?" Kenneth glanced at the line of men, with bowls in hand, standing at the entrance to the kitchen.

"Man, they serve slop in this place. You think just because I'm homeless I don't deserve a decent meal?"

Faith lifted the man's arm and showed Kenneth the needle marks. "This is the kind of food he wants. Trust me, I've been around this kind of stuff all my life." She released his arm. "Come on. I think I spotted my dad."

Stretched out on a cot, reading the newspaper, he looked as though he were taking first place in a relax-athon. His 'Go Rams' T-shirt and Docker shorts were Goodwill new. Legs crossed, no socks, his feet were clean. He had those same dope-fiend marks on his arm as the guy that had just asked for money. Kenneth hoped he was reading the HELP! I'm a bum, in need of a job section.

"Hey, James." Faith leaned down and kissed her dad on the forehead.

She addressed him by his given name. Kenneth understood. If you want respect, you've got to earn it.

"There's my buttercup." James reached up and kissed his daughter.

A man on the cot next to James leaned over and threw up.

"That's Pete. He's coming down off a serious high."

The smell of Pete's vomit mixed with the urine was a real treat. Kenneth gagged, then clamped his mouth shut. Throw-up man turned back over, wiped his mouth, and stretched out on his cot.

"Shouldn't he get something to get that mess up?" Kenneth asked James.

James waved his hand in the air. "One of the workers will clean it up in a little while."

"Oh," Kenneth replied calmly, but inwardly he was distressed over the disturbing images before him.

"Who's he?" James asked.

Faith beamed. "This is Kenneth. I wanted you to meet the man who introduced me to Jesus."

"Jesus, huh?" James looked at Kenneth. A smirk appeared on his over-traveled face. "You think this Jesus could make the government give back my SSI check? Can He stop those congressional dogs from cheating me?"

"Sir?"

"Yeah, you want to talk about organized crime? Well, I could tell you a thing or two about organized government. Them fat cats, in their two thousand dollar suits, paid for by the gullible US of A citizens, conspired to have me evicted from my home." He looked at Kenneth's cane. "They told me I'd have to maim myself if I wanted to keep receiving SSI benefits. Told me I wasn't disabled." He stretched his arms out so Kenneth could get a good look-see at the holes and scars in his arms. "Don't I look disabled to you? I'm a freakin' drug addict. How can you be more disabled than that?"

"Sir, I don't think your condition qualifies, because you can stop taking drugs if you wanted to."

James grabbed Kenneth's cane, shaking it. "Oh, and I guess you think your condition qualifies, huh? The government should give you the money just 'cause you walk around with a cane?"

"*James*," Faith said. "Leave him alone. I just wanted Kenneth to talk to you about the Lord. You need help. Why won't you let us help you?"

James turned back to face his daughter. "All right," he said. "Let me put my shoes on so we can get out of this place, and y'all can talk to me about Buddha if you want. Just get me out of here."

As they walked toward fresh air, Kenneth looked at all the beds around the spacious room. He saw all the faces that could have been him . . . that *would* have been him if crazy Debra hadn't taken him in. Even though she helped him for the wrong reasons, he was grateful that God hadn't allowed him to live in a place like this. Instead of being greeted by fresh air, when Kenneth exited the building, he smelled smog, urine, and poop. God bless America.

"We parked over there," Faith told her father as she pointed down the street.

They were about to walk down the stairs toward Faith's car, when a bearded man, sitting on the stoop, looked up at Kenneth. "Stop eyeballing me, boy."

Kenneth looked behind him.

"I'm talking to you," Beard Man, well, not just Beard Man—Stanky Beard Man told him.

Kenneth covered his nostrils with his finger, for the third time since arriving at this temporary home for the great unwashed.

"I'm on to you," Stanky told him. "You're not going to crack me. Keep sending your goons to beat on me if you want. I'll never give up my secrets."

Kenneth looked around and then back at Stanky. "What?"

James put his finger up to his head and made a circling motion. He rolled his eyes upward. "He thinks you're the FBI."

"Oh." Kenneth turned back to the man on the stoop. "Look, I'm not the FBI. Nobody's going to harm you here. Okay?"

Stanky stared Kenneth down. The silence ate up several moments. "I've stopped watching the TV news, so you can tell your FBI cronies to stop making the newscasters tell me to cut off my arms and legs. I'm not doing it," he spat. He stood and got in Kenneth's personal space.

"I've stopped going to the bathroom too. I do all my business right here." He pointed toward his pants.

Kenneth wanted to do the circle motion next to his head and suggest a dose of Prozac. Instead, he told Stanky, "All right, I'll tell them to leave you alone." Kenneth walked away with renewed gratitude to the Lord. He might have lost his memory and his family, but he wasn't running from the FBI, pooping in his pants, and calling it normal.

14

Elizabeth paced up and down the floor of her hospital room. Dressed in a chartreuse and navy blue St. Johns pants suit, she stood with her left hand on hip and her right hand holding the telephone. "I don't believe him. That is one triflin' man." She switched the phone from one ear to the other, listened some more, then hung up. Outraged, she turned to her brother. "Tommy was in a strip club last night. That's probably where he called me from, right before he left with some prostitute."

"Who was that on the phone?" Michael asked.

"That was the chauffeur we use from time to time. I asked him to keep an eye on Bad Luck Schleprock. Good thing. As soon as this nurse gets in here with my release papers, we're going to find him."

"I know you hate when I butt into your business, but I don't think you should go after him."

"Why not?"

Michael shifted in his seat. "Look, Elizabeth, I don't know how strong your feelings are for this man, but he's no good for you. He asked you to marry him while he was carrying on with a man, for God's sakes!"

"I understand that," Elizabeth said, her voice lifted in agitation.

"And now he's having sex with a prostitute."

"Hey, at least it was a woman this time. Do you have any idea how that felt, walking in his house catching him with a man?" She shivered. "I still can't think about it without wanting to vomit."

"That's exactly why I don't think you should go after him. For all you know he could have—"

Elizabeth raised her hand. "Tommy and I are *not* getting married. Any notion of that ended when I met Nigel. But that doesn't change what Tommy has been to me. When no one else knew how to help me, he gave me a lifeline. I won't turn my back on him now. I can't."

Kenneth didn't know what hurt more; seeing the outer beauty of his wife, all the while knowing that she was evil inside, or hearing this woman, his wife, pledge her loyalty to another man. He stepped away from the door of her hospital room, contemplating leaving the hospital, and the treachery of his wife behind. Why this knowledge hurt so much, Kenneth did not understand. He knew before he left New York that this woman's heart belonged to another, and that she had only caused him misery while they were together. But seeing that deep chocolate skin of hers—the face that needed no Fashion Fair, no Mac—the beauty of her natural face took his breath away. And though he wouldn't admit it—even if a gun were cocked at his head—he wanted her, all of her.

"Get a hold of yourself, man. Beauty's only skin deep, but her ugliness goes straight to the bone. Remember that," Kenneth told himself.

His children passed before his eyes. He was their only hope, and he would have to contend with the swamp thing to get them. Kenneth wondered about the powerful-looking man who sat in the leather chair next to the hospital bed as Elizabeth ranted and raved. He sat ramrod straight. Kenneth wanted to put his right hand to his forehead and scream, "Attention!"

He looked at the tabloid he'd brought with him. His wife looked angelic as she laughed at something the man seated next to her said. The man was Tommy Brooks. Deep dark chocolate, with a bald head and athletic build. The kind of man every unattached woman in America screamed for ever since *How Stella Got Her Groove Back* hit the big screen. Had Elizabeth grooved with Tommy? Was that why she had been all smiles and giggles for the camera?

He touched his scarred face. He didn't measure up. No way he could compete with this man's looks. He tore the tabloid and threw it in the trashcan. He would have his children. His wife could go to the devil for all he cared.

"Kenneth!" Michael exclaimed, standing up and pointing in the direction of the door.

"Kenneth, who?" Elizabeth asked, as she turned toward the door also.

His cane tapped as he walked closer to her. She noticed the cane, noticed the limp. She pointed at him as she turned back toward Michael. "It's Kenneth," she said just before her body fell unconscious to the floor.

When Elizabeth's body crumpled to the floor, Kenneth's protective instincts kicked in. He hobbled to Elizabeth, handed Michael his cane, then knelt down on the floor next to her. He lifted her head onto his lap. "Wake up, Liz. Wake up." He tapped her face a couple times. "Liz, can you hear me?"

When her eyes fluttered open, she stared at her husband. Her eyes focused on the left side of his face. She reached up to touch the scars. He pulled away and put his hand over the scars on his face.

"Oh, God, could this be? Has my husband come home at last?" Tears welled up and spilled over. She grabbed her husband and hugged him tight. She whispered sweet promises in his ear. Told him she would never let him go again.

If only he could trust her. He stood, lifting Elizabeth with him. The gentleman in Elizabeth's room gripped his arm as they rose. Kenneth was sure the man thought that he was going to drop Elizabeth. The idea of this man thinking he needed his help infuriated him. Kenneth reclaimed his cane.

Elizabeth turned to her brother. "Michael, can you believe it? My husband has come home!"

Michael put his hand on her shoulder. "Yes, Elizabeth, Kenneth is home."

More tears escaped her eyes. "I thought God had ignored my pleas." She brushed Kenneth's cheek with the back of her hand. Looking into his gray-green eyes she said, "Sometimes prayers are answered slowly. But God hears our prayers, Kenneth. He really does!"

He was momentarily caught off guard by the tenderness of her touch, the gentleness of her words. Her chestnut eyes sparkled with love. Could he trust her?

Michael put a possessive arm around Elizabeth and confirmed Kenneth's suspicions. Elizabeth didn't love him. But he would be strung up and whupped like Toby before he'd let this woman disrespect him.

"Get your hands off my wife!" Kenneth bellowed as his hand tightened around his cane.

Michael's smile disappeared. His eyes darted. Kenneth lifted his cane and swung at Michael. "Step away from her."

Michael took his arm off Elizabeth and rubbed his shoulder. "Hey, whoa. I don't know what your problem is, but I suggest you put that cane down."

"Kenneth, what's wrong with you?" Elizabeth screamed.

"Put your hands on my wife again, and I'm going to crack your skull with this cane."

Michael positioned himself in a defensive stance. "The first one was free. The next one will earn you these size twelves all up in your behind."

"Michael! Don't talk to him like that," Elizabeth said to her brother.

Michael turned to his sister. "Look, Elizabeth, you don't want no drama, and I don't want no drama. But if your husband hits me with that cane again, I'm going to wipe up the floor with him."

"Kenneth, put the cane down! Stop acting like a fool. You know Michael has had military training. Why in the world would you instigate a fight with him?"

"Shut up. I'll deal with you later," Kenneth told her and turned toward Michael.

"Aw, it's on. I know you didn't just tell her to shut up," Michael said with nostrils flaring.

They advanced like wolves, fangs extended, ready for the kill.

Elizabeth jumped in the middle and held her hands out, holding them back. "Stop it!"

"No, you stop it. How you gon' let somebody hug all up on you in my face?" Kenneth pushed her hands off his chest.

Elizabeth's mouth hung open. She held her hands in the air. "Am I missing something?" She looked from her brother to Kenneth and back again.

Kenneth continued his tirade. "Stay here with him for all I care. Just tell me where I can find my kids."

Michael eased out of his fighting position and studied Kenneth. "You don't know me, do you, man?"

"Where are my children?" he asked Elizabeth again, not wanting to admit that he didn't really *know* either one of them.

She grabbed Kenneth's arm. "We can talk about the kids in a minute. Where have you been, Kenneth? Why has it taken you so long to come home?"

"We'll talk later." He returned his gaze to Michael. "Who are you? Another one of my wife's prospects?"

Elizabeth gasped. "Kenneth!"

Kenneth had a sinking feeling that he had blundered big time. He let the anger and jealousy he'd felt after reading that tabloid get the better of him. He reacted without thinking and now the jig was up. He might as well throw up his hands, holler uncle, and ask them to tell him about his uncle, his mama, and his daddy too for that matter. Pride kept his mouth shut.

"Why have you been gone for so long?" Michael asked, putting his hands in the surrender position while sitting down. He rubbed his shoulder and kept an eye on Kenneth's cane.

Kenneth turned to Elizabeth. "Who is he, Liz?"

Elizabeth stepped back, clutching her hand to her chest. Kenneth's eyes were full of anger and contempt. She didn't understand him. She grabbed Michael's arm for comfort. "This is my brother, Kenneth. You've known Michael for years."

Kenneth sat down in the cloth chair opposite Michael. He put his hands to both sides of his head and rubbed his temples. "I want to see my children."

Michael tried again. "Where have you been, Kenneth?"

Michael was not a boyfriend but a family member—boy did he blow that one. "I was in the hospital for a long while, then I had a lot of physical therapy to get through." He squinted and looked at Michael.

Elizabeth moved in front of her husband. He could see the steam rising from her ears. "How long does physical therapy take, Kenneth? What, they don't have telephones in hospitals now? And why don't you know who Michael is?"

Evil E was boring down on him, ready to pounce if he didn't answer her questions. He would show her. He wasn't bowing and scraping to her whim. But she was going to answer his questions, or he would make her pay. "Where are my children?"

"They're at home. Kenneth, what's wrong?"

The jig was up, might as well fess-up. "I might as well tell you now. I didn't come home because I couldn't. I have amnesia."

"Do I look like Boo-Boo the Fool?" Elizabeth lifted her arms to the heavens. "Lord, please don't tell me that Kenneth has been shacked up with some woman all this time."

"Hah, you've got nerve."

She turned back to him, fire burning in her eyes. "Okay, Kenneth, how did you get amnesia?"

"The doctors don't know if my memory loss is due to something falling on my head and knocking me senseless, or if the experience was so traumatic that my mind has simply blocked everything out."

"Okay, Mister Amnesia Patient," she said, hands on hips. "How did you know to call me Liz if you've lost your memory?"

He shrugged. "Your name is Elizabeth. It wasn't a far reach."

"But everybody calls me Elizabeth. You're the only one that addresses me as Liz."

"What do you want me to say? I don't know why I called you Liz. It just felt right."

"Amnesia my eye. You've been off somewhere living your life, while I'm back here popping pills trying to die!"

Michael stared at his brother-in-law. He started to say something, changed his mind, then spoke up anyway. "You really don't remember anything, do you?"

"Not much, no," Kenneth answered.

Elizabeth started crying again. "Why me, Lord? Why can't anything ever be easy?" She went to Kenneth and sat down on the floor at his feet. "You really have amnesia?"

He nodded.

She put her hand on his leg. "You don't remember anything?"

"That's not completely true. I've had several visions of you these last few months."

"And you haven't been somewhere shacked up with some woman?"

Kenneth thought of crazy Debra. There had been no love connection. She just wanted a lucky charm, and was prepared to feed and clothe him to get what she wanted. "Not like you mean."

She laid her head on his leg and cried, "Oh, Kenneth. I'm so sorry. I'll help you. We'll get through this."

She looked into Kenneth's eyes and saw no love for her there. *Please, God, return Kenneth's memory. Lord, show him how things were between us—bring back to his remembrance the love we shared. Sweet love, that belongs only to me.* The frown that creased his brow as he looked at her indicated that this might be another one of those slowly answered prayers. Elizabeth decided to buck up, put her trust in God, and ride this storm. "I think we should have a doctor check you out before we leave."

"No. I just want to see my kids."

Elizabeth started to protest, but thought better of it. "All right, let's go."

The ride home was turbulent. Elizabeth wondered if she had made a colossal mistake by not having Kenneth thoroughly checked out by a physician before leaving the hospital. This was not her Kenneth. Her husband was kind and loving. This new Kenneth needed an attitude adjustment.

15

When they reached the house, Kenneth relaxed a bit. Who was he kidding? If this was a house, then the little cottage he was living in must have been a shoe. This was a sho-nuff-I-done-arrived-y'all mansion. Elizabeth's mother was at the house waiting on them. "Lillian Edwards," Elizabeth whispered to him. Kenneth didn't remember her either, but that didn't stop Mama Edwards from jumping up and down and falling on her knees in praise to the Lord.

She took off her blue-framed glasses, squinted at him, put them back on and stood shaking her head. "Kenneth Underwood, if you ain't a sight for these tired old eyes." She opened her arms to him. "Come here, boy and give your mother-in-law a hug."

Kenneth obeyed and Elizabeth let out the breath she was holding.

Michael told his mother that they needed to go to a hotel so Kenneth and Elizabeth could have some time alone. "That's fine," she told her son as she kissed Kenneth on the cheek. "I made dinner, so y'all just relax and eat whenever you get hungry."

Elizabeth had kept most of Kenneth's clothes and hung them in the bedroom closet of her new home when she moved from Dayton to Atlanta. So she laid out some clothes for Kenneth to put on after he showered. She then whisked his daughters into the sitting room to have a your-daddy's-not-really-dead talk with them.

After he showered and changed in the guest bathroom, Kenneth stood in the foyer looking up at the winding staircase. In his mind's eye, he saw a different staircase. He was running down the stairs with keys in hand. Elizabeth was at the bottom of the staircase waiting on him.

"Where do you think you're going?" she asked him.

"Out."

"Kenneth, if you open that door, I'll . . . I'll—"

"Elizabeth, why can't you accept the fact that we just don't work anymore?"

"There's nothing wrong with us. If you would quit sleeping around, you'd have time to work on your marriage."

He laughed. "Work on my marriage? Elizabeth, I don't want my marriage—I don't want you."

His hand on the doorknob, he heard his wife say, "Well, guess what, Kenneth, I don't want this."

"Nooo!" Kenneth screamed as Elizabeth and his daughters walked out to greet him.

The smile disappeared from Elizabeth's face.

"We had a staircase like this one in another house didn't we?" he asked.

She looked at the staircase. "Yes, we did. It's one of the reasons I bought this house."

"You busted up the vase my mother gave us." His words made Elizabeth's mouth drop. "See, I remember you."

He walked past her. Elizabeth grabbed his arm and turned him back toward her. "We were happy, Kenneth. We were in love."

"Your kind of love, I don't need," he told her as he snatched his arm from her grasp and knelt down in front of his children. "Hello," he said. His voice cracked a bit as he hugged his daughters.

The girls squeezed him tight. Tears ran down Erin's cheeks as she stepped back a bit. Flashes of questions danced across her face. "Where have you been, Daddy?"

"I've been away for awhile, baby girl," Kenneth replied, wiping away one of her tears.

Danae crossed her arms around her portly tummy. "Why didn't you take us with you?"

Instead of answering, he kissed them like he was trying to make up for two years of missed affection.

Erin held on to her father. "I missed you, Daddy. You'll never know how much I cried. I-I waited up for you so many nights."

"I know how you feel. I dreamed about you many nights, but I'm home now." He wiped her tear soaked face. "You can stop crying, baby."

Danae put his face in her hands and turned him to the left and to the right. "Somebody scratched your face, Daddy?"

He looked back at Elizabeth, sure that she would be giving his scars the once over. He expected a look of disgust. She was looking at his face, but she didn't appear to be disgusted. He was momentarily struck by the look of adoration in her eyes. The force pulled at him. He struggled hard to pull away. If he continued to look at her, drinking in her beauty, he would want her. But, a devil in a blue dress with a pretty smile was no less potent than the one with red horns and a pitchfork.

He turned back to Danae. "Yes, honey. My face was scratched and my legs were hurt when the building I was in fell down. The doctors tell me

I'm lucky to be alive. So, I guess I can't complain about a few scratches and a limp."

"Luck had nothing to do with it," Elizabeth announced. "Your daddy's alive because God wanted it to be so."

Danae left her daddy and walked over to Elizabeth. "God wanted you to live too, Mama."

Tears sprang to Elizabeth's eyes as she took her youngest child into her arms. "God is good like that, baby. He wants the best for us, even when we don't know what the best is." Why she had considered suicide a better option than raising her children, she couldn't explain. But now, she knew that she would spend the rest of her life making up the last two years to her children. She hugged Danae closer to her with one hand and reached out for Erin with the other. Erin fell into her mother's arms with fresh tears of her own.

"I'll make this up to the both of you. I promise," Elizabeth cried.

Erin lifted her head from Elizabeth's shoulder and wiped her tears with the palm of her hand. "It'll be okay now, Mama. You just missed Daddy more than you loved us. As long as he stays, you'll be okay with us again."

Elizabeth lifted her eyes to heaven and cried, "Oh, God, please forgive me for what I have done to my children!" She grabbed them and hugged them tighter. She couldn't deny Erin's words.

They had been right on point. How could she have put her children through such an ordeal? Nothing she could say would convince them that she wouldn't fall to pieces if Kenneth were to leave again.

She rocked them in her arms and whispered, "I'm sorry. I love you, Erin, love you, Danae. You don't have to doubt my love." More tears came and spilled over the backs of her children. "I'm so sorry. What else can I say?"

Kenneth took the girls out of her arms. "Enough of that crying. Come on, show Daddy your room."

They sat at the dinner table. Erin sat to the left of her dad. Danae sat closer to her mom. One big happy family.

"Ooo, Mama, Granny's mac and cheese is off the chain," Erin exclaimed, while stuffing her plate with a second helping of the cheesy pasta mix along with the sweet potatoes, collard greens, and fried chicken. All the good stuff that a heart attack is made of.

Danae lifted her plate to Kenneth. "Can I have another piece of chicken, Daddy?"

Kenneth looked at his daughter. Just as light-skinned and freckle-faced as he. His child, no doubt about it. He missed some vital years. Earlier, when they were in her bedroom, Danae had told him, "I'll be nine in a couple weeks." She pulled him down to her height and whispered in his ear, "But I won't mind if you still want to hug me like you used to."

Ah, she had taken his breath away. Gave him staying power. He would do whatever it took to be with his children. He took Danae's plate. "You want a leg?"

She nodded and smiled.

Kenneth smiled, put the crispy fried leg on his daughter's plate and handed it back to her. He turned his gaze to Elizabeth. "What church do we attend?"

Elizabeth frowned. "To be quite honest, Kenneth, my home church is still in Dayton. The Rock Christian Fellowship."

"How long have you lived in Atlanta?"

She frowned again. "Over a year."

He pushed his plate away. "Are you serious?"

"I'm not proud of it, Kenneth. I've been visiting the churches I sing at."

He turned his attention to Erin and Danae. "Are you full?"

"Getting there," they told him.

After dinner, Elizabeth let Kenneth spend some time alone with the girls. She went into her office to have a little talk with Jesus. Tell Him all about her troubles.

"Thank you for being with me, Lord. Thank you for loving me through a really tough time in my life. I can't thank you enough for bringing Kenneth home. You have given me everything. But I want to declare to you this day, that if you had given me nothing more than your undying love, I would have served you anyhow. I have fallen in love with you, Lord. I like where I am right now.

"Hard not to love a God as gracious and kind as you are. You know me, Lord. So you already know I have a few requests. Lord, please bring back Kenneth's memory. If not fully, at least help him to remember the good times. Our good times. And Father, my final request for today is for Tommy. Don't let Tommy leave this earth believing that you deserted him. Help him to walk upright before you. Help him to understand that you are holy, and you require holiness from your people. Help Tommy to come to terms with the feelings he has for men. Give him the ability to love one woman, and let that woman be his wife. In Jesus' name I pray, amen."

She read a little of her Bible, then went to the family room to claim her children. Kenneth and the girls were playing with the afrocentric Barbie dolls Elizabeth purchased last Christmas. She smiled as she watched Kenneth dress Brandy in one of her shimmering bright evening gowns, while Erin and Danae played tennis with Venus and Serena. Their laughter bubbled up a river of joy. Come what may, this was her family. She was blessed indeed.

The laughter stopped when Kenneth noticed her watching them. "Girls, your mother's here."

He might as well have sung, 'Here she comes to wreck the day,' as Jim Carey did in the movie *Liar Liar*.

"Time for your bath," Elizabeth said in an up-beat manner that her heart didn't feel.

"Nooo. Do we have to, Daddy?" Erin clung on to Kenneth's neck. "I want to stay up with you."

Kenneth looked from Elizabeth to Erin and back again. "Come on, I'll go with you." He stood and grabbed his cane.

Elizabeth was fuming. He had this I'm-calling-children-services look on his face. Like he actually thought she was going to harm *his* children. Maybe drown them in the tub like that lady in Texas did her five children. Or maybe he wanted to see if his children had any scars on them.

"I don't beat them on Thursday, Kenneth. Six days a week I beat 'em like Tyson on Bruno, but never on Thursday," she told him as she grabbed Danae's arm and headed for the upstairs bathroom. The tapping of Kenneth's cane told her that he and Erin weren't far behind. She didn't turn to see if he needed help getting up the stairs. Let him get up the best way he can.

Beloved, not this way.

She bowed her head and silently told the Lord, *I love you, Lord. I truly do. I don't know how to get Kenneth to trust me again. He doesn't love me anymore, Lord.*

Love Him anyway.

She received her rebuke from the Lord, then turned to watch Kenneth struggle up the stairs. She went to him, took the cane out of his hand, and replaced it with her arm. She felt his arm jerk. "Please, let me help you." He submitted. Elizabeth told the girls to go on and get in the tub and when thru bathing to put on their night clothes.

After the girls bathed, Kenneth and Elizabeth tucked them in and kissed them goodnight. Elizabeth walked down the hall with Kenneth toward her bedroom. "I kept all your clothes," she told him as she pushed open the door to her bedroom.

They walked into the parlor. A cream-colored chaise lounge was placed catty-corner to the wall. A Pulaski leather butler's table with a telephone was on the right side of the chaise and a ceramic floor lamp on the left. A brick fireplace was the focal point of the room.

"This is the parlor," Elizabeth told him as she opened the French door that led into the master suite. "And this," she did a sweeping motion with her arms, "is our bedroom."

Awestruck by the massiveness of the vaulted ceilings, Kenneth's jaw dropped. The walls were taupe. The crown molding was sage. Standing in the middle of this gigantic room, he eyed the four-poster king-sized bed. He walked over and touched it. "Pillow top mattress; nice."

A life-sized portrait of them hung on the wall, opposite the bed. No scars. No cane. "Did you burn my clothes before or after this picture was taken?"

"Why are you being like this, Kenneth?"

He smiled a wicked smile as he shrugged and pointed to the picture. "I seem happy with you in this picture. I just wanted to know if I was happy to have my clothes burned, or happy because I didn't know I was going to have my clothes served to me as my evening meal."

"We were happy, Kenneth." Elizabeth was frustrated, but she wouldn't give up. She had to help Kenneth understand who they once were.

His lips curved to one side, eyebrows arched.

His look made her feel small, less important. "There was a time when we were very unhappy," she admitted. "You did things to me, and I did hateful things to you. I changed Kenneth, and so did you. We learned to love one another again."

He turned from her soft words and looked around the room. "Where are my clothes?"

"This is your closet." She pointed to a door in the front of the room. "I have the walk-in closet next to the bathroom."

Kenneth laughed. "This bedroom is bigger than the entire house I had in New York."

"Would you like to talk about it, Kenneth?"

Did she really expect him to tell her how he discovered that his own wife allowed her manager to pay someone to keep him out of the way? "Not tonight. I'm tired. I just want to get a pair of pajamas, grab a pillow and blanket, and find a place to sleep."

"You sleep in here, Kenneth, with me. Remember?"

"I may have lost my memory, Elizabeth, but I know that I have never slept in this room with you."

"I didn't mean this exact room," she said. "We shared a bedroom together in every house we've had."

His visions had shown him a mean and hateful woman. However, the woman standing in front of him did not act like he expected. But if she wasn't evil, why did she decide it was better to pay his kidnappers rather than to bring him back home? He put his hand to his head and rubbed his temple. "I don't know, Liz. I'm trying to reconcile some things in my head. It might be best for me to sleep somewhere else for now."

Elizabeth gasped. "Kenneth, what about the girls? They're going to think something is wrong with us."

He shrugged.

Elizabeth sighed as she yielded. "At least sleep in the sitting room, Kenneth. That way the girls won't know you were in a different room."

"So you're okay with lying to them?"

Elizabeth gave her husband a weary look. "Haven't they been through enough, Kenneth? If we can minimize the trauma for them, I would appreciate it. That's all I'm saying."

"All right. We'll play the happy married couple in front of my children."

He took the pajamas that Elizabeth offered him and walked into the adjoining room. Before closing the door, he told her, "Maybe we should look for a home church on Sunday."

She nodded. "That's a good idea."

He closed the door without saying another word to her.

"We *were* happy," Elizabeth mumbled to herself.

16

Kenneth's homecoming was far from anything Elizabeth envisioned. She realized quick, fast, and in a hurry that God didn't grant her a cookie-cutter lifestyle. She wished she could model her family after that old *Leave It To Beaver* show.

God didn't take requests like that, so she started praying. When she prayed for Kenneth to regain his memory, he would remember some other horrible thing she'd done to him. Elizabeth had spent countless nights on the phone crying to Nina, trying to find out what had happened to her life. Neither she nor Nina had any answers for her current situation, so Elizabeth kept on praying.

Now, she sat on the cove of her bedroom picture window and looked out over her four-acre wooded lawn. Her life was in turmoil and she didn't know how to fix it. *Lord, can you rewind his brain to a happy time? Come on, I can't take much more of this.*

Ronda, the nurse from the hospital had invited Elizabeth to her church. So, that Sunday, just as Kenneth had requested, the Underwood family attended church.

They were a half hour late because of hair, make-up and clothes drama. But inside, an usher smiled as he told them, "Pastor Lewis has already begun his message, but I can seat you in the back."

As Elizabeth sat down, she looked around. Stained glass windows encircled the sanctuary. Wall to wall royal blue carpet covered the floors. *Faith Walkers* was inscribed in the marble wall behind the pulpit where the pastor stood.

"Turn in your Bible to Mark, chapter four, beginning at verse thirty-seven."

Pages turned, then Pastor Lewis began reading. *"A furious squall came up, and the waves broke over the boat, so that it was nearly swamped. Jesus was in the stern, sleeping on a cushion. The disciples woke him and said to him, 'Teacher, don't you care if we drown?' He got up, rebuked the wind and said to the waves, 'Peace! Be still!' Then the wind died down and it was completely calm. He said to his disciples, 'Why are you so afraid? Do you still have no faith?'"*

The pastor adjusted his microphone. "Did anybody catch what Jesus was doing during the storm?"

An old lady in a let's-go-to-church pink hat with silk flowers, hollered, "He was sleep."

"Thank you, Mother Mannin. Yes, Jesus was sleeping. And that indicates rest." Pastor Lewis smiled as he continued to address his congregation. "So why can't you rest during the storms that come into your life? Knowing that all Jesus has to do is speak a word into your situation, and the waves troubling your life will be still."

Elizabeth closed her eyes, wishing she knew how to put her trust in God and let that be that.

Kenneth nudged her. "I don't think we need to visit another church, do you?"

"You really like it here?"

"Yeah, I do."

Elizabeth shrugged. "Let's give it a try."

Kenneth relaxed in his seat and smiled.

By Monday, Kenneth was irritable again. Feeling confused and unsure of her place in her own home, Elizabeth stood, stretched her legs, and ran down the stairs. "Montira, can you stay with the girls for a little while?"

Montira served as cook, housecleaner, and at times, the babysitter. "Not a problem, Mrs. Underwood. You get out of the house for a while. Go shopping or something."

Elizabeth smiled as she picked up her keys and purse. Shopping was the last thing on her mind. Well, shopping for clothes was not on her mind anyway. She drove to Barnes & Noble, picked up a book on overcoming rejection, and drove to the address she had scribbled down, hoping she would be on time for the group study.

She rang the doorbell. "Hi, I'm Elizabeth. Is Ronda Bogen here?"

"Yes, she's here. I'm Barbara Smith. Welcome to my home." She opened the door and directed Elizabeth to her family room. "This is Mary and Patricia. Ladies, this is Elizabeth," she said as she pointed to each woman. "You already know Ronda."

Ronda smiled. "Glad you made it."

Elizabeth smiled at Ronda, then greeted the other women. "Nice to meet you."

"Don't worry about the formalities. Grab a seat and let's get started," Barbara said. "Whenever a new member joins our group, I go over the bylaws and read our covenant scripture. The first thing you need to know about us, is that we are people seeking deliverance. I do not accept members into this group who do not want to be delivered." Barbara pointedly looked at Elizabeth and asked, "Do you want to be delivered from your issues?"

Elizabeth thought about her family, her new relationship with God, and how she wanted to keep that relationship growing. "Yes. Yes, I do."

"Good. Turn in your Bibles to Jeremiah 50:6–7." Barbara flipped a few pages and began reading:

> "*My people have been lost sheep. Their shepherds have led them astray; they have turned them away on the mountains. They have gone from mountain to hill; they have forgotten their resting place. All who found them have devoured them; and their adversaries said, we have not offended, because they have sinned against the Lord.*"

Barbara lifted her gaze from the Bible and focused on Elizabeth. "You see, being delivered is all about finding your resting place. We all know that the resting place is in Jesus. But sometimes it's hard for us to put Jesus in the proper place in our lives—and that's why we meet here every Monday evening."

Pastor Lewis was talking about resting in God yesterday. Elizabeth felt like she was being set-up by the Holy Ghost. *Whatever you have to do, Jesus. Just help me through this.*

"However," Barbara continued, "I do not desire to become a crutch to God's people. So, once you find that resting place, we ask that you come to one more meeting—your graduation. On that day, we sit and listen while you tell us how you found your resting place. Okay?"

"I—I don't know what to say. This is all new to me."

"Say that you're willing to give it a try," Ronda said.

Elizabeth shrugged. "What have I got to lose?"

"All right then." Barbara clasped her hands together. "Tell us, Elizabeth, what do you need deliverance from?"

"I love the Lord," she said quickly, trying to spill her guts before she lost her nerve. "But I have never put Him first. I guess the first step is figuring out how I became such a mess—so I can heal."

The women in the group were silent.

"My husband's back home now and I'm scared. Basically, I want to learn how to give Kenneth my heart without giving away my soul." Elizabeth looked at the women imploringly.

There were no ready-made answers to heal a soul.

"Let's pray," Ronda suggested.

When they finished praying, the group turned to chapter five in *Overcoming Rejection* and studied some of the reasons women tend to put men before God. Did she walk in here on the right day or what? Kenneth had been first in her life, no question about it. Now that Kenneth was back, she still loved him—even with his miserable disposition. But things would have to be different. God had to be first in her life.

Elizabeth listened as they debated the reasons some women followed man rather than God. She was enjoying the lively discussion, but didn't feel comfortable participating.

"Women would rather be abused than loved. That's why they choose man first," Patricia said as she got up and filled her glass with iced tea.

"Yeah, but there's a reason why a woman would accept abuse from a man, rather than run to God and be healed. That's what we need to figure out," Mary said.

Ronda put her elbows on her legs and leaned in. "A lot of women don't have fathers in the home, so they want someone they can feel and touch. In fact, they make that man Daddy."

Elizabeth listened earnestly. They brought up some very valid points, but no one had touched on her issue yet. She desperately wanted to know why she had gotten lost in her love for Kenneth.

"I hear what all of you are saying, but I don't fall in any of those categories. I had a father at home, and he was a good man. My husband didn't abuse me—if anything, he loved me too well."

Mary laughed, and nudged Elizabeth's shoulder. "Girl, now that's a problem I'd love to have."

Yeah, I wish I still had that problem, Elizabeth thought, but said nothing.

"That's a tough one, Elizabeth. But if you keep seeking God, I believe you'll find your answer," Barbara said.

The women talked for a little while longer before Barbara closed out the meeting. "See all of you back next week," she told them as they headed for the door.

Elizabeth hadn't received her answer during prayer or during the discussion, but just putting her fears out there made her feel better. Now she had four other women committed to praying with her. She was going to call Nina and ask her to pray too. She was sure Nina had already figured out that she had a dependency problem. As she pulled her car in the garage and got out, she hoped God would deliver her soon.

"Where have you been?"

Elizabeth jolted. She looked up to see steam blowing out of Kenneth's nostrils. "Why? What's wrong? Did something happen to one of the girls?" She tried to run past him. She needed to get in the house to see about her girls.

Kenneth grabbed her arm. "The girls are okay. I just want to know where you've been." He got close up on her, sniffed like he had a cold or something, and gave her the evil eye.

She backed away from him. "What are you doing? You think you're going to smell somebody on me or what?"

"Did I say I was trying to do something like that?"

"Then why are you all up on me? This is the closest you've been to me since you came home." She pried his hands from her arm. "Honestly, Kenneth, I didn't know you cared so much."

"Don't flatter yourself. I just think that a mother of two small children should be at home with her kids."

"Well, I guess the amnesia didn't take *that* conviction from you." She walked away from him. Let him worry all night about where she had been. She didn't care. She was thirty-five years old and not about to report to him like a little schoolgirl asking her daddy if she could go out and play.

17

The phone was ringing.

Elizabeth opened one eye and glared at the clock on her nightstand. Three o'clock in the morning and some lunatic was ringing her phone. She thought about answering, then reminded herself that all of her people were present and accounted for. She would rather sleep.

The ringing stopped. She silently thanked God as she rolled over in bed. Kenneth opened the door and walked into her bedroom. "Tommy's on the phone."

Elizabeth sat up. "Why did you answer the phone, Kenneth? It's three in the morning."

"I wanted to know who would ring my house at this time of morning. And guess what? Not only did he have the audacity to call here, he called collect."

"What are you talking about, Kenneth? Why would Tommy call here collect?"

He rolled his eyes. "Three guesses."

She picked up the phone. "Tommy, Tommy, what's going on?"

"Who was that? Over there answering your phone like he's paying rent or something," Tommy said through the phone receiver.

Elizabeth rubbed her eyes. "He lives here, Tommy. That was Kenneth."

"What? Stop lying, girl. Wait a minute. Are you okay, Elizabeth? Should you be out of the hospital so soon?"

She yawned. "I'm not crazy, Tommy. Kenneth showed up at the hospital. He's had amnesia all this time."

"Yeah, right. And I'm chillin' with Tupac."

"Whatever. Why are you calling here this late, and calling collect at that?"

"Didn't your boy-toy tell you?" His speech was slurring more with every word. "I'm locked up. I need you to bail me out."

"Locked up? What did you do? Did they get you on a DWI?"

"More like a DWB," Tommy told her.

Driving While Black. She and Tommy had heard some comedian say those exact words not two months ago. It was funny then, but Elizabeth wasn't laughing now.

"The police are always trying to mess with a brother," Tommy continued. "Always trying to keep somebody down."

"You're drunk, Tommy!" she screamed into the phone. "They should have arrested you." She combed her hands through her hair. "Look, I don't feel like arguing with you. Go to sleep, I'll be there in the morning." She hung up.

Kenneth clenched his fist. "You're not going anywhere."

His eyes were cold and withdrawn as they bore into her. She massaged her forehead. His eyes still held no love for her. Contempt maybe, but no love.

"You ain't getting this one off on me." He crossed his arm and gave her an I'm-the-wrong-nigga-to-mess-with stare down. "I guess you're not tired of being front-page news."

Elizabeth swallowed hard. "So you read that tabloid, huh?"

"It's the reason I'm home."

She got out of bed and faced him. "I'm sorry about that, Kenneth."

The right side of his lip curved upward. "Whatever." He turned and started back to his room.

"Wait Kenneth, we need to talk about this."

He held up his hand. "This discussion is over."

He left her room, but not her heart. She lay awake long into the morning trying to figure out how she could make Kenneth sing the *When a Man Loves a Woman* song again.

Getting out of bed that morning, Elizabeth prayed that a change would come. She went downstairs and fixed some pancakes and bacon. The aroma must have snaked its way to the bedrooms, because one by one, each of her family members arrived at the breakfast table. "Eat up," she told her family as she put the plates on the table.

"Do you normally fix breakfast?" Kenneth asked.

"When we lived in Dayton, I cooked every morning. I didn't have a job then." She put a piece of bacon in her mouth. "No sooner than we moved to Atlanta, we started touring with the CD. I hired Montira."

"Where's the cook this morning?"

"I gave her some time off. I'm not touring now and since you're back home, I thought it would be nice if I cooked again. Might bring back some memories."

He took a bite of his food and cut up Danae's pancakes while licking the syrup from his lips. "Sorry I missed three years of these pancakes. They're pretty good."

"What happened, Kenneth? Why couldn't you come home?"

He started to respond to his wife, but Danae pulled at his shirt.

"Daddy, look." Danae put her face in her plate and began gobbling up her food. Syrup dripped from her face.

He turned toward his children.

"Disgusting," Erin said while pulling a comb and mirror out of her purse. "Look at her, Mom. She's a fat mess."

"Erin, that's enough," Elizabeth scolded, then turned to Danae. "Baby, you've had enough to eat. Go clean your face." Elizabeth then turned back to her husband to finish their conversation. She again asked, "What happened? I need to know, Kenneth."

He picked up his napkin and wiped his mouth. "Don't act like you don't know."

Elizabeth was confused. "Know what?"

He put the napkin down and pushed his plate away. "Okay, you want to play this game? Do you really want to know what happened in New York?"

Elizabeth nodded.

"There was this nurse named Debra at the hospital. She and her husband couldn't have children, so I prayed for them. Then one day she comes into the hospital and announces that she's pregnant and that I was the reason. I told her that it was God who helped her conceive. She must not have been listening.

"When the hospital put me out because I didn't have insurance or money to pay the bill, Debra and her husband took me in. I knew they thought of me as some sort of lucky charm, but they continued my physical therapy. So I thought, no harm, no foul. I couldn't have been more wrong."

Elizabeth put her index finger in her mouth and chewed on her fingernail. "Why, what happened?"

"Do you remember the flyers that you hung up at the family visiting area?"

Erin put her comb down. "I hung some flyers too, Daddy."

"Thank you, baby," Kenneth said as he smiled at his daughter.

"What about them?" Elizabeth asked.

Still smiling at Erin, Kenneth said, "Hon, can you go check on your sister so I can talk to your mother?"

"Okay, Daddy," Erin said as she threw her comb and mirror in her purse then left the table.

Kenneth turned back to Elizabeth and said, "Debra saw the flyers, but instead of telling me that I had a family that was searching for me, she stole the flyers. It wasn't until after you tried to commit suicide that she admitted what she did." He looked into his wife's eyes and continued,

"She brought the tabloid to my little cottage and told me that my wife tried to kill herself because she couldn't take knowing that her fiancé preferred boys."

"No, Kenneth that's not what happened."

"I don't want to talk about it."

She put her hand over his and gave him a tolerant smile. "Kenneth, I really want to help you remember the way things used to be between us."

"Things couldn't have been all that great, not if you could run off with another man without even knowing for sure that I was dead." He gnawed on some bacon and watched his wife skeptically. "Besides, I'm surprised you fixed breakfast this morning. I would have thought you'd have snuck out of the house this morning to go rescue your boyfriend."

Elizabeth put down her fork. "Why do you have to be like this?"

"Is that who you were with last night? Is that why you refused to tell me where you'd been?"

She closed her eyes and cursed her stupidity. If she had known that Tommy would call her house at three in the morning, she wouldn't have been so flippant with Kenneth the night before. "I was at Bible Study. Ronda invited me." "It took you all night to come up with a story like that?"

"I'm not lying, Kenneth. Why can't you stop thinking the worst of me and give us a chance?"

He turned from her, grabbed his plate and stacked on a couple more pancakes. He put on a plastic smile, and swirled the syrup on as if concentration was the key to the sugary sweet taste. She wanted to grab the syrup out of his hands, squirt him in the eye, and scratch the other side of his face. Something, anything, as long as it would get his attention. She clenched her hands around her plate, stood, and emptied its contents in the trash. She then stood, gripping the kitchen sink.

Lord, I love this man. Help me to not lose sight of that. Help me to think of his needs rather than the fact that I just want to slap him upside his nappy head right now. Silent prayers were just as effective as prayers stated out loud and bold.

"Kenneth, we need to talk," she told him as she reclaimed her seat at the table. "I love you, but I think your decision last night was wrong."

"What decision?" he asked, waving his fork in the air.

"I need to get Tommy out of jail. He needs to know that I care."

Silence filled the room as Elizabeth and Kenneth stared through each other. Kenneth ended the silence. "You're going to disrespect me like that?" He covered the scars on the left side of his face with his hand. "Go ahead, Liz, you deserve each other."

She might actually knock some sense back into his head if she cold cocked him one good time. "It's not like that, Kenneth. Tommy is a friend. I'm not in love with him, and I never was. He helped me through some tough times and—"

"Oh yeah, I know how he helped you."

"What's that suppose to mean?"

Kenneth wanted to tell her about Tommy giving twenty thou to Debra so that she would never contact Elizabeth again, but he didn't know how he would feel if his suspicion that his wife gave him that money to give to Debra was confirmed, so he said, "Forget it, just forget it. Go rescue the man."

To give her hand something to do, she put it on his arm and squeezed. "Come with me, please."

It cost a thousand dollars to bail Tommy's sorry behind out of jail. Elizabeth intended to take that thousand dollars out of his hide. He strutted out front to greet her, as if he'd just come from a Bahamas vacation. Tommy needed a dose of tough love. "All is right with your world I see," she told him, as he kissed her cheek.

"Why wouldn't it be? Am I supposed to be crying? Did you think that I would be shaken by that guy answering your phone last night?"

"Tommy, I told you that Kenneth is back."

He raised his hand. "Save it." He walked out of the police department with Elizabeth hot on his trail. "Thanks for bailing me out. I can make it from here."

"Oh, no. You are *not* getting off that easy." She grabbed his arm. They stood on the jailhouse steps and faced off. "I want to know what's up with this destructive behavior of yours?"

He shrugged.

"So you're not going to say anything, huh? Well, I already know that you were at a strip club the other night. And right before you got arrested for drunk driving, you were losing all your money in some crap game."

"Whoever your informants are, you tell 'em I said that they need to stop watching me and watch TV."

"You're out of control, Tommy. God only knows what else you've been doing."

"That's right," Tommy sneered. "God knows. He knows everything, but do you think He cares?"

"Yes, Tommy, God does care about everything you do."

"Really? Well, let's see . . . I was with Little Bo Peep the other night; God didn't say a word. The night before that I was with this redhead; never heard a peep from God. And you don't even want to know who I was with last night. But God knows, right?" He lifted his arms to the heavens. "No lightning struck me, no thunder roared. God does not care, Elizabeth."

"Well, I care, Tommy. And if you continue going down this destructive path, you can find someone else to manage."

Tommy's mouth gaped wide open. "You would *fire* me? After all we've been through? I've been here for you, Elizabeth. I stuck by you."

"And I'm here for you. You never have to doubt that. But I will not stand by and watch you destroy yourself."

He flung his hands in the air. "What do you want me to do, Elizabeth? You can't change me with threats. I was born this way."

"You don't believe that any more than I do."

"Hey, scientists have proven that our brains are wired differently."

Elizabeth crossed her arms. "Well, this won't be the first time I've ignored science. I choose to believe God. Every man is given a choice. You either choose to obey God or you don't."

"So that's it then?" He cocked his head and smirked. "This is where we part company." He started walking down the steps. "You've got your precious husband back, so you don't need me anymore."

Elizabeth reached out for him. "Tommy, wait. I do need you in my life. You're my friend. Let's talk about this."

He looked around. "Where's your husband?"

"He took the girls to the park." She tugged on his shirtsleeve. "Come on, let's go somewhere and talk."

He removed her hand from his shirt. "No. It's clear that you've got your family back. I'm going to do what you suggested earlier—go find myself some other group to manage."

"Weeeee. Higher, Daddy, higher."

Kenneth smiled as Danae kicked her feet, leaned her head back, and swung into the air with open abandonment. How he longed to join her. *Just forget about what was and concentrate on what is and what could be.* Liz claimed that they had been happy. She acted like she wanted them to be that way again. Maybe he was giving her too much of a hard time. But this morning, when she ran out of their house to go bail out her boyfriend, Kenneth could have strangled her.

Oh Lord, how do I trust this woman, when she keeps running after some other man? How can I work on my marriage, when I'm not sure if it'll last?

He stopped the swing. "Come on, Danae. You can get on the slide and then we've got to go."

Erin stood to the side looking bored. Danae got off the swing and ran over to the slide. She stumbled over some rocks as she ran through the sandbox. She was falling head first to the ground. Kenneth couldn't move quick enough.

A lady on the park bench next to the sandbox jumped up and grabbed the back of Danae's shirt. She stood Danae upright and gave her a toothless grin. "Almost got the wind knocked out of you, huh?"

Danae smiled up at the toothless woman. "Thank you."

The woman's clothes were filthy. She had holes in the sides of her shoes and she had her dirty hands on Danae.

Kenneth called, "Danae get over here."

Danae turned toward him. "Daddy, Daddy, this lady saved me."

He pulled Danae closer to him as he eagle-eyed the woman. "Thank you for catching my daughter," he finally said, then turned his girls in the direction of the slide and walked away.

"Hey, mister," she called out. "You got a couple dollars for a homeless, pregnant woman?"

"Come on. Hurry up, girls. Let's go," Kenneth said.

"Come on, mister. I'm not on crack. I just need something to eat." She followed behind them, rubbing her belly.

Kenneth turned back to the woman and shielded his children behind him. "Get a job. You can get all the food you need then."

Her blue eyes narrowed. "You think you're so much better than me, huh? Well, you ain't."

He held up his hand. "Look, I don't want to argue with you. I'm just trying to have a good time with my children."

"You go ahead and spend time with your children. Don't you worry at all that my children are starving."

Thanks for the permission to not have a sleepless night. "Okay, fine." He reached in his pocket and pulled out his wallet. "How much will it cost me to feed you and your children?"

"Thank you, mister, you don't know what this—"

"How much?"

She tapped her finger to her chin and squinted. Kenneth could just imagine her thoughts. *If you find a sucker, lick it.* Well, she wasn't about to find out what flavor he was. "Here's ten dollars—don't booze it up."

She looked at the money, then back at Kenneth. "I got five kids, mister. Ten dollars ain't gon' feed all them."

"Take it or leave it."

She snatched the money. "Next time I'ma let your daughter fall. Your crippled behind wouldn't have been able to catch her." As she walked away she added, "Shoulda least been worth twenty dollars."

18

Elizabeth sat on the floor in her home office with papers and envelopes scattered around her. She was crying. Her sorrow-filled eyes glanced up at Kenneth as he walked into the room.

He sat down on the couch near Elizabeth. "What's wrong, Liz?" She picked up one of the pieces of paper on the floor and handed it to him.

Dear Mrs. Underwood,

You were an inspiration to me. Your music really spoke to my heart. Well, all of it except one song that was on your CD. I didn't understand, then, why you put a song that didn't edify God on your CD, but now I know. That song came from your heart, and your heart has been turned black. You have been corrupted. I am very disappointed in you, Elizabeth. I bought your CD believing that you really loved the Lord. Now I feel like you stole my hard earned money—maybe I should ask for a re-fund. But that's *okay, you keep the money you stole from me and the thousands of others who bought your CD and use it to get some therapy.*

Sincerely, An X-fan

"What's this supposed to mean?" Kenneth asked, handing the letter back to Elizabeth. She wiped her nose and handed him another letter. "Oh, it gets better. My fans hate me."

Elizabeth,

I really enjoyed your first CD. But now I know that I really need to pray more before buying my CDs. You and your fag boyfriend are cursed. What in the world were you thinking? And to try to kill your-self over some confused man. Girl, I would have bust a cap in him and kept on step-ping. You are too weak-minded to be an idol of mine. God will judge you for all your wrong-doings. You and your boy-friend's days are numbered. When God gets through with you, you'll be sorry for even thinking about committing suicide over a man like Tommy Brooks.

Laquesha

"I have disappointed my fans."

Kenneth lowered his head and studied the ground. His eyes were cold and withdrawn as he shook his head. He got up to excuse himself.

Elizabeth grabbed his arm. "What's wrong?" Fresh tears explored her eyelids, then traveled down the familiar tear streaked paths on her face.

"Look, Liz. Maybe I'm not the best person to have this discussion with."

"But you're my husband."

He turned away from her. "That's why I don't want to read letters about Tommy Brooks."

"I'm a disgrace. I've disappointed you, my fans, everybody. Look at these." She handed him letters typed on church stationery. "All of my singing engagements have been cancelled. Nobody wants to associate themselves with me."

Kenneth frowned as he reviewed all the cancellation letters. "Liz, you need to look at this from their point of view. You did try to commit suicide."

"I know that, Kenneth. Don't you think I know that?" She grabbed some tissues out of the Kleenex box on her desk and blew her nose. "But some of these people were my friends. I've been to their homes, Kenneth. You would think they would have sent me a get-well card, or something. Instead, all I received is a letter from their secretaries telling me I'm not wanted."

"Look, Liz, these people aren't the only game in town. You want to sing?" She nodded. "Do you believe that this is the ministry that God has for you?" Again, she nodded. "Then you've got to believe that when one door closes, God will open another for you."

She tried to offer up a smile to his encouraging words, but her lips were still quivering from all the blubbering. Her smile didn't linger long.

Kenneth touched her face. "With your eyes. A smile from your heart shows in your eyes."

Elizabeth sucked in her breath and touched the hand Kenneth held to her face. "Kenneth, you used to tell me that whenever I gave you a half-hearted smile. Oh my God, you remembered."

He pulled his hand from her grasp and put it on his scars as he stood. "Liz, can I ask you something?"

She wiped at the tears on her face. "Shoot."

"What did I do? I mean, what was my job before I lost my memory?"

Subject changed. "You owned a technical consulting firm. It was called TechStar. You were very successful."

He lifted a bushy brow as he twirled his cane. "CEO, huh?"

She sat down on the sofa and smiled. "Yeah, baby, you were top dog."

"So what happened? Who's running my company now?"

The smile dropped from Elizabeth's lips. She had just let the cat out of the bag. Fur balls, too big to swallow, were getting ready to be coughed up. "Kenneth, I . . . I." She started picking up her X-fan mail. "Can we discuss this later, Kenneth? I really need to think about what I'm going to do now that I don't have any singing engagements."

"One thing you can do with all that free time is start talking. What happened to my company, Liz?"

She massaged her forehead, then faced her husband. "I sold the company, Kenneth."

He sat down and closed his eyes. His head was in his hands when he asked, "How could you do that, Liz? How could you sell something that belonged to me?"

She tilted her face and frowned up at him.

"How long after I disappeared before the 'For Sale' sign went up?"

She bent her head. "Kenneth, you don't understand. I was in no condition to—"

He towered over her. "How long, Liz?"

"Four months, okay! Four months! I had a nervous break down, Kenneth. I couldn't hold on to your business and regain my sanity. So, when the investors offered to buy me out, I jumped at the chance. Can't you see it was my only option?"

"Even Stevie Wonder could see plenty of other options besides selling off my company four months after I disappeared."

She closed her eyes. "Kenneth, I—"

"How much did you sell *my* company for?"

"When everything was done, I cleared three million."

"What did you do with *my* money?"

The frost in Kenneth's eyes chilled Elizabeth to the bone. She didn't miss the way he kept slinging "my" around either. Like this was his world, and she was on borrowed time in it.

Well, let the chips fall. She wasn't going to keep cowering to him. "I bought this house, Kenneth. You know, so *your* children would have a place to lay their heads at night. The rest of *your* precious money is in the bank." Getting off the floor, she stood to face him. "I couldn't stay in Dayton. I would have tried to kill myself sooner if I stayed in that town with all the memories of you. Don't you see I needed this? Can't you understand that?"

He lifted his cane like a sword and extended it toward her heart. His lips curled. "I ought to put you out!" He shook his head. "Scandalous. That's what this mess is."

The Arctic wind blew by her as he stormed out of her office.

Erin stepped in with fiery eyes. "Why do you keep upsetting Daddy?" she said to her mother.

Elizabeth put her hands to her head. "Not now, Erin."

"So, you're just going to let him leave? I guess you'll be walking out the door next."

She took a step toward her daughter. "Baby, no. I'm not going—"

"Don't come near me." Erin turned and stomped out.

Elizabeth flopped on the couch. What next? Tommy had dismissed himself from her life. Her fans and peers in the ministry wanted nothing else to do with her. Her husband was ready to toss her out of *his* house on her ear.

And now, her daughter was tripping. She looked to heaven as a single tear rolled down her face. "I won't crumble, Lord. All have left me, but as long as you are in my corner—I am never alone. I will fight, and with your help, Lord, I will win."

Kenneth sat in Elizabeth's SUV silently praying, *Lord, how do I get past this? How can I make a life with a woman who keeps showing her lack of respect for me?*

He glared at the house for which he had unknowingly spent over a million dollars. He slammed his fist into the steering wheel. Briefly, he felt bad for taking his anger out on Elizabeth's car. But then he thought that she had probably bought the SUV with his money too, and he hit the steering wheel again.

Your children needed a place to lay their heads, she had told him. What about him? Didn't he need a job, something to do? But Evil E had stripped that from him along with everything else. What was he supposed to do now? He was tired of sitting around. His body had done as much recuperating as it was going to do. He ought to go back in his house, get the name of the bank holding his money, drive over there, and make a one-time withdrawal. Then he would get on the road and never look back.

To think, he actually felt sorry for her when he first walked into the house. He wanted to hold her, rock her in his arms until her tears dried. But Tommy was between them.

I'm not needed at this house, Lord. Why should I stay where I'm not wanted?

A knock came on the window. Kenneth thought it was Elizabeth and snarled in her direction.

"What's wrong, Daddy?" Erin asked.

Your mother just gut-punched me. Kenneth rolled down the window. "Nothing, baby. I'm just getting ready to take a ride."

"Where are you going?"

No doubt about it, this was his child. She wasn't as light as he, but that was his round chin and box nose. How could he be thinking of leaving when everything he had—everything that would ever mean anything to him—was right here? "I'm just going for a ride, baby girl. You want to come with me?"

Erin ran to the passenger side of the car, jumped in and buckled up. Kenneth turned the key in the ignition and backed out of the driveway. He would ride I-285 and cool off, maybe grab a bite to eat, then come back home.

Kenneth and Erin drove out of the Sandstone subdivision, got on the highway, and took a wrong turn into the hood. The Black Mecca advertisements did not mention anything about this place. The ghetto in Atlanta was no different from any other ghetto—it and the inhabitants were broke, busted and felonious. He pulled onto one of the side streets and parked. Why had he driven down here? Maybe it was the shock of finding out he had 1.5 million collecting interest in the bank somewhere. Then again, maybe he was here because of the woman he was so rude to—the homeless woman who told him he was no better than anyone else.

Erin had fallen asleep. In no particular hurry, Kenneth parked his car and watched. A man in a construction hat and coveralls got off the bus and headed up the street. With shoulders slumped, his eyes told of the beat down the system had put on him. Probably had just gotten paid, tabulated his upcoming bills, and discovered what Chris Rock had already told America—he had just enough money to get his broke butt home. The good old USA. Where all were one paycheck away from being homeless. Well, not all. Kenneth, and countless others, had more money than they knew what to do with. He twisted his lip and tried to look away. He heard three little girls screaming, "Daddy, Daddy, Daddy," as they ran down the street.

The man smiled and reached deep in his pocket. He handed a coin to each girl. They turned and ran back the other way, and his smile faded. A woman opened the door to the third house from the corner. She said something to him. He shook his head. Her neck started moving, finger got to pointing. He pulled his pants pockets inside out and shook the lint out of them. She rolled her eyes and slammed the door in his face. He sat down on the porch step and let his head drop.

Kenneth closed his eyes and leaned back against his headrest. "Lord, what can I do for these people? How can one man correct such a huge problem?"

He opened his eyes just in time to see a couple of street-corner pharmacists approaching the SUV.

"What's up, man? What you need?" the drug dealer asked.

Kenneth put the SUV in gear and waved them away. Erin's eyes fluttered open. "Daddy, where are we going?"

He smiled and rubbed her hair. "Home, baby. We're going home."

19

Elizabeth sat in her bed trying to read her Word. Her mind, however, was plagued with two things: Kenneth's memory loss and the discussion at tonight's deliverance class.

The day of their how-could-you-sell-my-company blow up, Kenneth walked back in the house looking caged. House arrest hadn't drawn as many forehead creases from would-be criminals as the prospect of keeping house with Elizabeth had for Kenneth. She was determined to win back his heart and his trust. Elizabeth took Kenneth to see a specialist. Dr. Thomas did not promise a miracle cure after examining Kenneth. He told them that Kenneth's memory was locked somewhere in his mind. That's the kind of information three hundred bucks an hour will get you. Like they didn't already know his memory was on sabbatical.

Kenneth should have already regained his memory, instead of the few glimpses he'd managed to garner from the deep recesses of his mind. Dr. Thomas told them that Kenneth's inability to remember might be self-imposed.

"You see, there might be some traumatic experience that your husband wants to block out. To do that, he must block everything else as well," Dr. Thomas explained to Elizabeth.

Kenneth looked at her, as if she were the trauma he was trying to forget.

"Don't look at me. You've already remembered all the drama I put you through," she said.

She had to deal with Kenneth's hidden memory. Now, her deliverance group wanted her to deal with the hidden things in her heart. They were still delving into some of the reasons women clung to everything but God.

Elizabeth reluctantly admitted that she never believed she was good enough. She always thought she had to do more to get someone to love her, to want to be around her.

One night, while searching the scriptures, Elizabeth came upon Isaiah 66:2:

For this is what the Lord says: I will extend peace to her like a river.

Excited by the proclamation, Elizabeth scrawled the words on a piece of paper and taped it to a wall in her bedroom. She read her prophecy every night before she went to sleep.

Tonight, however, she couldn't sleep. She was drawn to the memories of her friendship with Nina. Nina had befriended her without receiving anything in exchange. Why would she do that? Elizabeth picked up the phone and dialed.

"Hello?" a groggy voice on the other end said.

"Hey, I'm sorry to wake you, but I need to know something."

"What? What's wrong?"

"I told you about the deliverance class that I'm going to, right?"

"Yeah."

"Well, one thing I've discovered is that I don't feel worthy of love unless I'm doing something to earn it. You never made me earn your love or your friendship. Why?"

"Hold on, let me sit up and turn this light on." The rustle of the sheets came across the line. "Okay, I'm awake now. What are you talking about?"

"Why are you my friend, Nina? I've never done anything for you."

"I just am. You don't have to do anything, but be who you are."

"You know that scripture in the Bible that says *it is by faith that we are saved and not of works, lest any man should boast?* That's how our friendship is. We love each other just because that is what we have decided to do. And when God decided to love me, He didn't wait on me to become perfect." Elizabeth smiled, thinking she had said something deep.

"None of us would be saved if God waited on perfection."

"I know, I know. But don't you see? I gave Kenneth everything I had so he wouldn't leave. I've tried to wow my fans so they wouldn't leave. But they left anyway."

"What are you talking about?"

"When people give you something, it should be free. I'm tired of paying!"

"Okay, okay. Stop paying, you sick puppy. Now go to bed and call me in the morning."

Elizabeth heard the dial tone then smiled. Okay, maybe Nina didn't get what she was trying to say. She had experienced a lot of that lately. Friends, family, and fans didn't understand her, but she was beginning to understand a few things. She hung up the phone and looked toward heaven. "Lord, I will accept your free gift of love. I will accept your friendship. Thank you for these precious gifts."

Joy was her companion, as she lay down to get a few hours sleep before morning.

"Wha—what's wrong?" Elizabeth asked, as she burst into Kenneth's room. He thrashed back and forth, eyes closed; asleep, but in torment. "Kenneth, wake up!" She shoved his shoulder. "Come on, you're having a nightmare."

Kenneth shot up, gasping for air. He looked around. Still gasping, he turned his gaze on Elizabeth. "Who—who are you?" Sweat dripped from his forehead as he searched the room. "Where am I?"

"I'm your wife, Kenneth. Liz." She shook him. "Look at me. Don't do this, you know who I am."

He wiped the sweat from his brow, sat up a little surer, and centered his gaze on the woman sitting in his bed. "Thanks for waking me up. That one was a doozy."

"Did you remember anything? The doctor said you should try to retain your dreams, even the nightmares. It might be the key to help unlock your mind."

Kenneth shook his head. He brought his knees up to his chest, rested his elbows on his knees, and put his hands on his head. "I'm sorry. I can't remember."

She grabbed his arm and pulled at him. "You've got to. I want you to come back to me. Tell me what the dream was about, Kenneth. Let's get it over with."

Three weeks had passed, since they talked with Dr. Thomas. Almost every night since, Kenneth had experienced tormenting dreams.

"Do you want me to stay in here with you?"

Yeah, he wanted her to stay. He wanted to pull that midnight black negligee off her mocha chocolate body and show her what else he wanted. But the way she asked to stay with him sounded maternal, like she wanted to chase his boogieman away. He was almost certain that he hadn't sucked his thumb since he was a child, and equally as certain that he hadn't needed a mama in his bed since that time either. No, he needed much more. But whether he liked it or not, Tommy was still between them. He wouldn't share any woman, and certainly not his wife.

"You go on back to bed. I'll be fine." He pulled the covers over his shoulders and lay down.

She started to say something, but got off his chaise—the bed he preferred to hers—walked over to the French door, then looked back at her husband. He was staring at her. "Sweet dreams," she said before closing the doors behind her.

A couple of hours later, they sat across the breakfast table, eating in silence; passing the salt and pepper while ignoring the issues between them. Kenneth put the last piece of bacon in his mouth, stood, and scraped his plate clean. "See you later," he said as he walked back to the table and kissed Erin and Danae.

Elizabeth puckered up and kissed the air behind Kenneth's back. He had on his power suit. The Brooks Brothers navy blue double-breasted number always made him look like the king of the hill. That yellow tie didn't hurt none either. She knew without asking that Kenneth was job-hunting again today. Every morning since their big blow up, Kenneth hit the pavement in search of a new gig. The economy was on a downturn and jobs for professionals were lean. Kenneth was a CEO minus the company. A tough sell to most Human Resource professionals.

"How long do you think you'll be gone today?" Elizabeth asked.

"Couple of hours. I want to stop at the church and speak with Pastor Lewis. Then I need to check on a lead I received yesterday.

Her eyes sparkled. "What kind of lead?"

"Two Fortune 1000 Companies are looking for vice presidents to run the IT department."

She wanted to hug him and wish him success with his hunt, but they weren't cool like that yet. "Will you be able to attend the benefit for the homeless with me tonight?"

All of Elizabeth's engagements cancelled on her. She had received an invitation to perform at a benefit. To her, it was a Godsend.

"What time do you need me to be ready?"

"By six."

"Not a problem," he said as he left the house.

Elizabeth stayed in her seat, marveling over the civilized conversation they just had. "It's a beginning," she said to herself as she picked up her tea and sipped.

Erin's brows furrowed. "Beginning of what?"

"What? Oh, nothing," she said, as if she'd been caught staring in the boys' locker room. "Eat up."

While Kenneth was out, Elizabeth cleaned the house and enjoyed her children. At five o'clock, she laid her dress on the bed and jumped in the shower. She towel dried, lotioned up, then squeezed into her evening gown. It was a remarkable dress. Red, with irregularly scattered sequins, and just a suggestion of cleavage. The knee-length dress was lined with red silk. Sexy, but in a respectable way.

Kenneth walked into her room. He fumbled with his bow tie, then threw up his hands.

"Here, let me help you." Elizabeth grabbed the tie from him and proceeded to fix him up.

"I like your dress," he told her as she stood close to him, putting the finishing touches on his bow tie. "Have I ever been able to put one of these ties on?" he asked as he covered the left side of his face with his hand.

"Never." She laughed. "But I've always enjoyed doing this for you."

He looked into her eyes, then stepped back. "Thanks."

"My pleasure. Oh, before I forget." She picked up a small box and handed it to him. "The stuff I ordered for you came in today."

"What's this?"

"Mudear's Herbal Salve. I surfed the net looking for something that might ease some of your pain." She gave him a half-smile. "Just rub it on your knees every night."

The cod, au gratin potatoes, and six green beans weren't bad. But, Kenneth kept eyeing her, sucking his teeth and clinking his fork on the plate. Good cause or not, Kenneth hated paying a hundred bucks a plate. Would have hated it, even when he had money to burn. And since she wasn't getting paid for singing tonight, he was probably calculating how much each green bean cost.

"So, Kenneth, what line of work are you in?" asked Roger McDaniels, a high-powered executive with a Fortune 100 Company.

Elizabeth put her fork down and lightly patted his hand. Betty, Roger's wife, put her elbows on the table, hands under her chin, and waited for Kenneth to speak. Clarence Johnson and his wife Sue were also all ears.

"I'm actually between jobs right now."

"I see," Roger said, then studied his food as if looking for bones in his cod.

Elizabeth wanted to scream at him and tell him that he didn't *see* at all. Kenneth wasn't avoiding the child support police, or selling dime bags on the corner like other men who claimed to be between jobs. He was a good man, with more talent and ability than all the Fortune 100 executives Roger McDaniel knew.

Clarence Johnson said, "Well, if you're looking for something to do while you're job hunting, I could sure use some help."

Elizabeth smiled. Kenneth pulled his hand from under hers. "What type of business are you in?" he asked Clarence.

"I run the Hope Center. It's a place where the homeless can get food, clothing, some Word, and a room for the night. I couldn't pay much, but God's rewards are much better than anything I could give you anyway."

"Let me think about it," he told Clarence, as Elizabeth stood to handle her business.

Sitting behind the piano, Elizabeth could feel the judgmental stares of the small crowd. She had sung in crowded coliseums, churches with ten and twenty thousand members. But tonight, as she readied herself to sing in front of two hundred fifty people, her nerves did a jig, and her palms got sweaty.

"I want to thank you for allowing me to sing tonight. You'll never know how much this means to me." She wiped her palms on her nine hundred-dollar dress. "It has been rough for me these last few years. I thought my husband was dead, and I didn't know how to cope with that. God was supposed to love me, so how could He have allowed such a tragedy to happen?" She looked at Kenneth, smiled sweetly, then continued. "My husband had been everything to me. When he was gone, I didn't want to live. But God has taught me how to live. He has taught me how to love Him. When all desert me, God is still my special friend. This song is my tribute to God. I hope you enjoy it.

She turned to the black and ivory keys and began to play:

"Sitting thinking about all of my yesterdays, Trying to find a reason for all the mistakes I made. Not knowing that it was your loving grace that spared my life. Now I'm daily learning how to totally trust in you, I've found that your love is—your love is really true, and Mighty good to know I can count on you— Lord, you are my special friend."

Elizabeth serenaded the Lord, as her audience, mesmerized, listened to her sweet, soulful melody.

"Pictures in my head of long ago memories and Failures from my past are continually haunting me, But I know, right here and now, You have delivered me—you've made me whole. Now that I've found you, you've given me liberty, Saved my sin-sick soul, set my spirit free—and, How I love you Lord, 'cause you first loved me, You are my special friend. Oooh, I adore you, I live for you. How you've blessed me. My confession is, you amaze me. You fulfill me. When I'm hurting you console and then you thrill me. How you've changed me—I'll never be the same. You are my special friend. Hey, Lord, you are my special friend."

Clarence leaned over and told Kenneth, "Your wife sings like Yolanda Adams."

Kenneth grinned like a schoolboy with his first crush. "You must be joking, man. She sings better than Yolanda Adams."

"And what a friend we have in Jesus, All my sins and grief He'll bear. What a privilege to carry everything to God in prayer."

Standing ovation, and pass the Kleenex please, were the responses when Elizabeth finished her love song to God. "Thank you. Thank you so very much." Elizabeth looked out into the small crowd. For two years, she had seen Tommy's face in the room as she did her thing. Kenneth's face was the one she looked into tonight. He stood and clapped with the others. For a brief moment, Elizabeth saw adoration and love swimming through his gray-green eyes. She smiled at her husband and he smiled back. *Thank you, Lord.*

Then she remembered Tommy and the smile faded. She hadn't heard from him in weeks. *Lord,* she silently prayed, *wherever Tommy is tonight, watch over him. Bring him home, Lord. Help him to know that you care for him.*

20

Tommy was into his third scotch. Looking at a ten and a five, hollering, "Hit me again!" A red lady, full of heart, was laid down on the table in front of him. "Dag. Where are all the tramps when you need 'em?" Tommy asked, as he threw his hand in. Blackjack wasn't his game anyway.

He was a craps man. In the mood to get paid and make some noise, he moved to the crap table, where he could do both. He placed a five hundred dollar, don't pass line bet and picked up the dice. He kissed them and cursed them at the same time. "Don't you dare be a seven or eleven." He threw the dice and waited. Around the table, everybody was yelling, cheering him on. Actually, they were drunk, but Tommy would take what he could get.

The dice hit the backboard and then bounced back midway of the table. "Two. Player wins," the dealer informed the rowdy group.

Cheers went up. Tommy took hold of the dice and worked his magic again and again. By the time he finished, he had twenty thousand in his possession. Pretty good. Especially since he had lost ten thousand at the tables the night before.

As he collected his bounty, Cynda Stevens strutted over to him like this was his lucky day. Tommy recognized her immediately. A face like Cynda's was not easily forgotten or dismissed. Her amber-colored skin, coal black hair, and beauty mark just above her pouty lips sent shivers through him. This girl would give J-Lo a run for her money. Beauty wasn't her problem; it was those cold black eyes. Eyes that carried pain. Eyes that knew too much, had seen too much. She used to be one of Isaac Walker's women. She'd come into the Belanté Club either with Isaac or looking for him countless times. But that was years ago.

"What brings you to Georgia, Cynda?"

"Oh, this and that. What about you?"

He lifted up some of his winning chips. "I came to gamble. Needed to clear my head, think some things over."

She cozied up to him. "Well, do you think best alone, or would you like a little company? Maybe have a party?"

"Who's having the party?"

Cynda put her hand on Tommy's thigh and squeezed. "We are. And I have two friends right over there." She pointed him in the direction of a woman with ample bosom, and a pretty boy showing off his Nautilus body in a tight muscle shirt. They both smiled and waved at Tommy.

So, Cynda was tricking. She needed her butt whupped, Tommy thought. But, he wasn't her daddy, so the butt whupping he contemplated was not about to make her keep her dress down and panties up. "How much?"

She grabbed a couple of his winning chips. "It won't break you, Daddy."

She had to go call him Daddy, and he had a good and thick belt on too. He licked his lips. "What about them?" He nodded in the direction of Cynda's so-called friends.

"Why don't we handle the negotiations in your hotel room?"

He wanted to thank God for his good fortune, then remembered he wasn't talking to God. "All right. Let me settle up, then we can go."

It took twenty minutes to settle up. Cynda and company waited patiently. When Tommy was finished handling his business, Cynda introduced him to Jasmine and Sam.

"Nice to meet you. Come on, let's go," Jasmine said.

Tommy opened the door to his room. Cynda spotted the two queen-size beds and pounced on them. She jumped in the air doing straddles, like a tenth-grade cheerleader for the winning team.

Tommy walked over to the bar and poured himself a drink. "Have a seat," he told Jasmine and Sam.

Cynda left her high school days behind and climbed off the bed. "Let's get this party started right." She pulled out a bag of white heaven and poured its contents onto the table. She pulled a couple of small straws out of her purse. She squatted on the floor, lined up the coke, and inhaled. She lifted the straw to Tommy with raised eyebrows.

A cokehead. Did he really want to deal with this mess tonight? What other options did he have? Tell the three of them goodnight and then turn on *TBN* and listen to some prophet or prophetess put him in his place?

Cocaine. Preacher. Cocaine. Preacher. He weighed his options as he took the straw out of Cynda's hand.

Jasmine and Sam joined the party too. Pretty soon, the room buzzed like a swarm of bees looking for honey. The honey was on the table and it was all gone.

Cynda stripped down to her baby-making suit. "Mm, mm, mm." Isaac must have been smoking that stuff to let all them curves go. Tommy told Cynda as much.

She just shrugged and asked, "Isaac who?"

He was about to ask her why she was trying to lie to him, but then Jasmine and Sam got butt naked too. "Thank you, Jesus," he muttered under his breath, then cursed loudly.

"What's wrong, baby?" Cynda asked with pouty lips.

"What? Oh, nothing. Don't worry about it." He put his drink down and consciously told himself to stop thinking about God and Jesus. They weren't interested in helping him. And they certainly hadn't gifted him with these three naked bodies on his bed. This act would secure his one-way ticket to hell, but he didn't care. Maybe he should thank the devil for his plentiful bounty.

A smile tweaked the creases of his full Mandingo lips. He walked toward the bed feeling as if he were in a Toyota commercial. Within minutes he would be kicking up his heels screaming, "Oh, what a feeling!"

"Just tell me one thing," Kenneth said, barging into Elizabeth's room. He startled her. She dropped the towel she was trying to wrap around her body as she walked out of her bathroom.

Kenneth let out a stunned gasp and put his left hand over the scars on his face.

"Why do you do that?" Elizabeth asked, picking up her towel and knotting it above her bosom.

"Do what?"

She walked over to him and pulled his hand away from his face. "Why do you put your hand over your scars?" She put her finger on his face and traced the lines of his scars. "Whenever I look at you, you cover your face."

He stepped away. Her hand fell. "I do not."

She raised her hand and gently stroked his face again. "Don't you know that this doesn't matter to me? The love I have for you is sealed deep in my heart. A few scratches won't change it."

He grabbed her arms and shoved her away. "It's more than a few scratches. Don't patronize me!"

She stumbled, grabbing hold of her four-poster bed. "Kenneth, what is your—"

"Stop it." He pointed an accusatory finger in her face. "Don't you stand there and tell me how much you love me, when you tried to kill yourself over Tommy Brooks."

"I did not."

"Stop lying! It was all over the news." Elizabeth sat down on her bed as Kenneth continued his diatribe. "Some homecoming, huh? Can't you just see the headlines?" He put his hand in the air like he was capturing each word. "Husband returns home to find wife in love with another man."

"Kenneth, you're not being fair."

"How fair were you when you sold my business? You didn't even wait a good four months before you ran off with *your manager*. Good grief, Liz. How can you call that love?"

"For the last time, Kenneth, I had a nervous breakdown after you disappeared. It was either sell your business and start my singing career or go completely crazy."

"All right, I can understand that. You needed to sell my business to help support my children and your new career—but I can't understand, nor forgive you, for falling in love with someone before my body was even cold."

Elizabeth flung her hands in the air. She slowly pulled each word through her teeth. "I am not in love with Tommy."

"Yeah, that's why you ran out of this house like the roof was on fire. *Got to go rescue Tommy*," he taunted.

Lord, when will I stop paying? She adored Kenneth, loved him with a passion. Only one thing had changed since he'd returned to her: he no longer owned her heart and soul. Oh, she'd gladly give him her heart—but her soul finally belonged to God, and she wasn't going to take it back. Not again, not ever again.

"I bailed Tommy out of jail because he is a friend of mine. I would have done the same thing for Nina if she had been in trouble." She stood and walked toward her husband. "I'm in love with you, Kenneth. I've loved you for as long as I can remember." She put her arms around his neck and pulled him toward her. "Let me show you what it was like between us." Her lips brushed against his. Her eyes implored him to give her what she wanted.

He inhaled her scent. "Mmh," he said as he put his arms around her and leaned into his wife. Opening his mouth to claim hers felt like coming home. There was nothing spiritual about this kiss. It was carnal. Flesh touching flesh and flesh begging for more.

He lifted his head and gazed into her eyes. He was trapped, but the honey was in the trap with him. "You make me want to remember."

"Aw, baby." She covered his face with wet smoldering kisses and pulled him toward the sanctuary of their bed. "Come with me. We'll make new memories together."

Elizabeth untied her towel and let it fall to the ground.

Tommy woke with a headache. He grabbed his head and reached for Cynda. He would have her get up and find him some aspirin. Cynda wasn't in bed. He lifted his head off the pillow and glanced around his hotel room. Empty.

He held onto his head and got out of bed. He looked around the room for his briefcase. It was on the floor next to the door. He really needed those aspirin now. His briefcase was empty. He shook his head. The trick had gotten tricked. What's new about this story?

He kicked the briefcase against the door and pounded his fists in the wall. He had a couple hundred in his wallet and about tripped over his feet getting to his pants. He picked them off the floor and examined his wallet. Cynda left no stone unturned. She had taken every cent. She didn't even have enough mercy to leave him bus fare home. Sure, he lived in Atlanta, but this casino was more than an hour away. "That mud-duck. No wonder Isaac dumped her." He wanted to dump her too. If he ever ran into that trick again, he would put his foot in her whoring behind.

He threw his pants down, walked to the bar and poured himself a drink. He gulped it down, then looked toward heaven. "I needed that money. Why are you always against me?"

Now he wanted to talk to God.

21

Kenneth grabbed a jar of peanut butter and smeared it on a couple of slices of day old white bread. He passed his handiwork on to Emma, the retiree who faithfully gave of her time at the Hope Center. Right now she was on jelly duty. Later, she and Kenneth would help make vegetable soup.

Yeah, okay. He decided to take Clarence up on his offer. With this slow economy, it wasn't as if he were doing anything else. And besides, he had talked to his pastor about the thought of helping the homeless. Pastor Lewis seemed to think it was a good idea.

The toothless woman from the park was standing in his line. Kenneth smiled at her and double swiped the peanut butter on one of the sandwiches. That was how Jamal, her youngest son, liked his sandwich. "How's it going today, Sandy?"

"Not bad. My mom agreed to take me and the kids in until I deliver this one." She rubbed her huge stomach. "Thanks for calling her."

"After you have the baby, come find me, okay? I'm sure we can get you a job somewhere."

A tear creased her eyes. "Thanks, Kenneth. You're all right."

When he was finished with his work, Kenneth sat on the steps and talked with a few of the men. He brought several Bibles that he purchased at the Christian bookstore on Peachtree. He passed them out and told the men that they could talk to him anytime and ask anything they wanted.

One of the men put his hand up, shielding himself from the Bible. "No thanks, man. I don't want no parts of the Bible."

Kenneth pulled the Bible back and put it on the step next to him. "No problem. Do you mind my asking why you're so against reading God's Word?"

"Naw, I don't mind." He opened his mouth to tell a story that made Kenneth want to crawl all the way home and suck the toe jam from Liz's feet. He'd even hand her another of his mother's vases, and cheer her on as she broke it.

Tyrone said that he had been married to one of them Bible-toting, long-dress-wearing sanctified sisters of the most holy church of God. "She preached hell and brimstone around my house all day long. Told me, if I didn't straighten up, that God was going to get me. I got tired of her telling me that I was no good. Acting like she was the sainted mother of the right way." He put his finger in his nose, pulled out a booger and wiped it on his shirtsleeve.

"Anyway, the minute I started going to church, she started skipping church. Skirt got shorter, make-up got redder. Come to find out, Mother Theresa had started dating one of the street hustlers she had tried to evangelize into God's kingdom. Before I knew it, this guy had turned her out. Had her turning tricks and calling him Daddy. She even tried to sell some of it to me when I was walking down the strip looking for her no good tail."

Silence filled the air. Every man on those steps had their own story to tell, but right now, Tyrone was king. Nobody wanted to top his story. If they could, they wisely decided to keep that lovely tale to themselves.

"Whew, I don't know what to say." Kenneth didn't know how to offer comfort for Tyrone's problems. Life wasn't fair; it was mean and hateful, and even spiteful at times.

"Don't say nothing. Just don't put that Bible in my face again."

Later that evening, Kenneth sat in the kitchen going over the details of the day with his wife. Six days had passed since he had made love to the woman seated across from him. Six long suffering days. But Kenneth was determined not to fall in love with this woman before he knew who she really was. Thus, his self-imposed celibacy.

He pulled his lower lip through his teeth as he studied her. She had on a yellow tank top that showed a little too much flesh, some form-fitting white slacks, and a white pullover apron. Ought to be a law against looking this good while grilling steaks and roasting potatoes. He was sure he could make a case for disturbing the peace. His peace. *Mmph, mmm*, he thought. "I don't know how much I'm helping those people. I'm down there slapping together peanut butter and jelly sandwiches, feeding the body, when their souls are still hungry."

"Not many people would do what you're doing for the homeless. You're doing your part, and that's at least something."

He put his hand on his head and massaged his temple. "I know. I just don't feel like I'm doing enough. You know?

I feel like I'm just giving them a fish when they need tools that will help them catch the fish for themselves."

"Kenneth, you have a very strategic mind. I've seen you at work." She reached over and caressed his hand. "I used to tell you that I was the reason you were so successful. The truth is, you were bound to succeed. You're a born leader. So pray, ask God to direct your path, then sit down and work out a strategy. Figure out what those people need, and go get it for them."

He looked at her for a stunned moment. Was this his wife? Was she really offering him sound advice, as if he mattered to her?

Elizabeth stood to tend to the steaks. Kenneth grabbed her arm and looked into her eyes. "I was upset when I found out you sold my company."

"I know," she answered with eyes looking into his, imploring him to understand.

"It wasn't the loss of the company that upset me. It was the fact that you didn't care what I would have wanted."

She ran her hand through her hair and lowered her gaze.

"I don't want you to feel left out," Kenneth continued. "Whatever idea or plan I come up with to help the homeless might cost us every cent we have left. Are you okay with that?"

"I don't know how I would feel about that, Kenneth. I think it's good to help those less fortunate, but giving up all of our money is a little scary."

He let her arm go. "You'd hate the thought of downsizing your lifestyle just to help a few unfortunates, huh?"

"I like my house, Kenneth. I like my lifestyle. Does that make me a bad person?"

"No. Look, Liz, I'm glad you told me how you feel. I'll keep it in mind."

"And I'll try to support whatever you decide. I can't promise anything though," she told him as she walked to the grill and pulled off the porterhouses.

Earlier that day, Kenneth had helped peel potatoes and chop celery for the vegetable soup the homeless shelter would serve for dinner tonight. No meat had been delivered to the shelter that day. So, while he, Kenneth Underwood, sat down to eat a thick porterhouse steak and roasted potatoes, the shelter would be serving vegetable soup, without meat, and day-old bread.

The Underwood family ate in silence. Kenneth tried not to feel guilty as he watched Erin pick over her steak and potatoes, and Danae flat out declare that she didn't like steak and wanted something else. For her, a thick cheeseburger and fries were produced. Kenneth tried to forget about the extra peanut butter on stale bread he gave to Sandra's little boy, and the smile that appeared on his face—but it was real hard.

Getting that food down was hard, too. To let it linger on his plate and go to waste, knowing that others would have given their left arm for the meal he had tonight, would have been harder. When he finally removed himself from the dinner table, he had a full stomach and a heavy heart.

Kenneth tossed and turned through the night. A sea of nameless faces passed through his mind, all begging him to help—to right the wrongs they had suffered. What could he do? He was just one man. He screamed back at the nameless faces. No answer came from the beggar brigade in his head.

The faces in his dreamland began to diminish. His tossing and turning became less frequent. His mind eased in the pillowy soft cushion of sleep. Then he saw the light—the same light that came to him just before his dreams turned dark.

Black, scaly fangs were extended. Jaundiced eyes were glaring at him like he was a rib dinner. Petrified, his breathing became labored. Jaundiced eyes opened his mouth and spat brown mucus on the ground.

Kenneth was safe though. Somebody was holding him. "No, no, no!" he screamed as he felt himself being laid down on the ground. Another bolt of light. This one was almost blinding.

"Wake up. Come on, Kenneth. Wake up." Elizabeth pushed and prodded. "Do you hear me? Wake up!"

Kenneth thrashed back and forth one more time, then his eyes opened. "Oh, thank God. Thank God, it's you."

"What was it? What did you see?"

"I . . . I . . ."

"What Kenneth? Don't let it go. Come on. What is this thing that you don't want to remember?"

He sat up. "I . . . I don't know what I saw." His eyes stared off into space. "The first thing I see is light, then I see some kind of animal glaring at me. I can feel how much he hates me." He looked at Elizabeth. "He wants to kill me. But somebody, or something is holding me."

She sat on the chaise next to her husband, rubbing his shoulder. "Sounds like you're just having a bad dream."

"No," he said with conviction. "This was real. Liz, I don't know when, and I don't know what was going on, but this happened to me."

With her index finger tapping against her chin she asked, "What else happened?"

"I don't know. I think I must have blacked out. I feel myself being laid down on the ground or something I guess. Then it all goes black."

"And there's nothing else? You don't remember anything else that happened?"

He put his hand to his chin, not to hide his scars this time, but to rub his chin as he thought. "Well, I didn't see it this time. But awhile back, I remember dreaming that I was lying on the ground, blacked out just as I was tonight. All of a sudden, this burst of light entered my darkness, and I heard a man's voice say, 'You've got too much to live for. Don't give up now.' I imagined that I was at Ground Zero and it was that voice that gave me the courage to live."

Tears danced around the corner of Elizabeth's eyes. She lifted Kenneth's covers. "Scoot over."

He gave her a questioning glance.

"I'm going to sleep in here tonight."

"I don't need you to protect me from the boogie man, Liz."

She gave him a tolerant smile. "I know you don't. Now scoot over."

Kenneth complied. Hard to argue with a determined woman. Anyway, he didn't feel much like fighting tonight. She cuddled up to him and rubbed his back. Whispering in his ear soft, sweet words of endearment. Kenneth closed his eyes as she began to sing.

"You are the one that I choose to share my life with, And you are the one that fills my heart

with so much joy. You are the one that makes my life feel so complete. There's no doubt in my mind—you are the one".

Kenneth's eyes jolted open; he lifted his head from his pillow. "That song, I've heard it before. What's the name of it?"

Elizabeth continued rubbing his back and arms. "*You Are The One.* It was our wedding song. Now lay back down." She continued, when he was comfortable.

"There's a peace that passes all our understanding, And it's the kind of peace that only God can give.

Now I know that I can say, without any reservation

That I will cherish you each day that I live.

For you are the one that I choose to share my life with . . ."

Kenneth slept. This time, his sleep wasn't infiltrated by fang-faced demons. He was enraptured with the thoughts of Elizabeth's love and the soft, sinuous feel of her body next to his. A few other thoughts of Elizabeth floated through his mind as sleep claimed him. They were R-rated and private.

22

Elizabeth sat in the living room reading her Bible, while Kenneth horsed around with the girls upstairs. She was reading the first chapter of Romans and finding no pleasure in it.

Although they knew God, they did not glorify Him as God, nor were thankful, but became futile in their thoughts, and their foolish hearts were darkened.

Professing to be wise, they became fools . . .

For this reason, God gave them up to vile passions. For even their women exchanged the natural use for what is against nature.

Likewise also the men, leaving the natural use of the woman, burned in their lust for one another, men with men committing what is shameful, and receiving in themselves the penalty of their error which was due.

And even as they did not like to retain God in their knowledge, God gave them over to a reprobate mind, to do those things which are not fitting.

She closed the Bible, sat on her comfortable Italian leather couch, and thought about Tommy. At the age of nine, Tommy's spirit had been broken. He spent his adult years acting out, daring anybody to challenge him; believing that his actions were justified. God wasn't there when he needed Him most, so why should he give a flying fig what God wanted now? She and Tommy had been friends for years, but she had not truly understood him. "Mind wired differently? Hah, it's different all right. It's reprobate."

She rubbed her hands over her Bible. "Your Word, Lord, it preaches judgment against Tommy. But I know that you are a merciful God. I'm asking you to take another look at my friend. Restore his soul, Lord. He has endured much pain. Show him your love."

She picked up the phone and dialed Tommy's number. It rang several times. No answer. She wanted to drive over to his house and shake some sense into him. After all, friends don't let friends live without Jesus.

It was her Christian duty to go see about Tommy. Donny McClurklin once sang, "We fall down, but we get up." Elizabeth was a firm believer in God's redemptive power, His ability to lift one of His children out of the depths of despair. He'd done it for her and Tommy's sins, although weighty, were no worse than the sins she had committed. In God's eyes, their sins were the same, and needed the blood of Jesus to cover them.

The theology sounded great. Now to convince her husband that Tommy needed someone to preach the Word to him. She put her keys on the table in the foyer and paced back and forth. She'd be thirty-six her next birthday, so she wasn't about to admit that she was scared to go upstairs and talk to her husband. She did, however, allow that she was a little hesitant.

So, while she cowered in the foyer, contemplating the words she would say, Kenneth whistled down the stairs. "Hey, Liz. I need to order some more of that salve. My knees are feeling better everyday."

"I ordered the product off the web."

He smiled as he conquered the last step. "Maybe one day I'll get rid of this cane." He stopped smiling when he glanced at Elizabeth. "What's wrong?"

She wrung her hands and pulled her bottom lip through her teeth. "I have to go do something."

"Can it wait until I get back? I wanted to talk with the director at the Hope Center before he gets too busy."

"Well," she began cautiously, "I need to make sure that you're okay with what I need to do."

He gave her a tolerant smile. "What is it?"

"Kenneth, I really need you to understand," she said quickly, holding up her hands to ward off any objection. "I need to go see about Tommy. I haven't heard from him in weeks. I'm worried."

The corners of his mouth tightened. "Why'd you lay in my bed last night, lullabying me, like I meant something to you—when you're still thinking about *him*?"

"Kenneth, be reasonable. One has nothing to do with the other."

"Do you even remember what you sang to me last night? You said that *I* was the one that you wanted to share your life with. That's what *you* sang to me, Liz. What happened between now and then?"

"Kenneth, I love you. I want to be with you. Plain and simple."

He pointed his index finger in her face. "Then act like it. Don't think I'm going to continue to let you live under my roof." He caught the look of surprise on her face. "That's right, I said *my roof*. You can't live here and hang out with Tommy."

She refused to cry. He would not see how much his words hurt. "What if God wants me to help Tommy? Can you honestly live with stopping God's work?"

"God wouldn't ask my wife to go sleep with some other man."

Elizabeth gasped then, without her help, her hand flew up and smacked Kenneth's face. "How dare you?" She stepped back. "I get it. You don't want me, but you take exception to anyone else wanting to be with me."

Kenneth rubbed his face and stepped back. "I never said I didn't want you."

Erin and Danae ran down the stairs. Elizabeth was too steamed to care.

"You don't have to say it!" She was screaming, arms flapping in the air as she tore into him. "You refuse to sleep in our bedroom. And last night, when I lay in bed with you—did you touch me?"

He didn't answer.

Danae hugged Elizabeth's waist. "No, Mommy. Don't yell at Daddy."

Erin stepped to Elizabeth like a grown woman. "Don't you hit my daddy. You're messing everything up, and I'm not going to let you."

Oh, somebody was going to get hit all right. The Underwood family was about to be news at eleven. Elizabeth reared back, getting ready to knock the taste of last night's corn-on-the-cob and pork chops out of Erin's mouth.

But Kenneth beat her to the punch. He grabbed Erin's arm and swung her around. He put his finger in her face. "Little girl, don't you ever disrespect my wife like that again."

A day late and a dollar short, but Elizabeth would take what she could get. *Go head on, boy,* she inwardly screamed. *Stand up for your wife.*

"But, Daddy—"

"Don't you *but Daddy* me. As long as you live under our roof and eat our food, you better act like Elizabeth and Kenneth are the best things since sweet potato pie. You got me?"

Erin lowered her head. "Yes, Daddy."

Elizabeth ran her hands through her hair, still wanting to reach out and touch her oldest.

Kenneth released Erin's arm. "Go to your room. You too, Danae."

Danae was still holding onto Elizabeth. "I didn't do anything, Daddy."

Kenneth pointed toward the stairs. "Go on anyway. I need to talk to your mom."

As the kids stumped up the stairs, Kenneth turned to Elizabeth. "I'm sorry that I got all that mess started. I just see red when you talk about Tommy."

Elizabeth's lip twitched and her hand itched as she crossed her arms.

He scratched his head. "Can't you understand, Liz? I just need to know that you are mine."

"You idiot! I *am* yours." She grabbed a piece of paper and pencil. "Look, I'm not going to argue with you about this. You don't want me to go see about Tommy? Fine. You do it." She scribbled Tommy's address and directions on the paper and handed it to Kenneth.

Tommy could go to the devil for all he cared. He started to throw the paper on the floor. His fingers twitched, lip tightened as he looked around for the trash can.

"Kenneth, this is important to me." She grabbed his arm, begging him with her sad eyes. "He needs to know that someone cares about him."

He shoved the paper in his pocket. "If I have time, I'll swing by there."

Kenneth walked out the door and Elizabeth walked up the stairs. The devil was running rampant through her house. Raising ruckus like his name was on the deed. Well, that freeloader was getting tossed out. As soon as she regained the strength to fight, she was going for the jugular. But right now, she needed to lie down and detox. *Lord, my family is hurting. Please help us.* Danae and Erin were in her bedroom.

Danae stood as Erin sobbed in Elizabeth's bed. "We've got to get out of here, Erin. You're going to get us in trouble again."

Elizabeth watched her children, then walked over to Danae and kissed her on the forehead. She sat on her bed next to Erin.

Erin lifted up. "I didn't mean it, Mama. I—I'm just s—so scared that he'll leave again."

Elizabeth pulled her daughter to her bosom and softly rubbed her hair. "That's all right, baby. I was scared for a long time too."

Erin continued to sob as she asked, "You're not scared anymore, Mama?"

"No, baby." Elizabeth situated herself on the bed and rocked her child. "Why should I be afraid? I serve a God who is more than able to deal with my problems."

Erin's voice quivered as she said, "I-I'm so s-sorry."

A single tear rolled down Elizabeth's face. She looked up, and once again read the words plastered on her wall:

For this is what the Lord says: I will extend peace to her like a river.

"Thank you, Lord."

"Clarence, these people need more than peanut butter sandwiches. There has to be more that I can do to help them."

Clarence Johnson put his elbows on his well-used desk.

He had been the director of the shelter for twelve years. "What do you think might help them?"

"What do you think about adding an independent living skills center onto this building?"

Clarence looked around his shoebox of an office and grinned. "Would I get a bigger office?"

"Yeah, whatever you want. I'm actually thinking of building a facility where unemployed and homeless people can learn to read, type, and any other skills that might help them get a job."

"That sounds great, Kenneth, but you've got to remember there are a lot of drug addicts on the street. They might be able to pass a typing test, but can they pass a drug test?"

Kenneth put his Bible on Clarence's desk. "That's why we'll offer them Jesus. He's cleaned up a few dope heads."

Clarence raised his hand. "I can testify to that, brother."

Clarence and Kenneth discussed avenues for fundraising. The center would be costly. They would need to hit local businesses. Appeal to their more benevolent side.

When they were finished plotting and planning, Kenneth was preparing to drive home when he heard the voice of God.

Son, do you love me?
Lord, you know that I love You.
Feed my sheep.
"But, Lord—"
Feed my sheep.

Kenneth turned onto Peachtree, headed toward the Aramore Apartments in Buckhead. When he parked his car in front of the building, he thought about putting the car in reverse and going home. But he couldn't leave, not until he handled his business. He got out of his car and walked into the apartment building. Loud music hip-hopped through the halls as he made his way down the corridor. The music was coming from one apartment. The neighbors were probably calling the police.

The door to the apartment was ajar. Tommy stood in the middle of his living room floor with a do-rag on his head, crust around the edges of his mouth, and from the way he was scratching, he probably had crabs. He screamed into the telephone. "No, I don't have your money! Look, you'll get yours when I get mine." He was squeezing the life out of a stress ball in his right hand.

Liz must have been crazy to trust her career to this maniac.

Tommy turned and saw Kenneth looking through the door. He lowered the volume and waved him in. "Well, get in where you can fit in, dawg. I've got someone waiting on me. I don't have time to argue with you." He hung up the phone and turned to Kenneth. "Are you here for the gold candle sticks or the stereo system?"

"Excuse me?"

Tommy gave him a frustrated glare. "Which are you here to buy, man? Come on, I don't have all day."

"I'm not here to buy anything. Elizabeth sent me."

Tommy eyed Kenneth, then turned up his nose as if he'd caught whiff of a stink bomb. "You look different."

"Having a building fall on you has a tendency to change things."

Tommy glared at Kenneth's cane, then at his scarred face, and sucked his teeth. "Don't come over here looking for a medal. You ain't no war hero, just a victim, like all the rest of us. I've got some scars too." He jabbed his chest with his index finger a few times. "My scars are inside though." He plopped down on his sofa, keeping his scorn directed at Kenneth. "Can't no plastic surgery fix me. So don't come in here looking for sympathy."

"Elizabeth wants to know if you're all right," Kenneth said, choosing not to be riled by this ignorant man.

Tommy put his feet on the coffee table, slouched down on the sofa, and smirked. "Tired of the cripple in her bed?"

Before Kenneth could respond, someone knocked on the door and let himself in. "I'm here for the candle sticks."

Tommy pointed toward the dining room table. The newcomer pushed his Kangol down tighter on his head and did the JJ strut over to the table. "These are nice, man, real nice. How much you want for them?"

"Fifty bucks."

JJ grabbed the candlesticks and pulled a fifty out of his back pocket. "Thanks, man."

Tommy opened the drawer to his coffee table and pulled out a joint. He lit it, inhaled, and blew contaminated smoke out of his mouth. "You sure you don't want to buy some of this stuff? It's all going at low, low prices."

Kenneth wanted to bust Tommy in the head with some of his low, low-priced merchandise. He took a step toward a crystal vase and was reminded of what God spoke into his spirit. He had been commanded to feed, not beat the sheep to within an inch of his life.

Tommy took another puff of the dragon and scratched himself. "You just gon' stand there or what?"

Kenneth's hands were still itching for that vase. He shook himself to get everything back under control. "Do you really think you should be smoking that?"

"It gives me something to do."

Kenneth looked around the room. "Why are you selling your stuff?"

"I got robbed. Why do you think I'm selling my stuff? Them hookers took all the money I had. I got to pay the rent somehow," he said while dragging on his weed.

"So, you choose to solve your problems with drugs?"

"Hey, I'm no crackhead. This ain't nothing but a joint.

Besides, I need a little pick-me-up since I lost the best woman I ever had." He put his hands up. "Wait, let me backtrack. You can't lose something you never had." He looked at Kenneth and tapped the ashes from his pick-me-up stick.

"You're one sick man. You know that?"

Tommy removed his feet from the coffee table, sat up, and focused a sneering glare on Kenneth. "You think you're something, don't you?"

"Excuse me?"

"You heard me. Just because Elizabeth thinks the sun rises and sets on your behind, does not mean the rest of the world is of that opinion."

"I don't know what you're talking about. Elizabeth does not think the sun rises and sets on me."

"Oh, pleasssse." Tommy put his joint in the ashtray and stood. "I couldn't touch her, man. You're gone for over two years, and she wouldn't let anybody near her." His hands flew in the air. "She wigged out on me about every other month. My God, I should have left her in that crazy ward the police checked her into."

That caught Kenneth's attention. "Why was Liz in the hospital?"

"She cracked up. No Kenneth, no stable mind for Elizabeth." Tommy gave Kenneth another scornful look and sat back down. "You've got Elizabeth thinking you're something special, but from where I sit, you're nothing. Just get out of my house."

Kenneth almost laughed out loud. He had despised this man, thinking that his wife was in love with him. Tommy held him in equal contempt because he couldn't get to Liz. She was still in love with her husband. His wife was in love with him. Kenneth wanted to do a jig right in the middle of Tommy's living room. He held himself in check and asked, "What should I tell Liz?" Kenneth looked around the apartment. Dirty socks and pants were scattered across the floor. Containers of half-eaten Chinese food covered the dining room table and floor, waiting on the roaches to finish the Asian cuisine. "She's worried about you. How are you doing?"

"I'll be all right. Just need to find another group to manage, that's all." He shook his pick-me-up stick at Kenneth. "That wife of yours told me I couldn't manage her career unless I straightened up. Ain't that some junk?" He chuckled. "*She's* the pill popper, but I need to straighten up."

"Do you need anything?"

"I'm in need of a lot of things. What do you have?"

Kenneth put his hand in his jacket pocket and pulled out a pocketsize King James Bible.

"Oh, now you're trying to save me."

"Just thought you might like to give the Lord a try."

Tommy smirked. "Man, if I had a nickel for every time somebody told me, 'Come to Jesus and all your troubles will be over'."

"I never said that all your troubles would be over once you came to Jesus." Kenneth stretched out his arms to give Tommy a full view of himself. "Look at me."

"Okay. Well, what can Jesus do for me then? Can He get my money back from them hookers?"

Kenneth laid the Bible down on the coffee table. "When you finish your joint, why don't you read a little. Nothing like reading God's Word when you're blowed, huh?"

"Get out!"

With pleasure, Kenneth wanted to tell him, but he simply turned and silently headed for the door. *Lord, don't you have sheep at the homeless shelter that need to be fed?* He opened the door and stepped out.

"Take this with you," Tommy said as he threw the Bible at him.

Kenneth turned back to Tommy as if a light bulb had finally come on. He said, "Elizabeth didn't give you the money that you used to pay off Debra, did she?" Kenneth didn't wait for an answer; he was now completely convinced that his wife was innocent. He closed the door and left for home sweet home.

23

Tommy sat on his sofa; well actually, the sofa didn't belong to him anymore. He sold his five thousand dollar camel-skin sofa to some freak down the hall for a mere five hundred bucks. She was going to pick it up tomorrow. Tommy sat on it thinking about Kenneth's last comment. Yeah, Tommy knew who Debra was, and yeah, he had gone to New York and handed that woman twenty thou to keep her mouth shut about Kenneth's whereabouts. So what? Like he was bound for the devil because of that one simple act. Mmph, the way Tommy saw it, plenty of people had wronged Him and hadn't had their life savings stolen from them for their efforts.

Tommy glared at the Bible Kenneth had left him, trying to figure out why everybody thought Jesus was the answer to whatever ailed them? Tommy could give all them Bible thumpers an earful of his sorrows. Jesus hadn't ever tried to fix anything for him.

That prostitute who stole his money was somewhere living high off the hog. Did Jesus bother to get his money back? No. Life was one big up-yours.

He was so tired of the 'Come to Jesus' spiel. The next time he heard it, he'd probably throw up. His mother's pastor preached that nonsense all the time. "If all my troubles would be over by coming to Jesus, why did one of your deacons rape me?" Tommy asked, as if the pastor of his youth was standing in his living room communing with him.

Tommy told his mother and her pastor what that fat, sloppy deacon had done to him. His mother told him to quit defaming the good name of one of Kentucky's prominent black citizens. His come-to-Jesus pastor prayed with him. He said, "If this abomination occurred, God will avenge you, son." In other words, he wasn't taking Mister Money Bags off the Deacon Board. Tommy promised himself that once he had a choice, he would never step foot in that church again. As far as he was concerned, his mother could rot in hell. He told the church secretary as much when he was twenty-five and she called to inform him that his mother had passed on.

"I'm disappointed in your attitude," the church secretary told him. "Your mother was a good Christian woman. She deserves to be buried properly."

"Where is the money from her insurance policy?"

The woman reluctantly admitted, "It lapsed. She hadn't paid it in a few years."

"Well, if she was so stupid that she didn't pay her insurance bill, she deserves to be buried in potter's field."

He heard the disapproval in her sigh. "Mr. Brooks—"

"Look lady, I'm not forking over a dime. You tell Deacon Gridley to pay for her funeral."

"We can't do that. Deacon Gridley has been dead for several years. He had a stroke. No, I'm sorry, it wasn't the stroke that killed him. He had a heart attack after the stroke. It was a very painful ordeal, I'm told."

"Good. I hope both their souls rot in hell. Don't call me anymore. If the church is so concerned about her casket, tell them to get up off that benevolence fund."

He hadn't seen the old biddy since his high school graduation. The minute the ceremony was over, he took off his cap and gown, grabbed his suitcase, and bolted. He stayed with friends throughout the summer. Come fall, he enrolled at Kentucky State University. He was only a hop, skip, and a jump from home, but during Thanksgiving and Christmas breaks, he stayed in his dorm and worked whatever jobs the University had for him. He'd even worn dirty drawers when he didn't have the money to do laundry. Anything to avoid going home.

To this day, Tommy still didn't know where his mother was buried. Nor did he care. That church, along with his precious mother, had made him the man he was today. They all should have their part in the lake of fire, and Tommy should be granted a front row seat to watch the agony they would suffer.

His phone rang, interrupting his thoughts. "Yeah, hello?"

"Mr. Brooks, this is Kim Dukes. I talked to you about purchasing your sofa."

"You haven't changed your mind, have you?"

"Oh, no," Kim told him. "I just wanted to know if I could pick it up today rather than tomorrow."

Tommy's gaze was on the Bible stretched open on the floor where he had thrown it. "Sure, why not? Oh, and I'll even throw something extra in the deal for you."

Tommy picked up the Bible, threw it on the sofa, and went into his bedroom to get dressed.

Elizabeth got out of the tub, dried herself, and put on her favorite hunter green silk nightgown.

She then knelt down and assumed her fighting position. She bowed her head. "Father, I thank you for the peace you've given me in the midst of my trials and troubles. Things aren't looking so good right now. I want to believe that everything will be all right, but I need your help. Lord, I just need a little encouragement to keep fighting. Please, Lord. Anything."

She got off her knees and walked out of the bathroom. Her skin was soft, supple and fragrant from soaking in bath oil—her one luxury after a day of pulling weeds, planting shrubs and nurturing children.

Kenneth was in her bed with the covers pulled just above his waist. "Are you tired?" he asked.

He had turned off the lights, lit a few warm vanilla scented candles and sprinkled rose petals on the floor and across the bed. Elizabeth's subconscious registered the ambiance because her eyes were only focused on Kenneth.

Kenneth is actually in my bed. Things are looking up, Lord. "Not that tired," she replied seductively. "Not if you have something other than sleep in mind."

He pulled the covers back on Elizabeth's side of the bed. "Come over here. Let me show you what I have in mind."

She turned out the bathroom light and walked over to the bed. "You're not upset with me anymore?"

He lightly brushed her arm with his fingers. Eyes danced over her silk nightgown. "Get in."

Elizabeth climbed in the bed, their bed. Kenneth kissed her lips, but it wasn't a peck. It was possession. As his hands glided over her body, he proclaimed that she was his.

She smiled up at him. "What's gotten into you?"

"I missed you today." His lips touched hers again; softly, at first. The kiss became demanding and she surrendered.

He told her all that was in his heart. Not with words, but in deed. Wrapped in this together groove, they motioned, I love you. I need you. I want you to be with me forever.

When their love was spent, Kenneth nudged his wife. "Sing to me."

She gave him a weary smile. "Now, I *am* tired."

He wrapped his arms around her and squeezed some love into her. "I just want to hear your voice. Come on, baby."

She was tired. A by-product of being well loved. But she managed to whisper:

Now I know that God has placed us together,
And I vow to let nothing tear us apart.

Starting today, I promise to love you forever,
Darling, right now, I give you my heart.

Kenneth sighed. "That sounds good, baby. Real good."

They slept in harmony, but not for long. Kenneth tossed and turned. He backhanded Elizabeth a couple of times, until she sat up in bed, turned on the light and shook him. She remembered the discussion they'd had with Dr. Thomas. Kenneth's memory was hiding behind his fears. If he could get past this thing that tortured his sleep, maybe he would be able to remember the love they shared.

Horror swept across his face. Elizabeth wanted to grab his arm and shake him, but she had a gut feeling that that was the wrong thing to do. "Lord, we need your help. Please God, deliver my husband from whatever this thing is that is tormenting him."

The bed rocked from the violence of his dreams. Sweat trickled down his face, as he let out a heart-stopping scream.

"Oh my God! Oh, my God! We need you, Lord! Please help us!" Elizabeth pleaded.

Kenneth stopped moving. He lay on his side of the bed completely stiff, as if momentarily paralyzed. His eyes flashed open. He looked at his wife and smiled. "I know, Liz. I know what happened to me."

"What?"

Kenneth sat up and grabbed her shoulders. "First, I've got to know something. Do you believe in the supernatural?"

"I'm a Christian, aren't I?"

"I know, but some Christians don't believe everything the Bible says."

She put her hand on his thigh. "Baby, please tell me. What happened?"

"Remember when I woke up from one of my nightmares and I told you that I saw some type of animal?"

"Yes, I remember."

"Well, it wasn't an animal at all. Hold on, let me start from the beginning." He was talking fast, breathing like an asthmatic patient. "We were in the World Trade Center, going over my financials, when the plane hit the building. Oh, and by the way, my business was worth a lot more than what you got out of it."

Elizabeth opened her mouth to defend her actions.

"We'll talk about that later," he told her, then continued his story. "People were going crazy. They were on the phone calling their families, letting them know they might never see them again. I tried to call you, but you weren't in your hotel room."

"I was on the street with thousands of other onlookers."

He kissed her forehead. "Now, you probably won't believe this, but right before the building fell, a cloud of smoke covered the windows of the tower. A hideous demonic face was in the cloud and everybody in the room saw it. Bob, my accountant, fainted. I tried to carry him down the steps so we could escape, but the building collapsed before we could get out."

Elizabeth was about to reduce his demonic face sighting to something he ate earlier in the day. Then she remembered the newspaper article and photos she had kept since the tragedy. She jumped out of bed and ran out of the room.

"Where are you going? I'm trying to tell you what happened to me."

"I'll be right back. I want to show you something."

When she returned, she threw the September 16th edition of the *New Jersey Daily Record* on the bed. The demonic face Kenneth described to her was front-page news. "Is this what you saw?"

Kenneth picked up the paper and stared into the hollow, evil eyes. He looked back at Elizabeth.

"Someone took those pictures the day of the tragedy. Don't you see, Kenneth? This is why you've been so tormented. You looked right into the face of Satan himself." She pointed at the picture. "That has to be who that is."

"Sit down. I have more to tell you about that day."

Elizabeth sat next to her husband, put her hand on his cheek and waited.

"Angels were there too, Liz. That's why I'm alive today."

"Tell me, Kenneth. What did you see?"

"As I said, the building collapsed while I was still in it. I was pretty close to death when someone pulled me out of the rubble." His gray-green eyes pleaded with Elizabeth to believe. "There were angels; two of them. That was the light I kept seeing in my dreams. When the demons approached, they drew their swords and they battled over my life."

"Wait, Kenneth. I don't get it. Why all this drama? They had taken plenty of lives already. Why fight over one?"

"I don't know, but that angel refused to give up on me.

And those demons didn't like that at all." Kenneth struck the bed. "Liz, do you know what this means?"

She gave him a questioning stare, but said nothing.

"All this time I've been angry with both you and God. I thought He'd forgotten me. Now I know that God doesn't forsake His people. But we stop believing. Stop trusting in His Word." He bowed his head in shame. "Oh, Lord, please forgive me."

Elizabeth pulled Kenneth into her arms.

"That's why we are admonished to pray. And that's why God tells us that our battles do not belong to us, they belong to Him. He sends angels to fight the battles we pray about," he told her.

"You did it, baby. You unlocked your mind."

"It feels good, Liz." He hugged her tight then pulled away smiling. "I've got me an angel."

That was great news, but she needed to know something else. Something he hadn't told her yet. "Do you remember anything else? What about us, Kenneth? Do you remember how we used to be?"

His forehead creased, eyes squinted. "Sorry, Liz. Not yet."

Tears sprang into her eyes.

He moved her closer to him. "It will come, Beautiful. Don't worry."

Her eyes were moist. "You used to call me Beautiful."

"You are." He kissed her. It was slow, wet, and hot. "I know you, Liz," he told her when their lips parted. "If my memory never comes back, rest in the fact that I know who you are. And when I visited Tommy, I also realized something else about you."

"What?"

"I realized that you really did want me to come back to you. And that you had nothing to do with bribing Debra to keep me away from you."

Elizabeth gave Kenneth a puzzled look. "Who bribed Debra? What are you talking about?"

Kenneth told her everything that Debra confessed the day he left New York.

"I don't believe that, Kenneth. Tommy knew how much I missed you. I had fallen apart—why wouldn't he want to see us back together?" But then Elizabeth answered her own question. Tommy wanted to marry her. "That idiot. I could ring his neck."

"Don't worry about it, baby," Kenneth said. "Tommy is bringing enough pain to himself."

But Elizabeth wasn't convinced that Tommy had suffered enough for what he had done to her. She would need to pray a long time before she would ever forgive Tommy Brooks for his sin against her.

Part Two

24

Two years later . . .

This Monday was special for two reasons. The first was that Kenneth had left a note pinned to his pillow for Elizabeth. When she woke up and read it, tears swam in her eyes.

Hey, babe. Just wanted to let you know that I went to sleep last night in love with you. I woke up this morning in love with you.

Despite the fact that some things are still locked in my head, when I think over my life, one thing is clear. I have loved one woman, twice in my lifetime.

Every time she thought about the note, a silly grin appeared on her face. Even in the midst of the second reason this Monday was special, she glowed with joy at the rekindled love and passion in her marriage.

Elizabeth was graduating from deliverance class. Although Ronda and Patricia had already graduated, and were now moving in their ministry for the Lord, they were in attendance for Elizabeth's graduation party. All the members of the deliverance group made a pact. They would show up to hear how each member found her resting place. Mary dropped out six months ago, but the group kept her on their prayer list. Three other women had joined the group: Vickie, Zee, and Michelle. Elizabeth promised to come back for their graduations also.

"Well, I guess this is it for me. I was a little slow getting to the finish line, but I finally found my resting place."

The group applauded Elizabeth's declaration. She had stood before tens of thousands singing her heart out. When she finished, the crowd would give her a standing ovation. At the time, she thought the admiration of so many was what she needed. She was happy when the crowd applauded. But sitting in Barbara's living room receiving cheers and hoots from six women was much more fulfilling than anything she could have imagined. She'd made it over. That was a good thing. No, it was a God thing.

Tears flowed down Elizabeth's face. Zee handed her a box of tissues. "Before I came here tonight, I was reading about Abraham and Jacob." Elizabeth blew her nose. "The Bible tells us that God came to Abraham and told him to move away from everything he knew. He was told to find a place whose builder and maker was God. And Abraham did it. He obeyed God without question or second thought."

"And then there was Jacob, the trickster. He knew exactly what he wanted out of life, and he went for it—didn't bother checking his agenda out with God. Consequently, his life was filled with misery and pain." The women were looking intently at her. "We all would like to be remembered as an Abraham. After all, he *is* listed in Hebrews as one of the heroes of faith." Elizabeth shrugged. "But I am a Jacob."

Zee raised her hand. "Me too, girl."

Elizabeth patted the tissue to her nose and continued. "I have hope in that knowledge though, because one faithful night, Jacob ran into an angel of God. He was tired of all his struggles. He wrestled with the angel, until he demanded to be loosed. Jacob said, 'I won't let you go until you bless my soul.'"

Elizabeth smiled as tears blurred her vision. "You ladies have been my angels. You have helped me defeat my demons. I just want to thank you, because I'm free."

"Well, for those of us who aren't free yet, tell us, Elizabeth, how did you find your resting place?" Michelle asked.

Elizabeth smiled again. She was doing a lot of that lately. "I guess what really helped me was that God sent Kenneth back to me scarred and bruised by the world. Before Kenneth and I were separated by the tragic events of 9-11, he had become my god. When he came back, I was able to see him as a man.

"You see, men have frailties and weaknesses. God doesn't. So, I chose to praise and pray to the One with the answers."

Zee leaned back in her chair and adjusted her blond wig. "That all sounds good, but when I pray, nothing happens."

Elizabeth patted Zee's hand. "Sometimes you have to wait on God. That's another thing I've learned."

Tears ran down Zee's caramel face. Elizabeth handed her some tissue. "I know you're right." She blotted her tears and wiped her eyes. "I want to trust God. It's just so hard."

Ronda and Patricia huddled close to Zee. They rubbed her back and whispered words of comfort to her. "It is hard, Zee, but think about our covenant scripture. When we started walking according to our own understanding, we left the place that God built for His people," Patricia told her. "We thought we were okay, because we could look back and still see God's place. As long as we knew where the resting place was, we thought we could just do our thing. We'd go back when we got tired." Sniffles were heard throughout the room. "But then we ran into an enemy and he whupped us so bad, we didn't know whether we were coming or going."

"And now the enemy stands guard over our resting place," Ronda added. "To get back to the place God has for us, we have to fight."

Barbara moved to the edge of the couch. "But you can win this fight, Zee. Look around. In this very room are four women who have won the fight. We may be a little bruised and battered for the effort, but we won. Just like Jacob. He walked away with a limp, but he also walked away victorious."

Elizabeth grabbed Barbara's hand and affectionately squeezed it. "When I started coming to these meetings, I didn't know if I was wasting my time or not. I soon discovered that I didn't like myself very much. I thought I had to do things to get others to love me. But guess what? I found out that God loves me for the person I am today, and for who I will be tomorrow."

Michelle raised her stubby fingers to the heavens. "I'm so glad I found this group. I don't know what I would have done without all of you."

"I know what I'd be doing," Vickie told them quietly. "I would be dead."

"That's why we're here." Barbara stood up. "We all know that the answer is to put our trust in God, but it's hard when you don't know how to do it. However, I am convinced that God will be found by the one who seeks Him. So, even when it looks like your efforts are in vain, don't give up. Keep reading your Bible. Keep praying. Get hungry for the Lord again. That's when He'll show up." She walked away from the group toward the dining room table. "Now who wants some cake?"

"I hope it's yellow this time," Michelle said.

"Girl, please. Strawberry. Now that's a celebration cake." Zee was now on her feet. "Did I tell you that we had strawberry cake at my wedding reception? The guests went crazy over it." Zee's groom was now locked up in the penitentiary for attempted murder. Three guesses who low-down tried to murder.

Elizabeth stood next to the cake. "You're both wrong. I picked chocolate." She wasted many years wishing she could change her complexion. Many hurtful and demeaning comments had been made about her chocolate-coated skin and full lips. It didn't matter now. She was free from public opinion. Free to be who she was. "It serves as a reminder to me. I am a chocolate sister, and I am sweet and divine."

"I heard that, girl." Ronda high-fived her.

Cake was passed around to the women. "Wait, wait, wait," Zee shouted. "Did I tell you that my low-down husband called me the other day?" She twisted her mouth in disgust. "Come talking 'bout he was sorry, and he wanted to make things right between us. Oh, and could I please put some money on his books?"

"You might as well untwist your mouth," Michelle told her.

"What do you mean?"

"There's no stupid stamp on my forehead, Zee," Michelle said. "That man is in jail. Somebody had to accept the collect call."

All eyes turned toward Zee. "I—I just wanted to hear what he was talking about."

Elizabeth laughed. "Mmph, that's why your silly self is still in deliverance class."

Barbara asked Elizabeth, "Can you make sure this girl gets the first copy of your new CD?"

Elizabeth nodded and said, "I sure will. I think it will really bless her soul."

God had allowed a Spirit-filled producer to cross Elizabeth's path. For the last six months they had been working on her CD. They talked about Elizabeth's goals and visions for her singing career and she had told him that she didn't want a career that didn't include God. Her whole life was now wrapped up in Him and she wanted to declare that fact to the world. And that's when they decided to call the album, *Life In Him*.

25

Kenneth stood outside the new extension to the Hope Center and gazed at the vinyl exterior, then checked out the foundation. Inside, carpenters were adding the finishing trim to the walls and windows. In two weeks, it would be complete. The culmination of a dream. Who was he kidding? This was the culmination of a lot of hard work. He met with investors, begged them to donate some of their corporations' hard-earned money. He met with contractors and suppliers. When the work wasn't moving fast enough, he laid a few bricks himself. The center would house fifteen homeless families. Its facilities were designed to provide life skills to its residents, and about twelve other families, whose providers were unemployed, but not homeless. He wanted to reach people before they lost everything, and teach them skills to help them get back on their feet. The overall plan was to avoid life on the street for the children.

He had enough beds for fifteen families, and two hundred were on the waiting list. The life skills classrooms accommodated about thirty people. Three hundred were on that list. That was the heart-breaking part of this business. So many were in need, but only a few would be served.

As if he didn't have enough to worry about, some crazy had started using the homeless for target practice. Two homeless men had been shot and killed last week. Another one, so far this week. The police had no leads. Kenneth guessed this was some sicko's idea of cleaning the streets.

"Hey, Handsome." Elizabeth closed the door to her SUV and walked over to her husband.

"Hey, Beautiful," he said as he leaned in to kiss her.

"What's with the sad eyes?"

He turned back to the building. "I was just thinking about all the people we won't be able to help. There's so many in need of our services, but we can only take about thirty at a time."

She gently touched his face. "Baby, do me a favor. Concentrate on the ones you are able to help. Okay?"

His gaze moved away from the building and centered on his wife. "Perspective. That's what you bring into my life. Thank you."

"You're welcome. Now, grab your coat and let's go. I came to rescue my husband from a day of do-gooding. You, sir, are going to enjoy a day of shopping with your wife. And you are going to spend some money on yourself, if I have to break your arm to get you to do it."

"I shouldn't let you get away with this." He smiled down at her. "Since our college days, you have been bound and determined to corrupt me."

"And you love every minute of it." She moved closer to his soft, wet lips and kissed him.

Kenneth hadn't fully regained his memory, but each day, a snippet of their past would creep up on him. He would tell her a funny story from one of their adventures, and they would laugh at the memory. Or sometimes, he would share a hurtful time during his childhood, like the day he learned his father cheated on his mother. He had idolized that man. He couldn't figure out what to do with his knowledge. If he admitted cheating was wrong, he'd end up hating his father. And how could one hate someone he loved and admired? "He was a good man," he told Elizabeth. "But I can admit that he was wrong." He then looked at his wife with regretful eyes. "I was wrong, too. I'm sorry I cheated on you."

Elizabeth wrapped Kenneth in her loving arms and let him know that he was all right with her. He was man; that meant he was human. Capable of flaws, just like the rest of us.

She smacked him on the backside. "Go get your coat so we can go."

He went into the Hope Center, grabbed his coat, and came back out. "All right, woman. I'm yours for the corrupting," he said as they walked to her midnight-black Escalade.

Before Kenneth could open the door, a man with torn jeans, dirty shirt, and a battered face ran up to him. Derrick was one of the men they regularly fed at the shelter. "Kenneth, man, it's Tyrone. He's been shot!"

Kenneth froze. He had been working with Tyrone. A slow, but steady process, trying to get him to see that not all Christians were like his ex-wife.

"The ambulance just picked him up. Ah, man, he didn't look good."

Please, God. Don't let him die before I can get your Word to him. "Where is he?" Kenneth grabbed hold of Derrick's shoulders. "Where did they take him?"

"I think they took him to County, man."

Kenneth turned sad eyes on his wife. "Get in," she told him. "I'll drive you to the hospital."

He let out a sigh of relief and covered her hand with his own as she drove down the street. "Thanks for understanding."

She hadn't always been supportive of his ministry in Atlanta or Dayton. Finding her resting place allowed her to let Kenneth handle God's business without whining and complaining about it. She dropped Kenneth off at the emergency room door, then found a parking spot.

When she walked into the hospital, Kenneth was barking at the receptionist. "I need to see Tyrone, now!"

"Like I said, I need a last name."

"I told you I don't *know* his last name. Why don't you go back there," he pointed to the double doors where the patients were being diagnosed, "and ask if there's anyone named Tyrone back there? Good Lord, lady, do your job."

The woman snarled at Kenneth. Elizabeth moved her husband aside and gave the woman a you-know-how-men-are smile. "Ms . . ." She looked at the woman's nametag. "Ms. Andover, my husband works at a homeless shelter. The reason he doesn't know Tyrone's last name is because he's homeless. The guy he's looking for was shot about an hour ago."

"Oh, well why didn't you say so?" She gave Kenneth a disapproving glance. "They brought a homeless man in here about an hour ago. He was DOA though."

"Excuse me?"

"Dead on arrival," Ms. Andover explained.

Kenneth wanted to scream. He wanted to shout. Oh, God, he wanted to curse. He held his emotions in check until they got inside the car. Then he whupped on the dashboard like Tyson. "This mess ain't right." He cried for Tyrone as they drove home. He then cried for all the Tyrones of the world; everyone that had been wounded by life's unfairness.

"It'll be okay, baby."

Kenneth used the back of his hand to wipe the tears from his eyes. "How will it be okay, Liz? Huh?" He pointed at the people on the street as they passed by. "There are countless people who need me, but I can't reach them. What do I do with that, Liz? How do I live with being so inadequate?"

She pulled the car into their driveway, and turned to her husband. She lifted his chin with her finger, wiped a few tears from his face. "Find strength in the souls you are able to save, baby."

"But I—"

She put her finger to his lips. "No buts. Jesus wasn't able to save everybody He encountered. As His servant, you are going to suffer losses.

Don't give up. This world needs someone caring and compassionate like you."

He turned his face from her, and sat starring out the window. God had told him to feed His sheep, but he was too inadequate for the job. There had to be someone more qualified than him. Someone with more compassion for the lost, who could really shake things up.

"Baby, when you get to heaven, I would love to be a fly on the wall. I want to see how many jewels are put in your crown. And when Jesus says, 'Well done my good and faithful servant,' I just know there's going to be a special inflection in His voice, meant only for the goodie-two-shoes servants like you."

Kenneth laughed. He couldn't help himself. His wife always seemed to be able to find a way to make him smile. He lifted her hand, gently squeezed it, then kissed her palm. "Thanks for being my perspective."

26

Tommy woke up hungry, wet, and irritable. One of The Dells' old songs rang in his head. *Nights like this, I wish that raindrops would fall.* Well, last night, when it rained on him, he figured The Dells must have been smoking crack when they came up with that song. He would be lucky if he didn't catch pneumonia. He was going to have to sleep in a shelter tonight. That was all there was to it.

The past year hadn't been kind. He'd managed two non-singing groups. Lost his shirt in both deals. Snorted enough coke to bleed a hundred noses. When his money ran low, he downgraded to crack. That's when the sheriff put his belongings on the curb. So now, here he was, sleeping on a park bench, holding onto a duffel bag that held his life story. Matt, Elizabeth's old chauffeur, offered to put him up for a few days. Tommy rang his phone 'til two in the morning. No answer. That's life. When you're up, everybody takes your call. When you're down, they get caller ID.

That's all right. He would be back on top. He just needed to get this monkey off his back. Nobody wanted to hire him. They had this new thing called drug tests. The hypocrites. Like the crack he smoked was any worse than the dirt they did behind closed doors.

If Tommy ran into a corporate tycoon, he'd probably spit on him. But not too many corporate types walked the parks, or came near the park bench he'd slept on last night.

Even Burger King asked him to pee in a cup. Now, if a grown man had to say, 'Would you like fries with that?' he should at least have a good buzz on while he's doing it. Boy, if he had a gun, he'd show them all. Huh, who was he kidding? If he had a gun, he'd probably sell it to get more crack. Tommy folded his blanket. What was he going to do about his growling stomach? The bleeding hearts down at the House of Love were serving chicken and passing out Bibles. But the Hope Center had beef stew. The cook was pretty good too.

He hadn't shaved in days. Maybe he could find a shelter that was giving away razors. After he finished shaving, maybe he'd slit his throat. There was talk on the street about some crazy that had killed four homeless men within the space of two weeks. What was wrong with that guy? If he wanted the homeless to suffer, let 'em live. After life got finished kicking them in the head, they'd willingly commit suicide and save him a bullet.

"I need a drink," Tommy said to no one in particular. He reached into his coat pocket, pulled out a pint of gin, and took a swig. He stood and started walking "Aaaah." Nothing relieved like strong drink. Of course, he did not state it out loud. Only the crazies talk to themselves.

His stomach was talking now. Telling him it was time to find one of them cheese and butter places and separate his guts from his ribs.

He got in the meal line at the Hope Center. The fellow inhabitants of hell took the bowl of stew like it was lobster and steak. They humbled down to the ladle holder like he was God. Tommy refused to humble down for a lousy bowl of stew. When his turn came, he stuck out his chest, lifted his bowl and his eyes to the ladle holder. Tommy wanted to let the man know that it was his job to serve him. Some government agency was probably paying him for his time anyway. Another cup-peeing-don't-want-no-drug-addicts-on-the-payroll agency.

"Tommy?"

Just his luck. Kenneth was the ladle holder. He averted his eyes and held up his bowl and shook it.

Kenneth filled the bowl, then took a business card out of his back pocket. "Look, Tommy, please call me at the number on this card. I want to help you, man."

Tommy put the card in his pocket, walked away without a word, and turned his face from Kenneth's inspection. He pulled up a seat next to Little Man, June Bug, and Skeeter. He had met these guys yesterday. The funny thing was, last week, he would have called them bums and told them to get out of his face. Now, they were his best buds.

"Hey, did y'all hear about the fourth victim? Man, these streets ain't safe for people like us," Skeeter told the group.

"Yeah, I heard about it. The newscasters say it's a white guy," Little Man informed them.

June Bug dipped his cornbread in his stew and said, "Man, I don't know what those yuppies feed them kids that makes 'em go crazy and start killing everybody that even looks like their mama. At least when a black man kills you, he's got a reason."

"He's got a reason all right. That Negro wants the fifty-cents in my pocket," Little Man told them as he pulled a small kitchen knife out of his coat pocket. "I got something for that serial killer though."

June Bug laughed. "What you think that little butter knife gon' do against a nine millimeter?"

"All I know is, I'm not going down without a fight," Little Man told them.

Tommy just wanted to wolf down his stew and get out of that place before Kenneth came over trying to sell him Jesus again. He might even run and call Elizabeth and have her come and cry all over him. No, he was going to have to find another place to sleep tonight.

When Kenneth got home, Elizabeth was just pulling a meatloaf out of the oven. Erin was sitting at the kitchen table completing her homework. Danae was waiting for her dinner. Kenneth put his briefcase on the kitchen counter, walked to Elizabeth, and put his arms around her waist.

"Welcome home, baby."

"Mmm." He squeezed tighter. "I'm glad to be home. Woman, your man is t-i-r-e-d."

She turned to face him—her man! She put her arms around his neck and pulled him closer to her. The kiss was intense. A kind of welcome home. The rest would come later. "Now, sit down. Let me feed you, then I'll tuck you in so you'll have the strength to serve another day."

He went to his children and kissed them on the tops of their heads. "Hey, princess. Hey, baby girl."

"Daddy, look." Danae stuffed a boatload of green beans in her mouth.

"Yuck. Y'all need to do something about her. She's disgusting." Erin put her books in her book bag and left the table.

Kenneth ate dinner, then sat and talked with his children until their bedtime. He wouldn't give that up no matter how tired he was.

"You ready for bed?" Elizabeth asked Kenneth as she tucked Danae in.

"Yeah, baby. Take me to bed," Kenneth said.

She smiled as they walked hand in hand to their bedroom. Their life had not been smooth sailing. In fact, there had been so many bumps in the road of their love, Elizabeth thought she should wear a helmet.

In bed, Kenneth pulled her close and told her about his day. "I think I saw Tommy today."

She sat up. "Where?"

"He was in the food line at the Hope Center."

"I don't care. I don't want to hear about Tommy Brooks."

He put his hands up to halt her explosion. "Now, hold on, Liz. If that was Tommy, he's really hit rock bottom. Maybe we need to help him."

"Why would you want to help him, Kenneth? After what he did to us, you should be just as upset with him as I am."

"I was upset with him, Liz. But I put all that to rest when I realized that Tommy hadn't stolen your love away from me." Kenneth shook his head. "I don't know, maybe I was wrong for telling you the whole story about my captivity in New York. I was just trying to get you to see that I believed in you; but I never thought it would cause you to turn your back on someone that was in need of help."

Elizabeth got out of bed and knelt on the floor. She stretched out her hands to Kenneth. "Pray with me, please. If Tommy is in need, I want to help him; but God has to release the anger I have in my heart toward Tommy first."

Kenneth bowed down next to his wife. Understanding that where two or three are gathered together, God is in the midst. Tommy would need God tonight. Kenneth felt it in his bones. But Elizabeth would also need God to help her to forgive a friend in need.

27

By the time Tommy arrived at the other shelter, all the beds were taken. He walked away feeling humbled and dejected. No room in the inn. No wonder Joseph and Mary took refuge in a stable. Beggars can't be choosers, and neither could he. It was back to that hard, but reliable, park bench.

He was beginning to shake, and not from the cold. Tommy needed to score, but with one dollar to his name, what could he afford? Maybe if he found a crap game, he could win enough money to get his buzz on and forget about the fact that he was using a park bench for a bed.

Felons usually congregated in alleys to shoot dice. He stayed on the path toward his bed, but kept an eye open for a back-alley crap game. A white dude followed him. Dirty blond hair sat scraggly and unkempt on top of his head.

What the devil? Why was this white boy following him? He turned another corner and picked up his pace. He was still being followed. He turned to face his stalker. "Look, weirdo, I only have a dollar to my name." He went in his pocket and pulled out the only dollar he owned and threw it at the man.

Tommy fast-walked through a field. The field dead-ended into an alley. He would have been happy to see this alley about twenty minutes ago, but with the white-boy stalker on his trail, an alley was the last place he wanted to be. Footsteps clattered behind him. He looked around and prayed for the earth to open up and swallow his stalker. Or maybe a tidal wave would sweep him away. Any catastrophe would do. Tommy wasn't picky—just do something. Do you hear me, God? Wake up and finally do something to help me for a change.

Tommy thought he'd found refuge in an old rusted tool shed. But a pit bull chased him out. He slammed the door shut, chest pounding, as he propped himself against the door. The footsteps were coming around the shed. Tommy was tired. He had walked several miles today, all on one bowl of stew. If his ribs weren't sticking to his guts, he might have found the energy to run.

"Turn around, nigger." The man grabbed his arm, spun him around, and shoved him against the shed. "Empty your pockets right now, before

I cut your heart out." The knife in the man's hand convinced Tommy that he just might cut his heart out.

Either this was a practice run, or this guy needed Remedial Robbery 101. He was sure the first page said something like, FIND A PIGEON WITH SOME MONEY. This guy must have slept during the training sessions. Tommy wanted to clap and tell the guy how good a job he did. He had scared him, real good. Now run along and find your real victim. Instead, he tried wiggling out of his hold. "What do you want, man? I ain't got nothing. Leave me alone."

"This is a sweep, dirty boy. I'm cleaning the streets of America, one bum at a time."

Didn't he already feel bad enough about not showering the last couple of days? He smelled bad, but that wasn't reason enough for name-calling. What if Tommy called him crazy-boy, or commented on how he looked like Norman from that *Psycho* movie?

He put the knife to Tommy's throat. "Time to die."

Tommy's eyes bugged out. "Come on, man. Haven't I been through enough?"

"Shut up, nigger. Empty your pockets like I told you."

28

Kenneth rolled over and grabbed for Elizabeth to pull her close to him. She wasn't in their bed. He couldn't sleep when she wasn't next to him. He forced his eyes open, turned on the light, and searched the room. There was his baby, sitting in the recliner, feet in the chair, knees pressed to her chest. Worry etched its grimace throughout her perfect face. Kenneth pulled back the covers and got out of bed.

"Look at you," he said as he noticed the dried tear stains on his wife's face. He attempted to bend down on the floor in front of her, then realized that his bad knee wasn't going for that. He stood, picked up his wife and put her on his lap as he took her place on the recliner. "I miss you when you're not in bed with me."

She leaned her head into his chest. Her sob vibrated through him.

"Baby, it will be okay."

"Will it, Kenneth?"

"How can you doubt it, baby? You've been pray-ing. I've been praying. We've got to trust God on this one." Funny thing—his wife was in his lap, crying over another man, and he wasn't jealous. He hoped his mature attitude stemmed from the trust he and Elizabeth had built, and not from the fact that Tommy was homeless and the only thing he was probably attracting right now was fleas.

She lifted her head and looked at her husband. "Don't you see, Kenneth? I made Tommy what he is today. Me and every other fake Christian he ever ran into."

"You're not a fake. You love the Lord."

"Today, yes, I do, with all my heart." She grabbed some tissue off the table next to the recliner and wiped her nose. "But when Tommy managed my career, I wasn't in love with Jesus. He was the last thing on my mind." She cleared her throat and continued, "I didn't tell you this before, and I really hope you don't take it the wrong way now."

"Baby, just spit it out."

"Well, you read the tabloid, and I also told you that I caught Tommy with a man. Right?"

"Right."

She put her index finger in her mouth and bit off her nail. The same nail that took three months to grow in the first place. "I went over to his apartment to sleep with him."

Now Kenneth was jealous of Tommy again. He tried not to show his disappointment, but Elizabeth saw it anyway.

She cupped his face in her hands. "Baby, I'm sorry. I don't want to lie to you about this, okay?"

He didn't have a problem with her lying. Liars didn't gut punch you. They smoothed things over, helped it go down like butter. Matter-of-fact, some of his best friends were liars. But he bent down and kissed her forehead like a fool in love. "It's okay. Keep talking."

"Tommy knew why I had come over that night. He also knew that my actions had been less than Christ-like the entire time we were working on the CD. Every so-called Christian he's run into has probably given him a reason to doubt God."

Kenneth massaged her back. "That might be true, but every man, woman, or child is still given a choice. You can either become what you see, or you can seek God's will for your life. There are no excuses, Liz."

She leaned her head back and let it drop on the arm of the recliner. "Yeah, but then I turned my back on him. These last two years, I've been so angry with Tommy that I wanted nothing to do with him. And look what my anger has done. Tommy needed us, and we were nowhere around."

"Stop it, Liz. You are going to get rid of this gloomy mood right now." He looked at the clock on their dresser. It was just after five in the morning. "You've got to meet with your back-up singers in three hours."

Elizabeth rubbed her eyes. "I know. If I weren't practicing for your celebration, I'd cancel it."

"Ah, Liz. I still can't believe it. In just three weeks, we will be celebrating the opening of the new and improved Hope Center. There were so many days when it didn't look like this was going to happen."

She stood and walked over to the bed. "Well, it's happening." She held up three fingers. "In three weeks. So, Mr. Underwood, you open the doors and I'll sing my heart out. How does that sound?"

"Sounds perfect."

The phone rang. Something was mentally wrong with a person that could ring somebody's house before daybreak. He snatched up the phone. "Yeah!"

"Is this Kenneth Underwood?"

"Who else would be answering my phone at five in the morning?"

"Be nice," Elizabeth instructed, still standing.

"I'm sorry to have disturbed you. This is Dr. Corney. I work at South Fulton. A man was brought into the emergency room an hour ago. He had no identification on him, just your business card."

Kenneth turned to face the opposite wall. "Oh, my God. What happened? Is he all right?"

"He was stabbed six times. He just came out of surgery. Look, we were hoping you could come down and ID him."

Kenneth's breath caught in his throat. He looked back at Elizabeth. She had a tell-me-what's-going-on look on her face. He turned and whispered, "Is he dead?"

"Not yet, but it doesn't look good."

"I'll be there in an hour." He hung up and walked toward the closet.

"Who was that? What happened?"

He pulled on a pair of stone washed jeans. "Get in bed, baby. One of the homeless men from the shelter got into a bit of trouble. I'm going to the hospital to see about him."

Kenneth walked into the hospital, hoping he was wrong. He kept trying to remember who else he'd given his business card to. Unfortunately, his question was answered the minute he walked into the intensive care unit.

It was Tommy all right. How was he going to break this news to Liz? At least he didn't have to report that Tommy was dead, although he looked like death warmed over. He didn't just get stabbed, they must have beat on him awhile. His right eye was swollen shut, lips busted, cheeks black and blue. The priest was doing the death-watch. But if Kenneth had anything to say about it, Tommy wasn't going out like this.

Looking at him, Kenneth saw Tyrone and every other down-on-his-luck brother he'd tried to save but couldn't. He thought of the angel that whispered in his ear at Ground Zero. That angel gave him hope, a reason to keep on breathing. Maybe he could do the same for Tommy. He walked to the head of the bed, bent down, and whispered, "Don't give up. Don't you ever give up."

Tommy's eyelids fluttered. The left side of Tommy's lips curved into a half smile. A cinnamon-brown nurse walked into the room carrying official-looking papers. Her sandy brown hair barely touched the nape of her Winnie-the-Pooh smock. Kenneth turned to greet her.

She returned the salutation, then asked, "Are you related to the patient?"

Kenneth shook his head.

"Do you know any of his family members?"

"No, sorry."

"Not half as sorry as our patient will be." She looked at Tommy and shook her head. "Mmph, mmph, mmph."

"What? What's wrong?"

She bit her lip. "I guess we'll have to move him to Grady Hospital."

He shrugged away her concerns with a wave of his hand. He and Elizabeth had invested the money they had left at the time of his return. They were doing all right. "I've got it covered. My wife and I will pay his bill ourselves. Just get him better."

"Look, do you mind signing these papers? I will have to get approval from the administrative office. Hopefully, they won't give us any problems."

Kenneth took the papers in one hand, then stretched forth his other. "I'm Kenneth Underwood."

She took his hand and shook it. "I'm Taijah Hughes."

Kenneth sat down to fill in as much information as he could. Taijah snapped her fingers, "Hey, you're the one that's building that center for the homeless, right?"

He had been in the newspaper two Sundays in a row. He was becoming quite famous in his community. Kenneth's eyes moved from the papers to Taijah and smiled. "Yeah, that's me."

"Oh my God!" Taijah screamed. "You're married to Elizabeth Underwood."

The smile dropped just a bit. His wife was the famous one in their house. He was going to have to roll over and accept it. "That would be me also."

"Oh my God!" She jumped in the air, putting her hand over her mouth and looking back at Tommy. "Oops." She grabbed a chair, sat next to Kenneth and whispered, "I bought her CD. It was so awesome, I went back to the store and bought three more. I gave those copies to friends of mine. I've been waiting on another CD from her. What gives?"

"Wait no longer," Kenneth said proudly. "Her new CD, *Life In Him,* releases next month."

"Oh my God!" she repeated, then clamped her mouth again, before whispering. "I can't wait."

"I'll be sure to tell her that. She's hoping that this CD will be well received."

"Well, of course it will. Why wouldn't it? What took her so long anyway?"

"Even *God's* wounded need time to heal."

To Taijah's credit, she didn't pretend to not remember Elizabeth's attempted suicide. After all, it was front-page tabloid news for several weeks straight. She shook her head and patted his hand. "That was a bad time for her."

Kenneth was grateful for people like Taijah. They weren't the stone throwers. No, people like Taijah extended God's grace, and allowed Him to be the judge of His people.

Kenneth pointed toward Tommy. "Your patient's name is Tommy Brooks. He used to be my wife's manager."

Once again, Taijah didn't pretend to be unaware of the circumstances. "He's the one, huh?"

"Yeah, he's the one, and he needs our help. Somebody has to convince this man that Jesus loves him, before it's too late."

Taijah stood and walked over to Tommy. His face was battered and bruised. She lightly touched his bumpy skin. Her compassionate eyes kept searching as she stood over him, praying. "It's like you said." She turned back to Kenneth. "Even *God's* wounded need time to heal. I'll help out as much as I can."

Kenneth's voice was caught in his throat. This nurse wasn't like the one he'd had. Doing good deeds with selfish motives. Taijah believed in God. He could feel it all the way through his bones. "You are a beautiful person, Taijah Hughes. Both inside and out."

"Aw, shucks, now you're making me blush."

Kenneth laughed as he finished filling out the forms. His insurance would not cover Tommy, but he could write them a check without feeling too much pain. With the money he and Liz were going to make once the CD dropped, they certainly could afford to spread a little of it around.

29

Elizabeth arrived home about five minutes before Kenneth, kicking off her shoes and plopping on the couch. She rehearsed the same song for five hours but either she or one of the backup singers kept messing up. She leaned back on the couch just as Kenneth hit the garage door opener.

Jumping up, Elizabeth ran to the garage. She had to make sure her husband was all right, and not losing his mind over yet another victim of the streets. Tyrone's death hit him hard, but her man was a survivor and she would help him remember that. "Hey, baby, let me take your jacket. How did everything go at the hospital?" she asked, as she hung his jacket in the closet.

"He's still alive," Kenneth answered.

"That's good, right?" She coaxed him toward the family room. "Come on, baby. You need to get off your feet for a while."

Kenneth sat down and Elizabeth stood behind him. She massaged his aching shoulders with great care. "You're all knotted up. You can't allow these things to stress you out so much."

"What else can I do, babe? Some days I feel like I'm making progress and then something happens to knock me right back to square one."

Her husband's voice was angry and full of pain. The pain was for the victim, and the anger for the perpetrator. She was proud of him. His work with the homeless was his ministry. He really cared about them. They weren't nameless, faceless people to him. When he discussed his day with her, he talked about the people he dealt with and called off their names like family members. "Have you ever mentioned this guy to me, Kenneth? What's his name?"

He put his hands over hers to stop the massage. "Do we have anything to eat, honey? I'm tired of talking. I just want to eat and take a nap."

Elizabeth started to say something, then let it go. "All right, let's see what's in the kitchen."

Kenneth followed her.

She made him a turkey sandwich and kept him company. While he ate, she told him about her rehearsal, and he told her about Taijah.

A tear formed in the corner of her eye. "You're not kidding, are you?"

"No, babe. She said she couldn't wait for your next CD. She was genuinely excited. She'll probably end up being the president of your fan club."

Elizabeth wiped the tear as it dropped. "I don't want another fan club. They just turn on you in the end. When they hear my music, let them think of Jesus—that's more than enough for me."

He leaned over and kissed her. "No doubt this new CD is all that. If they don't end up on their knees with arms lifted to God, they probably don't have a soul worth saving anyhow."

She nudged his shoulder. "Finish eating your sandwich. Leave the pep talks to me, okay?"

When Kenneth finished, they went upstairs and napped.

Kenneth left the house at seven that evening to check on Tommy. When he got to the hospital, Taijah was in the room praying for him. "How's he doing? Any change?"

"He woke once, moaned, then went back to sleep."

Tommy's face was still swollen, eye clamped shut. The fist that smashed into his face must have come from some big, hold-my-mule kinda farm-working dude.

He looked at his watch. "What are you still doing here?"

"Somebody's got to pray for Tommy," Taijah told him as a tired smile crossed her lips. "If he survives the night," she continued, "he should be out of the woods, and on his way to recovery."

And then what? What would Tommy do once he recovered? Go back on the streets? Continue taking drugs? Was he tired of the life he was living? Would he be willing to give God a try? No, when Tommy woke up he would curse Kenneth and God. *What was he doing here?*

Feed my sheep.

How, Lord? I don't know what to tell him that will change his situation. He rubbed his head with his hand. *I don't know what to tell any of the people that come to me needing help.*

Tell them about my love and mercy.

"Well, goodnight. I'm going home," Taijah said, breaking Kenneth from his trance.

"What? Huh? Oh, okay. Don't worry about our patient. I'm going to sit with him for a little while." He patted the Bible that was in his hand. "Maybe I'll read the Word to him." Kenneth watched the door close behind Taijah's exit and then sat next to Tommy's bed. "Feed your sheep, huh?" he whispered to God while fumbling through the pages of the Bible. "Well, help me out a little bit here. What part of your Word do you want me to feed to your sheep?"

Kenneth didn't tell Liz about Tommy when he went home that night. He should have, but he didn't worry about that now. If Tommy survived through the night, then he'd have something to report. He wasn't going to upset his wife with the news that Tommy was in the hospital, only to have her be devastated by news of his death. No. One blow was better than two.

The next day, after tying up some loose ends at Hope Center II, he went back to the hospital. Tommy was half sitting, half lying in bed. He couldn't move much, though. His body violently conveyed that message, when he tried to adjust his position.

"So, how's our patient today?" Kenneth asked cheerfully.

"In pain."

"I'm sorry to hear that. If it helps any, you look better today than you did yesterday."

"You should see the other guy." Tommy pointed at the Bible in Kenneth's arm. "Did you read that to me yesterday?"

"Yes." Kenneth sat and scooted his chair closer to Tommy's bed. "Would you like me to read some more today?"

Tommy's face contorted as he shook his head. "When I was a kid, there was this deacon who would read from the Bible before offering every Sunday." Tommy turned toward Kenneth. "Guess what he did on Saturdays?"

Kenneth sat attentive, waiting for Tommy to elaborate.

"He was a mentor. He'd pick little boys up and take them to baseball and football games. Then he'd take them to his house and rape them."

Kenneth grunted.

"He raped me," Tommy continued. "Nobody cared either. Not my mother, not the preacher. They just expected me to deal with it. Let it go. 'Quit lying on the good deacon,'" he mimicked his mother.

"I don't know what to say, Tommy."

"You don't have to say anything. I'm just letting you know that all that Bible thumping don't mean a thing to me." Tears rolled down his face. "I know first hand what a Bible-toting pervert can do."

Kenneth put the Bible down. He silently prayed for wisdom. "Tommy, I understand—"

"You don't understand nothing," Tommy spat. "You don't know the half of what has happened in my life."

And please don't tell me, Kenneth wanted to scream. Instead he said, "You're right. I can't possibly understand the hurt and the humiliation of what you've gone through."

"Darn right, you can't."

Kenneth stood. "Even though men are supposed to represent God on earth, we are not God. Some men make mistakes, others can't be trusted. You found that out first hand. But God is different, Tommy."

"Don't you preach to me about God. He has never been there for me. I pray and He sits in the heavens laughing at me."

"You're alive, Tommy. Don't you credit God for that?"

"Naw, that psycho stalker was too stupid to puncture any vital organs."

Kenneth threw his hands up in frustration.

Feed my sheep.

"Whether you want to believe it or not, God loves you. He's waiting for you to come back where you belong," Kenneth told him.

"Yeah, God loves me so much that He sent His Son Jesus to die on a cross so that I might be saved, right?"

Kenneth nodded. "Just answer this for me, why couldn't God stop that man from raping me, huh? If He loves me soooo much, why didn't He do that?"

Kenneth put his hand on Tommy's shoulder, then remembered his bruises and pulled away. "Okay, so you blame God for what happened to you when you were a kid. But tell me, Tommy, who will take the blame for the way you've lived your life as an adult? Honestly, I don't know why bad things happen to people." Tears filled Kenneth's eyes. "And I don't know why you choose to live in torment, rather than fight your way back to God."

"What are you crying for?"

"For you, man, I'm crying for you. I'm tired of seeing brothers broken down by situations and issues they had no control over in the first place. Don't you understand? The things that have happened to you, those are not your issues—they belong with Jesus. Give them up and let Him heal you."

"I've tried. Don't you think I've tried?"

"No, you didn't. All you did was go to church. But you hid your true self—your problems, from the Lord. Don't you know that you can trust God?"

"I stopped trusting God a long time ago, man."

Kenneth wiped at a tear as it rolled down his cheek. "Do yourself a favor. Give God a second chance." He offered his Bible to Tommy. Tommy hesitated, then took the Bible and laid it on the nightstand next to his bed.

30

"Kenneth C. Underwood, you must have a death wish."

Kenneth put his arms up. "Now, now. No sense getting all upset. Sit down and let me talk to you."

"Sit down!?" Elizabeth screamed as she scanned the room. "I ought to find something and bust you upside your head!"

"Now, baby, you're going to regret this kind of talk later."

"Maybe later, but right now I can't see regretting telling you about yourself. You are just wrong, Kenneth." She strutted up and down their bedroom trying to make sense of her husband's deception. If anger was fire, whew wee, call the fire department quick. Kenneth opened his mouth and she put the five-finger disconnect in his face. "You are wrong and you know it. I don't want to hear anything you have to say." She walked over to the closet and rummaged around.

"Look, there's nothing we can do about it tonight—"

"You made sure of that." The sista-sista neck
was going as she interrupted him. "Yeah, tell
your wife at ten o'clock at night that one of her
friends has been in the hospital for three days
from six stab wounds." Elizabeth's voice caught
on the last three words.

"Baby, what do you want me to say?"

"Do what you've been doing for the last three
days; don't say nothing." She walked out of the
closet with pillow and blanket in hand. "Just
take your behind downstairs and sleep on the
couch."

Kenneth stood back and folded his arms. "I
know you're not putting me out of my own bed."

Elizabeth put the bed linen atop his folded
arms. "Guess you don't know everything. Do
you?"

"So, what are you saying? Some *friend* of
yours means more to you than I do?"

"You're not going to make me feel bad." She
pointed a loaded finger at him. "You're the one
that's wrong. And you're the one I don't want to
see for the rest of the night."

He threw the pillow and blanket on the floor
and poked at his chest. "I'm also the one who
paid Tommy's hospital bill. Liz, I told them

that we would do that because he is a friend of yours. I also talked with his nurse. She's Spirit-filled and told me she would take good care of Tommy."

She twisted her lip and finally said, "Well, at least that's something."

He held out his arms. "Ah, come here, baby. I hate it when we fight."

The five-finger disconnect went up again. Her other hand pointed at the door. "The couch."

Kenneth ignored the bedding on the floor and pulled the blanket and pillow off his bed, all the while mumbling about the unfairness of the situation. He was just trying to protect her from hearing bad news twice. He walked out of their bedroom and turned to face-off one last time. "I thought you'd be happy with my news. My God, Liz, the man is alive. You don't have to be so evil. You act like I stabbed him myself."

She very calmly walked over to the door and slammed it in his face. She went to bed mad, woke up mad, fixed breakfast mad.

"Good morning," Kenneth tried as she brought the plates to the table.

"Can you watch the girls this morning so I can go to the hospital?" she asked without returning his salutation. No sense being a hypocrite. She wanted him to have a bad morning, and a horrible day.

Before Kenneth could answer, Elizabeth turned to walk out of the kitchen.

"Where are you going?" he asked.

She tried to smile at him, but just couldn't. "I need to go pray. I just had a vision of me smashing the breakfast plates over your head."

"Hey you," Elizabeth said from the door.

Tommy's nurse was giving him some medication. Tommy was cheesin' and trying to get his mac on. Ain't that some stuff? No job, no car, no place to lay his bald-head, but he was trying to come up.

He turned from his nurse to Elizabeth and smiled. "I was wondering when your husband would turn you loose."

Elizabeth was not going to discuss that sore subject with Tommy. She walked into his room. The nurse was on the right side of his bed, so she took the left. "Hi, I'm Elizabeth Underwood," she told the nurse. "Me and this nut," she pointed at Tommy, "go way back."

"I know who you are, Mrs. Underwood. I have your CD." She extended her hand and Elizabeth took it. "I'm Taijah Hughes."

Elizabeth held Taijah's hand a little tighter before releasing it. "My husband told me about you." She almost called him a ratfink husband, but controlled herself.

"I can't wait for your next CD to release."

"Thank you. I appreciate your support."

"So, your man just now letting you out of the house?" Tommy jested.

She would not debate Kenneth's actions with friend or foe. "It's nothing like that. Kenneth just wanted to make sure you were up to a visit from me because I came here to knock your head off." She muffed him on the side of his baldhead.

"Well, I've got to make my rounds," Taijah said.

Tommy lifted his bandaged arms and hunched his shoulders. "So you just gon' leave a brother? Ain't you supposed to report violent acts when you see them?"

Taijah turned to Elizabeth and winked. "I didn't see anything, Tommy."

"Oh, it's like that, huh?" Tommy said.

"Let's just put it this way. Elizabeth isn't the only one who thinks you need your head knocked off." She turned to Elizabeth. "Now, when you knock his head off, just make sure you shake out all the junk that's in it before reattaching it to his neck."

They laughed and Taijah left.

Elizabeth turned back to Tommy. "What's wrong with you? Why are you always doing something stupid?"

He nestled in the cushion of his pillow and stretched out his legs. "Oh, so I guess I kicked my own behind? It's all my fault that I'm in the hospital, right?"

"Yeah, it's your fault," she told him as she slapped him upside his head again.

"Ouch." He rubbed his head. "I'm trying to recuperate, you know."

"You wouldn't need to recuperate if you had just contacted me when you lost your condo."

"I didn't want to be a burden."

"Do you want me to hit you again?" He shook his head. "Then stop talking stupid. Friends are never a burden."

He looked away. "What's this I hear about a program you and Kenneth are throwing for the homeless?"

"Are you planning to come if you're out of the hospital by then?"

"Can't make any promises about that, but tell me about this new CD."

She smiled. "Tommy, I'm so excited. This CD is anointed. I know that God is truly pleased with the songs I have written."

Tommy's eyes shifted downward. "I'm sorry you didn't feel the same about the CD we did together."

Open mouth. Insert foot. "It wasn't your fault, Tommy. I was in a different place with God when we did the first CD."

"Taijah liked the first CD."

"I'm glad, but I didn't come here to discuss what I'm doing or my music or—"

"No, of course not. You wouldn't want to gloat to a bum like me."

Tommy was taking her words the wrong way, and she didn't know what to say to help him understand. Maybe Kenneth was right. Maybe she and Tommy weren't ready to see each other. What could she do for him? She'd been praying for him a long time. He only seemed to be getting worse.

She tightened her hold on her purse. "Look, Tommy, maybe I should go." She smiled to ease the tension. "I usually don't like to talk to anyone with a worse disposition than my own, so I'll see you tomorrow. Okay?"

"Go ahead and run out on me. That's all you're good for anyway."

She stood. "You know what? You need to stop blaming other people for the choices you've made. Yeah, some bad things have happened to you, but you need to stop letting life whup on you."

"Whatever," he said as he rolled his eyes and turned away from her.

She slung her purse over her shoulder. Tommy turned back to face her. "Your husband's not so bad. I can see why you love him so much."

She just stood there clutching her purse. Not trusting herself to speak. Her words kept coming out wrong.

"He cried for me. Nobody's ever cried for me," he told her, while shaking his head.

She would go home now and eat crow. *Crow isn't so bad*, she told herself, as she walked out of the hospital. *Not if you use the right spices.*

31

Kenneth had asked him to give God a second chance. Tommy wasn't sure if he wanted to do that. But reading the Bible he'd left couldn't hurt anything. His body was on the mend, but he was still in a hospital bed with little else to do. He read through Genesis and Exodus. He skipped over a couple of books he considered insignificant, and then started back up in Joshua. He had a puzzled looked on his face when Taijah came in to check on him.

"What's wrong?" she asked him.

"I don't understand this." He pointed at the Bible, then looked up at her and explained. "There's this harlot named Rahab in the book of Joshua." His hands danced in the air as he told the story. "God tells Joshua that they are going to destroy Jericho and everything in it. Somehow Rahab finds out about it. She asks the servants of God to spare her life. And they did. Well, not only did they spare her life, but one of the Jewish men married her."

"What part didn't you understand?" Taijah asked, changing his bandages.

"The whole thing!" he shouted. "I would have thought for sure that ol' Fire and Brimstone would have murdered her right along with the rest of the people in that city. But He spared her. A prostitute."

"That's what this Christian walk is all about. God gifting us with His grace and mercy, even though we don't deserve it."

Tommy was silent. He let Taijah finish fiddling with his bandages and doctoring him up. When she was gone, he put the Bible back on the nightstand and lay down. Before he drifted off to sleep, he mumbled, "I've never received any grace or mercy."

The next day, he took on I Kings and I Chronicles. It was in I Chronicles 4 that he found hope:

Now Jabez was more honorable than his brothers, and his mother called his name Jabez, saying, "Because I bore him in pain."

And Jabez called on the God of Israel saying, "Oh, that You would bless me indeed, and enlarge my territory, that Your hand would be with me, and that You would keep me from evil, that I may not cause pain!" So God granted him what he requested.

Tommy closed the Bible and held it close to his chest. As he pondered this indeed blessing that Jabez asked God for, Kenneth walked in.

"Hey, what's going on?" Kenneth asked.

Tommy sat up. "Ain't nothing changed but the date. What's up with you?"

"Nothing much. Just thought I'd check on you, see how you're doing." Kenneth pointed at the Bible. "So, what were you reading today?"

Tommy shrugged. "I was just reading in First Chronicles. Sounds like Jabez had a triflin' mama too."

"Why would you say that?"

"Come on, man. What good mother would name her child something that means pain?"

Kenneth laughed. "You've got a point there."

"Hey, do you think Jabez had one of them angels you told me about?"

"Jabez became a great man. He would have needed God to dispatch angels of protection."

Tommy shook his head. "You really believe that stuff don't you?"

Kenneth shrugged. "It's no great thing that I believe. I witnessed angels protecting me. I wish I could have believed without having to see them in action."

"With a name like pain, the angel probably had to help Jabez out of some tough spots."

Tommy turned away. "I wonder what my name means."

"Is your first name Tommy or is that your middle name?" Kenneth asked him.

"Actually my name is Thomas. Everybody just calls me Tommy."

"I'll look up the meaning of your name," Kenneth told him.

And being true to his word, Kenneth returned to the hospital the next day. "Your name means twin."

Tommy rubbed his goatee with his thumb and index finger, then he turned to Kenneth. "What do you suppose that has to do with who I am and what I've become?"

Kenneth pulled his lower lip between his teeth. "I don't know. What do you think of when you hear the word twin?"

"I think of two, or double." Tommy snapped his finger. "That's it." Tommy laughed. "For as long as I can remember, I have led a double life. I have been dealing with women and men, but I tried to keep both sides of my life separate."

Kenneth's mouth hung open. He sat down and asked, "Are you prepared to do something about this double life you've been leading?"

"You know," Thomas said as his hand rubbed his chin, "I guess if Jabez could ask God to bless him so that he would not cause pain, I could ask God to give His grace and mercy to me so that I could stop living a double life."

Kenneth rested his hands on the bedrail and smiled.

Tommy picked up his Bible. "I read in the ninth chapter of Romans today how God said that He would show mercy on whomever He chose." He looked at Kenneth. "But how do you know if God has decided to show you mercy or not?"

"By faith, Tommy. Begin to believe that even you are worthy of God's mercy. Trust God and see what happens."

"Even me, huh?"

32

Kenneth and Elizabeth were setting out folding chairs in the back of Hope Center II. "Are you ready for tonight?"

Elizabeth unfolded the last chair, then stood to face her husband. A look of uncertainty was on her face. "We'll see."

Kenneth walked to his wife and put his arm around her. "This is your thing. Baby, you were born to serenade the Lord."

She smiled at her husband. The passing years didn't change a thing for her. She still loved that man. "I know you're right, Kenneth. It's time for me to get out there and do what God has called me to. So, ready or not, I'm going to set that stage on fire tonight."

"All right now, baby. That's what I want to hear," Kenneth said with a big grin on his face.

They finished getting the area ready for the service that was to take place later that evening. Enough seats for two hundred people covered the space. Tonight they would give the dredges of society information about a new center for the homeless and downhearted. Before doing that, though, Kenneth would preach the Gospel and offer Jesus to the hearers of it.

He stood behind the pulpit and breathed in deeply. "This feels a little strange. Am I doing the right thing, Liz? I mean, I'm no preacher."

Elizabeth was knelt down praying over the seats. When the people arrived, she wanted to make sure that their seats were already warmed with the Holy Ghost. She turned and looked up at her husband. His stance was regal and authoritative. "You've had the itch for a long while now. It's where you belong, baby."

"You really think so?"

"I know so," she told him with a smile. Kenneth flexed his muscles, doing a couple of strong man stances behind the pulpit. "And besides, if you start preaching, maybe you'll let me get some sleep at night. And I won't have to hear every revelation God gives you."

Kenneth twisted his lip. "Oh, so I've been bugging you? Is that it?"

She laughed. "I was just kidding. Don't get all weepy on me."

After a moment, the smile left her face. Kenneth asked her about it.

"I was just wondering if Tommy will show up tonight."

Tommy had been released from the hospital a week ago. Kenneth found a rehab center willing to accept him, so there he was. When Kenneth had brought him to this place, he had said, "Cheer up. It's better than living on the street."

Tommy wasn't sure about that. Nobody searched his bags or asked him to pee in a cup on the street. Tommy shook his head, still amazed at the downward spiral his life had taken. "What happened?" he asked out loud. "God wasn't there for me, that's what happened," Tommy told himself. Now, Kenneth wanted him to believe, wanted him to trust that God's mercy would be there for him.

Tommy put his head in his hands and for the third time that day, he thought about what Kenneth had said to him: "*Don't you know that you can trust the Lord?*"

Tommy stood and paced around the room. How could he trust in the Lord when he had issues with the Lord? Or maybe it was like Elizabeth had said: he needed to stop blaming others for the choices he had made.

Tommy wished he could trust God. Wished he could turn over his life to the Lord and start fresh. But he knew firsthand that God didn't care. Tears rolled down his face. He and God had irreconcilable differences. Just as Tommy's own dad had been missing in action, God had also played the absent father role in his life. "You weren't there for me," Tommy repeated.

He stood in the middle of his room, half expecting to hear God apologize for His absenteeism. But that would be admitting wrong, and of course, the Almighty was never wrong.

On his nightstand was a flyer announcing the grand opening of the new Hope Center. It invited the downtrodden to come out for a night of enlightenment, food, and fellowship. If God wouldn't provide answers for His neglect, Tommy was going to get it from Kenneth. He put on his shoes, snatched up the paper and left the rehab center.

33

Kenneth looked out at the sea of hungry and dejected faces. For two years, he had fed and ministered to them. Nothing had changed. Not much, anyway. Oh sure, a few souls gave their lives to Christ here and there, but that was only a momentary fix. They usually ended up right back on the streets and farther away from God.

Was he doing the right thing? Was this really the ministry God had for him? If so, why was he so ineffective? The people that came to him were the walking dead; corpses just waiting on a casket. He felt like Ezekiel in the valley of dry bones. Dead men didn't listen. What was he doing behind this pulpit? Maybe he should just scream, "Soups on," and line them up for dinner. That's why they came to this grand opening anyway. He was just about to turn away from the pulpit, when he heard his Lord.

Son, can this situation be turned around?

He lifted his eyes toward the crowd again. They had given up. The world had pimp-smacked them one time too many. Shoulders slumped, eyes downcast, hands always out. That was the posture of the homeless. And for the first time, Kenneth wondered what each one of these people used to be. Had the man seated in front of him, with the patched-up coat and holes in his tennis shoes, once been an executive or maybe a doctor? What about the woman seated to the left of the podium—

Son, can this situation be turned around?

Okay, Lord, I know that with you, all things are possible. So yes, I do believe that this can be turned around. But am I the right man for the job? I don't know what to do.

Speak to their situations. Speak to their problems. Son, feed my sheep.

Kenneth smiled as he opened his Bible and flipped the pages. He had fed God's sheep soup and peanut butter sandwiches. Today, he would feed them the Word.

"Turn in your Bibles to John, chapter four. I'd like to introduce you to a woman from Samaria, who came to draw water from a well while Jesus rested there. Let's start at verse seven.

A woman of Samaria came to draw water. Jesus said to her, "Give me a drink."

*Then the woman of Samaria said to Him,
"How is it that You, being a Jew, ask a drink
from me, a Samaritan woman? For Jews have
no dealings with Samaritans."*

*Jesus answered and said to her, "If you knew
the gift of God, and Who it is Who says to you,
'Give Me a drink,' you would have asked Him
and He would have given you living water."*

Kenneth lifted his head just as Tommy walked
in and sat down in the back. He smiled, Tommy
nodded, and Kenneth continued reading the
story of the Samaritan woman. He told his congregation how this woman asked Jesus to give
her a drink of the living water He talked about.
And Jesus instructed her to call her husband.

"She told Jesus that she didn't have a husband. Jesus affirmed her statement. She didn't
just have one husband, but five. And the man
she was with now, wasn't her husband." Kenneth
looked out at the crowd and moved to the side of
the pulpit. "Why do you think Jesus asked her
to go get her husband when He knew that she
couldn't produce one?" After a sufficient pause,
he continued, "This woman had a problem with
men. She had had five husbands, and the man
she was currently with wasn't even her husband. It's possible that she had a lust problem
or maybe she was lonely, and that caused her to

run from man to man. But what Jesus was really saying to her was, 'Go get your issue.' Go get the problems and situations that have kept you away from me."

Kenneth walked down the aisle. He stood in front of Tommy. Their eyes locked as he said, "God wants you to bring your issues and problems to Him. The things that keep you up at night, the very issue that has kept you on the wrong side of salvation." Turning away from Tommy, he scanned the crowd.

As Kenneth walked away, Tommy mumbled under his breath, "My issue *is* with God." Then he boldly looked to the heavens and mouthed, "You were never there for me."

"Remember," Kenneth was saying, "sin entered into the world, and it must run its course. Bring your problems to God. Let Him wipe away your past."

Unrestrained tears ran down Tommy's face.

Kenneth continued, "Do you think crack is too big an issue to bring to God? What about the spirit of failure that looms over your life? Do you think that God can't provide a place for you to live and put your family back together? What about sexual immorality?"

Tommy lifted his eyes.

A man in a raggedy overcoat, shabby shoes, and pin-striped bell-bottom pants stood and advanced on Kenneth. "Shut your mouth! You don't know what you're talking about!"

Kenneth turned and looked at him. His countenance reeked of evil. The man stood several feet away from him, as if a force field stopped him from coming any closer. "Please sit down."

"No," he growled. "I'm tired of you lying!"

Elizabeth stood. She was on the platform, but was willing to take her shoes off and get busy with anybody that messed with her husband.

Kenneth turned to Elizabeth. "Let me handle this."

Remembering that angels protected Kenneth, Elizabeth sat back down. If she had a stool, she would've kicked her feet up.

Kenneth held up his hands. "What am I lying about?"

The man wobbled as he pointed an accusatory finger at Kenneth. His pores reeked of alcohol. He jerked a couple of times, then vomited all over his bell-bottoms and passed out.

Kenneth's congregation ignored the vomit on the floor and the man who lay next to it. They continued to listen as Kenneth expounded on the goodness of God that leads men and women to repent. They amened and high-fived each other.

He turned to Elizabeth and asked her to grab the mic and stand by him. He wanted to implore them to come to the Lord. He was willing to promise them the moon and then some. But instead, he opened his mouth and told the people, "I don't want to sell you a bill of goods. You all have been through enough storms in your life to know when to come out of the rain. So, I'm not going to tell you that if you come to Jesus all your troubles will be over." He smiled at the people. "I do believe that Jesus will wash away your sins and your troubles. But it might not feel like it has happened right away. You might have to struggle to hold on to what you believe, but you'll never regret turning your life over to Jesus. Come my friends, come to the Lord."

Elizabeth began to sing:

"Whosoever will, whosoever will, let him come. Jesus said come unto me all you who are weary And heavy-laden. You will find rest for your soul . . ."

Two ladies in the front stood and walked toward the altar.

God had surrounded Tommy with His love. No matter how he moved, he still felt the gentle presence of the Lord. It was pulling him, asking him to come to Jesus. Kenneth's words had struck cords of emotion. Yes, Tommy had a lot of issues. He didn't think the Lord could deal with all his problems. But maybe, that was God's job. Maybe God could mend the broken places in his heart, he thought.

So, as Elizabeth serenaded the Lord and enraptured her listening audience, Tommy stood. He'd tried everything else; now he was willing to give God a try. Maybe God would have mercy on him just as He did with Jabez. Tommy took a step toward God's mercy seat, then fear gripped him.

What if he was not a Jabez, but an Esau? What if God had already reviewed his sins and found him unworthy of forgiveness? Could he live with that? No, he could not. Better to reject God, than to be rejected. Tears cascaded down his face as he turned away. His shoulders slumped from the weight of his world, his troubles. But he kept walking to what he knew—his comfort zone.

Elizabeth watched Tommy leave. She didn't get disheartened or become disillusioned. She had learned some tough lessons during her walk with God, one of which was that sometimes prayers are answered slowly. She looked to heaven with a partial smile, tears in her eyes, and a confident heart. Tommy would find peace. She knew this because she wasn't going to stop praying until he did. "I trust you, Lord," she whispered, then continued her serenade. *"Whosoever will, whosoever will, let him come."*

Kenneth and altar workers from his church were busy leading each person in the sinner's prayer.

Sandy and her children walked to him and asked for prayer.

The prayer was not, *now I lay me down to sleep, I pray the Lord my soul to keep.* Kenneth asked a series of questions:

"Do you believe that you have sinned? And that God can forgive and deliver you from a life of sin?"

Sandy bowed her head. "Yes. Yes, I've sinned."

"Do you believe that Jesus Christ is the Son of God and that He died and rose again so that you could be saved?"

She raised her hands in submission to God. "Yes. Oh, Lord, yes."

"Then enter into the kingdom of life."

Tears ran down Sandy's worn face. She embraced her children. "I'm free," she told them.

Elizabeth searched the crowd for Kenneth. He was praying for a woman and her small children. She smiled. She and Kenneth were in this thing together. Their mission in life was about loving God, loving each other, and saving souls. She would have it no other way.

EPILOGUE

The smell of death and decay ruled the air. Fire licked the walls as smoke carpeted the floor. Satan fueled the fire with his lust for revenge and anger. He stalked his domain. Eyes ablaze with unshed fury. "Assassin!"

The hulking figure trotted into the evil one's presence with the confidence of one who had wielded many victories. The notches on the belt that held his well-used sword were many.

Satan opened his mouth and spewed out fire. It consumed Assassin and licked his pockmarked flesh, until nothing but ashes remained.

"Destroyer!"

Destroyer's bat-like head hung low. His flesh-devouring fangs scraped the ground as he bowed down to Satan. "How can I serve you, my lord?"

Satan towered over him. "Assassin disappointed me. You are now the captain of the hosts."

Green slime dripped from his crust-laden lips. "You won't regret this, my lord."

Satan's lip curled as he trampled over Assassin's ashes. "Assassin lost a very important battle last night. He sent the wrong demons. See that you don't make the same mistake."

"No, my lord. I won't." Destroyer stood.

Satan kicked him in the stomach, sending him across the room, smashing into the wall of the lost. "Who told you to stop bowing?"

Destroyer rubbed his ribs. "No disrespect intended, my lord. I—"

"Call your demons!"

Within minutes, thousands of menacing spirits were snarling, howling, and scratching the tunnel walls. Blood drizzled down the walls, as demons poked through the muck and mire that incased lost souls.

Satan oozed evil as his troops stood before him. The angels that were kicked out with him were changed into the howling, snarling demons that stood before him—God's little way of allowing Satan to see inside himself.

"Quit drooling," Satan told one of his frontline warriors. "It makes me sick to look at you."

The demon backed up. He didn't stop moving until he reached the ninth row. Satan smiled as he strutted before his troops. "You have been brought into my presence to tear down, kill, and destroy. I will accept no excuses for failure. Do you understand what I am saying?"

A unanimity of "Yes, my lord," filled the polluted air.

"Now, bow down before me while I tell you about a human I hate."

The loud sounds of the trumpets, guitars, flutes, and drums could be heard throughout heaven as angels lined up on the streets of gold. They were getting ready to get their party started with music and dancing. Shoot, the Electric Slide was invented in heaven. The angels rejoiced over the sinners that repented when Kenneth and Elizabeth had reached out to the homeless.

God was seated on His throne. His omnipotence glistened through the emerald rainbow arched above the magnificent throne. The twenty-four elders surrounded Him, also seated on thrones, and clothed in white radiant robes. They wore crowns of gold on their heads.

Seven lamps of fire were burning and a sea of crystal lay at the Master's feet. In the midst of the throne and around it, were four living creatures with eyes covering their entire bodies. The first living creature was like a lion, the second, a calf, the third, a man, and the fourth, a flying eagle. Each of the creatures had six wings. They do not rest day or night, as their massive wings enable them to soar high above the thrones. Generating cool winds throughout heaven, they bellow continuous alms to their King crying, "Holy, holy, holy. Lord, God Almighty. Who was and is and is to come!"

The twenty-four elders fell down before Him and worshipped, saying, "You are worthy, O Lord, to receive glory and honor and power, for you created all things, and by your will they exist and were created." They threw their crowns before the throne in adoration.

Michael stood in the back of the throne room. He clasped his jewel embedded sword against Aaron's. "Your men have done well. They not only kept Kenneth and Elizabeth alive, but aided them in finding their purpose."

Aaron put his sword back in its sheath and chuckled. "Yes, Nathan is quite pleased with himself."

The voice of thunder and lightning crackled from the throne. Michael excused himself. When he returned, he handed Aaron a scroll.

Aaron opened it and smiled. "Davison has done an excellent job protecting this one."

Michael put his hand on Aaron's shoulder. "Davison will need help. Satan has launched a massive attack against him."

"Why is the evil one so interested in Isaac Walker?"

Michael smiled. "Isaac was born to bring in the last day harvest. The world has yet to see what he is capable of doing."

Aaron assumed the warrior position. "My General, you have my word. We will protect him."

Please turn this page for a bonus excerpt from

LATTER RAIN

the third book in the
RAIN SERIES
by Vanessa Miller

PROLOGUE

Isaac lay on his cot rubbing his chin. This was his final wake up. His last morning as a federally mandated, underpaid license plate maker. Most would have been elated. But Isaac needed time to think. Time to put together what his new life outside of prison would look like. So as the morning bell shook the prison walls, and hundreds of men stood to be loosed from the cells that held them bound, Isaac continued to rub his chin and ponder. He stretched his well-toned chocolate body and exhaled. Isaac was in an uncomfortable place. He'd given his life to Jesus and meant every word of his declaration. But did he really have what it took to live for the Lord outside the confines of prison?

Two things Isaac wanted—no needed—more than the air he breathed: to walk upright before the One who claimed his soul, and to be forgiven by the one who had claimed his heart oh, so many years ago. Sweet Nina Lewis, his baby's mama. He thought he was strong, until she taught him how to withstand the storms of life. Thought he had all the answers, until she taught him how to bow his knee, and wait on God to bring the answer.

The bell stopped ringing and his cell unlocked. In about an hour, he would be released. Time for him to teach Miss Nina Lewis a few things. Isaac made up his cot, then got on his knees. Most of the inmates joked about Isaac's morning routine. But Isaac could find nothing routine about his relationship with Jesus.

"Oh Father, here I am, the one you cleansed. Thank you for being so faithful. Thank you for loving me in spite of all the things I've done. You're great and mighty, Lord. Help me to walk upright before you—you are a holy God. And you require your servants to be holy. May my life bring you glory. May I never grieve the Holy Spirit you have placed in me."

For some odd reason, he looked at his hands. Hands that had caused mass destruction. Hands that had destroyed not-so-innocent lives. "This is my pledge to you, Lord. I will never use these hands to destroy your people again. In Jesus' name I pray. Amen."

After communing with his Savior, he walked through the morning mechanically. Didn't even notice the plaster falling from the walls, the scratchy soap as he showered and shaved. He said his final goodbyes without catching a whiff of the mixture of urine, humidity and sweat that clung to the air. "You keep walking with Jesus," Pete, his old cellmate, told him.

T-bone strutted over to him. "Don't worry about the prison ministry. I'm in this joint for another year at least. I'll hold it together."

Isaac picked up the Bible and an assortment of workbook material the chaplain had given him. "You'll need this stuff."

He walked away. No looking back, no regrets. He'd served his time and done God's will. Time for a new chapter. He'd received letters from countless preachers over the last year. Many had heard about the revival going on in this place.

He was grateful for all that God allowed him to do while in prison. But right now his son, Donavan, and Nina were on his mind. He wasn't sure if Nina could let go of the past and accept him back into her life. But he would do anything to make that happen. He tried to convince her that he was different every time she brought his son for a visit. But Nina made it clear that she wasn't interested, and was only there to provide Donavan a ride home.

He picked up his two-hundred dollar check for five years of service. Yeah, that would go a long way toward all that back child support he owed. His hand tightened around the check. He wanted to ball it up and throw it in the guard's smug face, but that would go against his pledge to God. The prison doors opened. He felt like Mel Gibson in "Braveheart," screaming FREEDOM!

He put the check in his pocket and walked out. Walking up the street toward the pick-up zone, the brisk March wind swirled around him. He zipped his jacket and stuffed his hands in his pockets, all the while hoping that Keith would not be late. Entering the pick-up zone, Isaac spotted a broken down Ford Taurus, a red Lincoln Navigator with spinners and a black and gray Cadillac Seville. Keith was in none of them. The guy in the Navigator got out and headed over to him.

His smile showed off his gold plated mouth. His jeweled hands seemed out of place with his baggy Nike jogging suit.

"Isaac, my man. How's it going?" He offered his hand. "I've been out here over an hour waiting on you to pop that spot."

Isaac glanced at the outstretched hand, then sucked his teeth while sizing up the hustler in front of him.

The hustler conceded. He put his hand down, rubbing it on the side of his pants. "You don't remember me? I'm Mickey." He put his hands in the air, indicating someone about chest level to where he now stood. "Remember little Mickey Jones? I worked for you on Williams Street."

Mickey had gotten taller, but Isaac made the connection. With recognition came a flood of memories. The Williams Street turf war was the source of Isaac's nightmares. The whole thing was wicked from the start. Isaac had been losing money on Williams Street. A quick investigation told him that a hustler named Ray-Ray had moved in on his turf. By the time the episode was over, Isaac had been shot, Valerie, one of his girls, and Ray-Ray were dead. The only good memory he had of that night was of Nina birthing his son.

"Yeah, Mickey, I remember you." They did the black man's handshake. Isaac's head nodded in the direction of the Navigator. "I see you've come up in the world."

His gold teeth glistened as he smiled. "Well, you know, I couldn't be a runner forever. You taught me better than that."

"You can't stay in the game forever, Mickey. The game gets played out, one way or another."

Mickey shook his head. "Nobody ran them streets like you did. You ain't played out, Isaac. That's why I came to get you."

A silver Mercedes pulled up next to the Navigator.

Mickey continued. "I already got you a house." He handed Isaac the keys to the Navigator. "I bought it for you. You don't have to worry about a thing. Me and you, Isaac. We will own the city of Dayton."

A suit stepped out of the Mercedes. Armani down to his shoes, with a Sunday-go-to-meeting hat on his self-assured head. He trotted his well-to-do self in Isaac's direction.

Isaac looked at the keys, studied the jewels on Mickey's hands. "Looks like you already own Dayton."

Mickey lit up the friendly skies with his smile again. "Man, there's room enough for the both of us. I started in this business because of you."

Isaac flinched. Life would be so sweet if only he didn't have to think about how many dead men walking he had started in this business.

"Isaac Walker?"

Isaac turned toward Mr. Well-to-do. Maybe *I'm getting a Mercedes next. How much of this do you think I can take, Lord?*

"That's me."

The man extended his hand.

Isaac glanced at it, but his hands still felt like resting at his side. Something about shaking a man's hand. Isaac didn't take it lightly. Shaking a man's hand connected you with him. It said, "I agree with you." And Isaac wasn't agreeable all the time.

"I'm Bishop William Sumler. Your friend, Keith, asked me to come and pick you up."

Isaac shook his head. *I've got to work on my trust issues.* He took Bishop Sumler's hand and shook it gladly. "I thought Keith was picking me up."

"He had some car trouble. I told him that I wanted to meet you in person anyway. So I made the trip for him."

Mickey got fidgety. Started looking around. "Look, Isaac, can we get going? I really don't want to hang around this place any longer than necessary."

Bishop Sumler eyed Mickey as he moved a little closer to Isaac. "Is this young man a friend of yours?"

"Yeah," Isaac told him. "Me and Mickey go way back. As a matter of fact," Isaac lifted the keys in his hand. "Mickey just brought me a car to roll out of here in."

Bishop Sumler's high yellow cheeks reddened. "So you don't need a ride?"

"That's not what I said." Isaac plopped the keys back in Mickey's hand. "Thanks for the offer. But I'm a new man now. I can't go back to life as usual."

Bishop Sumler put a possessive hand on Isaac's shoulder. "God is pleased with you. Just keep looking to Him for answers."

"That's what I intend to do." Isaac smiled at Mickey. "Thanks for looking out for me. I'll catch up with you another time—shoot the breeze or something."

Mickey backed away. "All right, man. But if you change your mind, you know where to find me."

"Didn't I always?"

Mickey gave a small, nervous laugh. "Yeah, I guess you did." He opened the door to his Navigator. "Well, keep holding it down. I'll see you on the other side."

"I sure hope so." But Isaac knew they were thinking of two different sides. Mickey wanted to see him back on the gang-banging drug dealing side. While the side Isaac hoped to see Mickey on had pearly gates and streets of gold.

"You ready?" Bishop Sumler asked.

Isaac hesitated for a moment. Something in Mickey's eyes, in his nervous laughter, made Isaac uneasy. He wanted to catch up with him and tell him about life after the game. Let him know that there is a man named Jesus who could change his whole world in the blink of an eye. But he let it go. "Yeah, let's get out of here. I'm ready for something new."

1

Five years later

Nine long hours on the road had beaten him down. All Isaac wanted to do was grab hold of his pillow and power nap himself into the land of the unconscious. Opening the door to his two-bedroom roach motel never felt better.

Actually, he didn't have roaches, but Isaac expected them any day now. Oh, how the mighty have fallen. If anyone had told him that accepting Jesus meant giving up everything and starting from scratch, he would have rebuked that devil. But here he was, suffering for Jesus.

Three steps into his apartment the floorboard creaked. Another five steps, creak. Two more steps, creak, creak.

His slumlord promised to fix that months ago. Isaac pulled at his tie as he shook his head. "You can't trust nobody but Jesus."

Isaac set his mind to endure the lean years. He knew that once he was pastor of his own church, things would get better. Bishop Sumler had promised him that. So, he went from town to town with Bishop, learning the ropes.

On the road, he was king. Traveling with Bishop Sumler gave him privileges a young struggling preacher wouldn't have normally had. Bishop Sumler wasn't a Motel Six kind of man. When a congregation put him up for the night, they had to dig deep in their pockets. And if meals were included, even Isaac, the armor bearer, had steak that night.

Unbuttoning his good as new, but-still-used-to-be-somebody-else's Italian knit shirt, he stepped into his bedroom and flicked on the lights. He'd asked Cassandra to check on his apartment while he was away, to make sure the TV and DVD player stayed where he'd left them, and to water the one lonely plant that had bothered to stay alive in this dump. But he did not ask her to warm his bed.

"Cassandra!"

She jumped. The cover fell off her body as she stretched and yawned. "What took you so long?"

Had he given a nutcase the keys to his apartment?

Something had to be wrong with her. She was in his bed, acting as if this was where she belonged. Talking 'bout,

'What took you so long' like they had been married for ten years, and had five kids already. "Um, Cassandra, can you tell me why you slept over?"

She wiped the sleep buggers from her big brown eyes, then looked at him as if to say, you know what's up. "I've been waiting for you, baby. Now, I know you're tired." She pulled the cover back as she scooted over.

His eyes feasted on her black silk, low cut negligee.

"Climb on in, baby. I warmed that spot just for you."

Isaac's mouth opened. No words escaped, but a little drool did swim down his chin. Wiping his unsanctified mouth and turning toward his bathroom, he told her, "I'll be right back."

He buttoned his shirt as he stepped into the bathroom.

Looking to heaven he asked, "Lord, why have you allowed this? How much temptation does one man have to endure?"

He fell to his knees, elbows touching the toilet seat lid, hands entwined, head bowed. "Oh God, my Lord and my King, You know that I am just a man. I can't handle this kind of temptation, yet it keeps coming my way.

"You know me, Lord. I want to go out there, toss Cassandra up and repent later." He waited a minute to hear what God would say to that. No answer came, but Isaac knew. He was born to do God's will, even when it conflicted with his own.

He stood, shook off the old man and slowly opened the door. He hated feeling like a peeping Tom in his own house. But there he was, door cocked open, peering out at the woman sprawled across his bed. Lying on her stomach, the roundness of her backside was in full view. He closed the bathroom door like a punk and fell back on his knees. "I can't do this, Lord. How can you allow me to suffer like this?"

Isaac closed his eyes as his mind turned to Jesus, bruised and beaten. Hanging on a cross for the sins of the world. "I am not worthy to suffer with you." He hung his head low. "But if you could endure death by crucifixion, surely I can crucify my body."

This time when he stood, his old nature was truly under subjection. He opened the bathroom door with boldness.

"Cassandra, you've got to go."

Cassandra jumped as Isaac's words vibrated off the bedroom walls. "Wha . . . what's wrong?" She giggled nervously.

"It's still dark out, Isaac. I can't go now."

Isaac grabbed her ankle length skirt and turtleneck off the dresser and threw them at her. "Get your clothes on, you have got to go." She opened her mouth to protest.

"I'm not throwing out jokes, Cassandra. But I will throw you out, if you're not dressed and gone in two minutes."

She rolled her eyes and got out of his bed. "Whatever, man. You're the one missing out."

Isaac shook his head as he watched the praise leader at his church squeeze into her long conservative skirt. He thought Cassandra was different. But she was just like all the rest, trying to get in his pants. That thought almost made him burst out laughing. All his life he had been a sexual predator. But he was doing this thing for Jesus now. No room for compromise. Straight and narrow was the only walk his Lord would accept. He had slipped once. He vowed never to let it happen again.

"Denise said that you used to love for her to surprise you like this when you returned home." Cassandra put on her shoes and continued pouting. "What's wrong? You don't think I'd be as good as Denise?"

"Just give me my key and get out." She took his key off her key ring and threw it at him. Isaac sat on his bed, shoulders slumped, and allowed his heart to fill with shame as Cassandra slammed his door. "I don't know how I got caught up again. It had been two years since that thing with Denise. But every time he thought about how he'd messed up Denise's life, he remembered Cynda Stevens.

For a time, Cynda's beauty outweighed the defects of her personality. Isaac had used her to make Nina jealous.

But that had been years ago. He'd also passed Cynda on to his old friend, Spoony, when he was done with her. The guilt of that still ate at him. Spoony had turned Cynda out.

He looked to heaven. "I thought you cast sins into this great sea and stop thinking about them. When will I stop paying for the mistakes I've made?"

To whom much is given, much is required.

Isaac fell back on his bed and sighed. "I'm sorry, Lord. I never meant to hurt you. I'll get this thing right, if it's the last thing I do." He wanted to talk to his Lord a little while longer, plead his case. But his eyelids won the battle and sleep consumed his soul.

Dreams were much better than reality anyway. When Nina was the star of the show playing in his head, Isaac could sleep for days. She was wearing that hand-me-down blue jean dress that looked so good on her. She walked toward him smiling. No, she didn't just walk. Baby-girl strutted with purpose. Confident of who she was and what she wanted. He always did like a woman who had her mind made up.

"It's time, Isaac," she told him with fire in her eyes.

He gave her an 'I got you now' smile, as his dimples dipped into all that chocolate. "You ready for this?"

Her head bobbed.

He reached out for her, but it wasn't Nina anymore. His mother was now in front of him. She was falling. Oh, God!

He couldn't catch her. Her head hit the table. The glass shattered and his sweet mother lay in a pool of blood.

"Nooooo!" Isaac bolted upright, panting, as sweat drizzled down his face. He ran his hands from his forehead to the back of his head.

Bam. . . bam. . . bam.

Before he could calm his nerves, Isaac realized that some lunatic was trying to knock his door down. The half moon that still clung to the sky told him that it was way too early for visitors. The sound would have normally irritated him and curled his fists. But right now, he was grateful for anything that would pull him out of bed.

He trodded through his bedroom and the creak, creak, creak of his living room. The bamming stopped once he stepped in the living room. He'd never be able to sneak up on a burglar in this mug. Rubbing his eyes with the palm of his hands, he looked through the peephole then flung open the door. "Man, it's five in the morning. What's the emergency?"

Keith stepped in, clothes wrinkled—hair hadn't seen a brush. "I've been trying to call you."

Isaac plucked a fur ball out of Keith's low-cut fade.

"You must have been dialing the wrong number. I've been home since about two."

Keith picked up Isaac's phone and put the receiver to his ear. "No dial tone."

"What do you mean there's no dial tone?" He grabbed the phone to investigate. "Man, I know I paid this bill."

Keith raised his hands. "Calm down. Maybe something's wrong with your line." He walked away from Isaac.

"Let me check the phone in your bedroom."

Isaac looked to heaven. "This suffering for Christ stuff is getting old."

"Here's the problem," Keith hollered from the bedroom.

"You had the phone off the hook."

Isaac clenched his fist. "Cassandra must have done that. I'm so tired of these Holy Ghost filled jigga boos. I'm gon' have to get me a woman off the street. Maybe she'll respect the fact that I'm trying to live saved."

"Another one trying to give you the midnight special?"

Isaac shook his head. "I ain't gon' lie, Keith. I almost took it." Keith smiled, then his expression changed, like something was wrong. Real wrong. "What's up, man? Why you stalking me at this hour?"

Putting the phone back on the receiver, Keith sucked in his breath. "Sit down, Isaac."

"Just tell me what's up." He got in his mac-daddy stance. "I can take it."

"I'm not joking, Isaac. I really think you should sit down for this."

Isaac folded his arms across his chest. "Look, I'm a man. I can take your news standing up."

Keith opened his mouth, then closed it. He stood there contemplating his options. He shook his head. Sometimes there was just no reasoning with Isaac. "There's been a shooting."

Isaac unfolded his arms. "Someone at the church?"

Keith shook his head.

Isaac hunched his shoulders. "Don't just stand there.

Who got shot?"

Moisture creased the edges of Keith's eyes. "I-Isaac, can y—you please sit down?"

"Just spit it out."

"Someone drove by their house about one o'clock this morning. Nina must have been waiting up for Donavan.

As soon as he stepped on the porch, she opened the door.

The neighbors said she was yelling at him when the shooting started."

Isaac's knees buckled. "Are you trying to tell me that my family is dead?"

The moisture escaped Keith's eyes and ran down his cheeks. Isaac's legs gave out and he fell to his knees. "The last I heard they were in surgery."

"Oh, God, not my family." Isaac pulled at his shirt. Ripping it, just as his heart was being ripped.

Keith wiped his face with his shirtsleeve, then tried to pull Isaac up. Isaac yanked away from him. "Come on, man. Dayton is hours from here. We've got to get going."

Isaac didn't hear him. Couldn't hear anything from the turmoil going on in his head. For as long as he'd known

Nina, his life had been about loving her and their son. A decade plus, hadn't changed that. Nina's unwillingness to come back to him, hadn't changed that. And now, some bullet was supposed to end the dreams he had for his family?

He looked toward heaven, where his help came from.

"God, do what you want to me. I can take it. But not my family. Please don't destroy my family like this."

About the Author

Vanessa Miller, of Dayton, Ohio, is a best-selling author, playwright, and motivational speaker. Her stage productions include: *Get You Some Business*, *Don't Turn Your Back on God*, and *Can't You Hear Them Crying*. Vanessa is currently in the process of turning the novels in the Rain Series into stage productions.

Vanessa has been writing since she was a young child. When she wasn't reading, writing poetry, short stories, stage plays and novels consumed her free time. However, it wasn't until she committed her life to the Lord in 1994 that she realized all gifts and anointing come from God. She then set out to write redemption stories that glorified God.

To date, Vanessa has written the "Rain Series" and the "Storm Series." The books in the "Rain Series" are: *Former Rain*, *Abundant Rain*, and *Latter Rain*. The "Storm Series" is comprised of: *Rain Storm* and *Through The Storm*. These books have received rave reviews, winning Best Christian Fiction Awards and appearing on numerous bestseller's lists, including the *Essence* Bestseller's List. Vanessa believes that each book in these two series will touch readers across the country in a special way. It is, after all, her God-given destiny to write and produce plays and novels that bring deliverance to God's people.

Vanessa self-published her first three books, then in 2006 she signed a five-book deal with Urban Christian/ Kensington. Her books can now be found in Wal-Mart and most all major bookstores, including African American bookstores and online bookstores such as Amazon.com.

Vanessa is a dedicated Christian and devoted mother. She graduated from Capital University with a degree in Organizational Communication. In 2007 Vanessa was ordained by her church as an exhorter, which of course, Vanessa believes was the right position for her because God has called her to exhort readers and to help them rediscover their place with the Lord.

A perfect day for Vanessa is one that affords her the time to curl up with a good book. She is currently working on a new novel outside of the Rain and Storm series. She is also preparing the stage production for the *Former Rain* novel. Go to: *www.vanessamiller.com* for more info on Vanessa and her books.

Discussion Questions

Elizabeth

1. Elizabeth's dependency on Kenneth caused her to forsake all and attempt to take her own life. She finally came to understand that she could give Kenneth her heart, but not her soul. What does God's Word say about placing man above Him? Read: *Old Testament New Testament* Exodus 20:3–5 I Corinthians 8:5–6 Leviticus 26:1 Colossians 1:14–29 Isaiah 40:6-8; 12–31

2. Although Elizabeth was called and anointed to sing, she initially moved without allowing God to lead her. As a result of being in ministry out of season, her career was turbulent and plagued with scandal. How can we know that we are walking in our purpose at our appointed time? Read:

Old Testament New Testament Job 14:14
Matthew 23:12 Proverbs 16:18 I Peter 5:6
Proverbs 25:6–8; 20; 27 I John 2:15–17

3. Elizabeth realized that some prayers are answered slowly. What things can hinder your prayers? Read:

Old Testament New Testament
I Samuel 15:23 Matthew 17:20
Psalm 66:16-20 Romans 10:1-4 Proverbs 6:16–19 James 1:5–8

4. While in the garden, Elizabeth made peace with God's direction for her life. How can we usher in peace and calm in the midst of our storms? Read:

Old Testament New Testament
Psalm 34:11–14 Luke 12:22–34 Isaiah 26:12 John 16:31–33 Jeremiah 29:10–14 Romans 12:17–21

Kenneth

1. Throughout the book, Kenneth encountered supernatural beings, both good and evil. What does the Word tell us about the spirit realm? Read:

Old Testament New Testament

Exodus 23:20–23 Matthew 9:32–33 Job
1:6–12 Luke 4:33–35 Psalm 91:11 Ephe
sians 6:11–12

2. Kenneth asked Elizabeth "What is one
man to do?" expressing his feelings of inad-
equacy in ministry. How could you encour-
age someone to reach his/her full potential
in God? Read:
   Old Testament New Testament
   Exodus 4:10–12 Matthew 18:19–20 Deu
   teronomy 32:30 I Corinthians 12 Judges
   6:11–16 Philippians 4:11–13

3. Kenneth had to dig deep to forgive Debra
of her betrayal and Elizabeth of her per-
ceived betrayal. What are we to do when it
comes to forgiving others? Read:
   Old Testament New Testament
   Genesis 45:1–15 Matthew 6:9–15
   I Samuel 24:8–22 Matthew 18:21–35
   Psalms 103:12 Mark 11:26

Tommy
1. Tommy attributed his homosexuality to
his childhood experiences with the church
deacon. How does God view sexual immorality? Read:

Old Testament New Testament Genesis 19:5 Romans 1:26–32 Leviticus 20:13 Ephesians 5:1-7 Deuteronomy 23:17–18 Colossians 3:5–9

2. Tommy was ready to give his life to the Lord, however, comparing his life to Esau and Jabez caused his faith to waver. Do you believe that you are an Esau or a Jabez? Why? Read:

Old Testament New Testament I Chronicles 4:9–10 Romans 9:11–16 Malachi 1:1–3 Luke 14:25–27 Genesis 25:20–34

3. Given the opportunity to repent of his sins, Tommy chose to reject God. What hope does he have for salvation? Read: *Old Testament New Testament* Genesis 3:14–15 John 10:7–18 Proverbs 28:13–14 John 14:1–6 Isaiah 53:1–6 Romans 10:9–14

UC HIS GLORY BOOK CLUB!

www.uchisglorybookclub.net

UC His Glory Book Club is the spirit-inspired brainchild of Joylynn Jossel, Author and Acquisitions Editor of Urban Christian, and Kendra Norman-Bellamy, Author for Urban Christian. This is an online book club that hosts authors of Urban Christian. We welcome as members all men and women who have a passion for reading Christian-based fiction.

UC HIS GLORY BOOK CLUB pledges our commitment to provide support, positive feedback, encouragement, and a forum whereby members can openly discuss and review the literary works of Urban Christian authors.

There is no membership fee associated with UC His Glory Book Club; however, we do ask that you support the authors through purchasing, encouraging, providing book reviews, and of course, your prayers. We also ask that you respect our beliefs and follow the guidelines of the book club. We hope to receive your valuable input, opinions, and reviews that build up, rather than tear down our authors.

WHAT WE BELIEVE:

- We believe that Jesus is the Christ, Son of the Living God.
- We believe the Bible is the true, living Word of God.
- We believe all Urban Christian authors should use their God-given writing abilities to honor God and share the message of the written word God has given to each of them uniquely.
- We believe in supporting Urban Christian authors in their literary endeavors by reading, purchasing and sharing their titles with our online community.
- We believe that in everything we do in our literary arena should be done in a manner that will lead to God being glorified and honored.

We look forward to the online fellowship with you. Please visit us often at:

www.uchisglorybookclub.net.

Many Blessing to You!
Shelia E. Lipsey,
President, UC His Glory Book Club